The TREE of LIFE

Fredelle Bruser Maynard

VIKING

VIKING

Published by the Penguin Group
Penguin Books Canada Ltd, 2801 John Street, Markham, Ontario, Canada L3R 1B4
Penguin Books, 27 Wrights Lane, London W8 5TZ, England
Viking Penguin Inc., 40 West 23rd Street, New York, New York 10010, USA
Penguin Books Australia Ltd, Ringwood, Victoria, Australia
Penguin Books (NZ) Ltd, 182-190 Wairau Road, Auckland 10, New Zealand
Penguin Books Ltd, Registered Offices: Harmondsworth, Middlesex, England

First published 1988

Copyright © Fredelle Bruser Maynard, 1988
Printed and bound in Canada

Canadian Cataloguing in Publication Data

Maynard, Fredelle Bruser.
  The tree of life

ISBN 0-670-81023-1

1. Maynard, Fredelle Bruser. 2. Jews — Canada — Biography. 3. Authors, Canadian
(English) — 20th century — Biography.* 4. Teachers — Canada — Biography.
I. Title.

FC3549.B57Z49 1987   971.004924   C87-094088-0
F1074.5.B5M39 1987

American Library of Congress Cataloguing in Publication Data Available

For Sydney,
who brought the most important gift

Acknowledgments

I am grateful to the Canada Council for support,
and to my good friend and editor, David Kilgour,
for understanding, patience and a firm hand with
the pruning shears.

Some portions of this book have appeared, in
different form, in *Maclean's*, *Chatelaine*, *Reader's Digest*, and
Woman's Day.

The Tree of Life is a traditional metaphor for the Torah, the five books of Moses which incorporate the Jewish moral law. When the ark is closed after the reading of the Torah on Sabbath and holidays, this prayer is sung to a melody plaintive and hopeful, in minor key:

It is a Tree of Life to them that hold fast to it…
Its ways are ways of pleasantness, and all its paths are peace.

CONTENTS

The TREE of LIFE

Introduction

A vast blue sky, sunshine, snow, frosted breath, and my father in his shaggy buffalo coat moving just ahead through a white silent world — these are my earliest memories. When, long after, I recalled this impression, my mother nodded. "You were two years old the winter Papa made you that sled. There wasn't a child in town had anything like it — rock maple, with a curved railing all the way round, so you could lean back. We used to bundle you up in a sheepskin and away you went like a little princess with Papa pulling the droshky." It was December 1924, a moment that seems to encapsulate my prairie childhood in its meld of comfort and bitter chill.

Foam Lake was the first of the many towns we lived in; we seldom stayed long in one place. My father, a Russian painter turned country merchant, opened one store after another — in Birch Hills, Gretna, Plum Coulee, Altona, Grandview. In every town but the last, our store failed, a casualty of poor crops and uncollectable debts; in every town we lived as the only Jewish family in a community Lutheran, Mennonite, Anglican or Russian Orthodox. The world around me I experienced always as alien if not actively hostile, but our house was a safe haven — my father in his leather armchair, playing Chaliapin records on the Victrola; my mother in the kitchen making magic with butter, eggs and cream.

So it is that when I look back at my beginnings what comes to me most powerfully is not the experience of outsiderness, or the small playground persecutions inspired by my Jewishness. What I remember is *home*. My mother was, in the truest sense of a now debased word, a homemaker. Whether rolling a pie-crust, cool-sponging a fevered child, repotting a fern or embroidering a linen tablecloth, she moved with common sense, efficiency, conviction and good cheer. She performed by hand all the tasks now governed by an electric switch. She pumped water from the cistern and collected, in a special barrel, rainwater to wash our hair. She did her own dry-cleaning with solvent that reddened and stung her hands. She beat rugs with a wire whisk. She made her own cottage cheese and her own noodles, rolling and cutting dough, then drying strips in the sun. The only operation my mother did not perform from scratch was making soap. That she wouldn't do: it required lard (unclean) and lye (dangerous where there are children). For the rest — she baked bread, cleaned and plucked chickens for the Sabbath meal, produced a constantly changing assortment of delicate pastries, set an elegant table. She had the town's best garden, the greenest plants. When, as a grown woman, I visited our old house in Birch Hills, I was surprised to find it cramped and dark. My mother had made the space ample, bright.

Birch Hills, where we lived for six years — I was nine when we left — is the town of my important firsts. I started school there, made my first passionate friendship, began my career as a child elocutionist and child poet. In Birch Hills I saw my first airplane, heard my first radio broadcast, a program featuring a female singer. As we gathered reverently round, my father rose and — no doubt to show his mastery of exotic machines — turned up the volume. The soprano sang louder. "Don't, Papa," I pleaded. "Somebody in Kinistino might turn the knob *down*. Then what'll she do?"

That moment holds the essence of my Saskatchewan child-hood: its isolation, its simplicity, its radiant and tender inno-cence. We were all, parents and children alike, new hatched to wonder. We had some notion of a world beyond our shells, but we neither divined its nature nor imagined its extent. I know I believed for years that telegrams were physically attached to overhead wires and then sent zooming to their destinations.

It is hard to imagine an eight-year-old in the world today so grass green, so prairie buttercup as I was. I didn't myself wholly believe in fairies, though I wanted to. But I had friends who had seen them, and friends whose mothers forbade the wearing of green, lest their offspring be carried away by the little folk. I knew that toads gave warts (which could be cured by application of raw meat, first buried in the ground). I walked carefully on cement sidewalks, knowing that stepping on a crack might break my mother's back. Magic was real to me. Phrenologists and spiritualists and Chautauqua lecturers held keys to special revelation. What was printed in books was infallibly true. (If it weren't true, how could it be printed?) At sixteen, an entering university student, I was honestly puzzled to find in the library books that contradicted each other.

As for sex — like any country child, I had plenty of opportu-nity to observe the facts of barnyard life. But I never imagined that told me anything about *people*. I knew a few off-colour jokes, mostly scatological. I had never read a dirty book and wouldn't have understood if I had. At seventeen I stammered my way into an "Adults Only" movie, wearing hat and gloves as proof of maturity and was, I think, not greatly surprised to find that the climactic incident took place in a canary's cage. That must have been my first encounter with symbolism as well as with sin. A boy and girl, not married or even engaged, sat side by side on a couch. He kissed her. She protested, but without conviction. Meanwhile, high above, a canary trilled on its perch; a cat watched below. The camera panned back and forth a bit, faces to bird to feline. The boy looked upset. We caught a last glimpse of the lovers in decorous clutch, then a shocking view of the empty cage, door swinging, and the cat's complacent smile. I remember being puzzled. Who opened the door?

The net effect of my severely limited experience was that I had an unusually long childhood. In the prairie towns where I grew up, doll play was tea-parties and pushing the babies in carriages. As late as the fifth grade, on special occasions we took our dolls to school. *The fifth grade.* I don't know how it is now on the Canadian prairies, but in cities from Halifax to Vancouver, when ten-year-olds buy a nickel bag it is probably not candy.

In the late twenties and early thirties, we played a lot. Toys were not important or necessary, there was so much, every-where, to *do*. Every house had an attic, a basement, a cellar door, a clothesline, a rain barrel, a well, a shed, a woodpile, an outdoor toilet, a climbable fence with swinging gate. Fascinat-ing. Few of us had lawns, but of course a dirt yard makes a better play area. You could dig a hole for Peggy, scuff wildly about in Prisoner's Base, and no one ever said, "You're ruining the grass." We peeled birch-bark and wrote Indian messages on it, made kites and butterfly nets. A good stick was a treasure — spy glass, sword, gun, cane, drawing implement (in sand) and pointer for playing school. We knew literally dozens of games and played them not just at birthday parties, as the young do now, but every day. There were dramatic games like Statues (some versions revolved around an enchanter whose potent glance froze players in weirdly distorted postures) and Miss Jenny Jones, a song-pantomime that swept us from domestic trivia to a region of ice. No matter how often we played it, I experienced real chill as we moved through the dialogue like steps of a dance.

We've come to see Miss Jenny Jones,
Miss Jenny Jones, Miss Jenny Jones,
We've come to see Miss Jenny Jones,
          And how is she today?

We never got to see Jenny. She was washing, baking, ironing, scrubbing, sick…and dead.

There were games of risk, games testing speed and strength, games where winning depended on quick reflexes, games of pure chance — in short, all the games of real life. Children today have toys (plastic gas stations and beauty parlors) that reproduce the adult world in miniature. That is not what I mean by real life. Our games — centuries old, some must have been — were initiation rites for the human experience. Poison Tag: touch, association infects. London Bridge: choice has consequences you can't predict. Giant Steps: you move at a rate determined by others — unless you're very shrewd. Many games were a kind of exorcism, a deliberate courting of terror and mock death. Did we catch dim, prescient insights as we played in those green meadows? Some girls, at eight or nine, shone at Post Office, getting all the mail. The games I, as a Jew, really understood — though I never got to be good at them — involved a circle of linked hands and a breathless figure outside, trying to break in. Or musical chairs where, when the piano stopped, there were never enough seats to go round.

The prairies gave me a long childhood, and an instructive

one. Though my father did not farm I grew up close to the soil, aware of elemental forces. Sun, rain and the land: those were the ultimate realities. Long before the word became fashionable, I was an ecologist, aware of the intricate interdependence of all living things. I breathed the rhythm of the seasons and watched the weather. To this day I judge summers as "good for crops," "bad for crops." I cannot imagine a life in which one does not plant in April, harvest in September. For me, now, it may be only a patch of dill. But sowing it is a ritual. When the heads mature, I gather and dry them as tenderly as if I were five hundred miles from the nearest store.

The processes that sustained life were everywhere in evidence around me when I was a child. I saw the soil prepared for planting, the wheat sown, and all summer grain and grain elevators were the ground of my consciousness. I saw the wheat cut and stooked, and prayed for no rain while the stooks stood vulnerable in the field. Rain lowered the grade. Threshing, hauling, milling and baking were all familiar sights. I knew how the loaf of bread came to our table. In contrast, I think of the time I pointed out a green field to my three-year-old daughter. "Look," I said, "that's corn." She studied the phenomenon. "Ah," she said. Then, with interest, "Does it come from cornflakes?"

I learned young that survival requires effort (and so have been perpetually surprised ever since at the number of people who expect that the tide will carry them safely into harbour). Except for hoboes and gypsies, the moths and butterflies of our world, everyone I knew worked hard. Laundry meant scrubbing, and butter churning. Cooking began, in effect, at the woodpile, splitting wood and gathering kindling. Ironing involved two heavy flatirons, one heating while the other hissed and sizzled over cloth. I remember, from the late thirties, a scene in my father's store: two maiden ladies — we called them, unblushingly, "old maids" — describing the delights of their first electric iron. One gloved hand sweeping the air, the older sister summoned up the marvel. "You just plug it in and go back and forth — *and it irons!*" She might have been describing a moon landing, so amazed she was, and so proud.

Remote as we were from "civilization," always hard up, we took nothing for granted. Waste of any kind was unthinkable. We had a neighbour who saved the water with which she rinsed out the milk bottles and then used it for soup. That was carrying economy a bit far. But apart from rinse water, we didn't throw out much. When a shirt became shabby, the collar was turned. When the collar gave out on both sides, the shirt made smocks and blouses. And when we outgrew those, there would still be a few quilt patches to salvage — at the very least a dustcloth. I have thought of those austere disciplines often in the years since I left Saskatchewan. From my children's growing up, two moments suggest an immeasurable distance travelled. One occurred when I reached into my six-year-old's sweater drawer. (My mother wouldn't have believed that drawer, *I* owned one suit of winter underwear, washed nights and dried before the kitchen stove to be ready for school next day.) "Here," I said. "A nice red sweater." "I don't like that colour," my child announced. "Okay," I said. "Here's a yellow one. Same style." Rona frowned and peered over my shoulder. *"Does it come in blue?"*

The other moment occurred in a department store when one of my daughters paused to look at a dress. "Do you really need that?" I asked. She looked honestly puzzled. "What has *need* got to do with it?"

I learned on the prairies to make do — and to be alone without feeling restless or bored. The world was full of marvels. Because it was an essentially safe world. I was able to explore it, unsupervised, at a very early age. I knew every wild flower, every kind of tree; I could identify birds by their calls or by a single cast feather. I learned that beauty has little to do with conventionally beautiful elements (daffodils, pink sunsets); a grain elevator against the sky can be most awesomely beautiful. So is a stalk of Indian paintbrush.

I left the prairies fifty years ago — marked for life. Of all I took with me, I value most a kind of double vision: the feeling that one must do for oneself, and along with that the certain knowledge that some things are beyond human control absolutely and must be borne.

What I didn't know — couldn't have known — when I left was how radically the circumstances of my life were to change. *The Tree of Life* takes up where an earlier memoir, *Raisins and Almonds*, left off. It is, however, a very different book. Partly this is a matter of circumstances. I did not set out, fifteen years ago, to write my life story. What happened was that a small, painful experience of anti-Semitism intensified my sense of outsiderness. I wrote one story, "Jewish Christmas," about a child excluded from the joys of the tree. To my surprise, the act of writing triggered a flood of memories — childhood friendships and betrayals, Canadian schoolrooms, the Eaton's catalogue, my father's country store, the ambiguities of university life. For some time, these remained a folder of fragments. Then my father died. Grief and irrevocable loss shattered a composure carefully maintained throughout a difficult marriage; the fragments flew together and became a book, originally called, after a Housman lyric, *The Blue Remembered Hills*.

> *Into my heart an air that kills*
> *From yon far country blows:*
> *What are those blue remembered hills,*
> *What spires, what farms are those?*

That is the land of lost content,
I see it shining plain,
The happy highways where I went
And cannot come again.

Because *Raisins and Almonds* is an account of the happy highways, it involved some simplification and some deliberate exclusions. I did not write about my sister; an honest picture of our conflicted relationship would have distressed her and wounded my mother. I did not really write about my mother, who appeared briefly in domestic scenes; she would have misunderstood any attempt to present the rich complexity of her character. I did not write about my marriage because I could not.

Shortly after *Raisins and Almonds* appeared, my husband and I separated. There was no accident in this timing: for Max, frustration as an unrecognized, failed painter was exacerbated when both his wife and his younger daughter published books. For me, writing about my childhood released sorrows long held in check. The shock of divorce created a new perspective on everything that had gone before; I began to rethink my life. If *Raisins and Almonds* is a kind of sundial book ("I count only the happy hours"), *The Tree of Life* is chiaroscuro, less lyrical and less blithe. Because Max and my mother are dead, and my sister is lost in the fog of Alzheimer's disease, I have written more freely of my family. This account is tougher, coming as it does not out of random childhood memories but out of an attempt to make sense of my adult life. It is also, I think, truer.

Fredelle Bruser Maynard
Toronto, January 1988

That
Sensual
Music

◇ ◈ ◇

> ... *The young*
> *In one another's arms, birds in the trees*
> *— Those dying generations — at their song,*
> *The salmon-falls, the mackerel-crowded seas,*
> *Fish, flesh, or fowl, commend all summer long*
> *Whatever is begotten, born and dies.*
> *Caught in that sensual music all neglect*
> *Monuments of unageing intellect.*

It wasn't until high school that I really became conscious of my sister Celia. That seems, on the face of it, absurd. We had eaten at the same table and shared the same bedroom for years. In the photographs documenting our childhood we stand always side by side — and yet, to a close observer, not *together* at all. A snapshot taken one distant summer is typical. We pose on a swing. It is not tree-hung (our parents were too careful for that)

but what is now called a lawn swing: two slat benches facing
each other, suspended in a frame and moved by energetic foot-
work at the sides. I, the footworker, brace myself against the
posts, legs straddled, grimacing so that the gap between my
two front teeth yawns into the camera. Sunlight cruelly illumines my sparse crop of hair. (Five years old and still just
wisps! "Is it a boy or a girl?" strangers asked.)

Celia stands behind me, leaning between the opposite posts.
Already she knows about placing one leg slightly forward to
get the best angle. *Her* hair is a Dutch bob — thick, lustrous,
silky. She looks down, to prevent an unbecoming squint. Though
we wear identical costumes, the effect is most unidentical.
Those blouses were made from Mama's wedding train, and the
gold velvet jumpers from a trousseau suit. How can they look
so different? It is not just that I am four years younger and
running to fat. Somehow Celia is composed, a fashion queen, a
little princess waiting for the coach that must unquestionably
sweep her away from this bleak landscape to a setting more
appropriate. As for me — my neck bow is askew and flapping,
my stockings sag.

If I could believe in the primitive magic of names, I would
think we were stamped from the beginning. She was named
Chia Ziesele, and I *Chia Freidele*. *Chia* is Hebrew for *life*. *Ziesele*
and *Freidele* are Yiddish diminutives: little sweetness, little joy.
The sweet one, the graceful one, the delicate one…Celia moved
more and more deeply into that role as she grew, and as I
embraced the robust virtues decreed by physique and name.
Other separations developed or were imposed by family legend. She was difficult, I was easy. Mama often told us how Celia
was born crying and wailed throughout her sickly babyhood.
"For months," Mama would say, "we walked her night and day.
I couldn't even comb my hair." As a little girl, she was thought

to be tubercular and taken daily to a nearby farm for a most extraordinary cure — a dipper of unpasteurized milk, still foaming from the cow. All through her school years she fainted easily. I remember her brought home by cart, by car, and once in a teacher's arms. I, on the other hand, weathered accidents and illness with equal fortitude. My legend includes the tale of an occasion when, still in my pram, I was pushed down a long flight of stairs by a mischievous cousin. Mama ran screaming after, plunged through the tumble of blankets and fished me out — smiling.

But the deepest division was one that followed — or led — us through the years. Celia was the pretty one and I the clever one. How this division became absolute puzzles me still: I was a pleasant-looking child, she was intelligent. But we accepted our separate destinies and even learned to enjoy them. We never played together and, to a degree unusual for a small, close family, we seem in memory to have blotted each other out. My recollections are mostly unkind. I remember how she took me for a ride in her wagon one day, pulled it up short under an overhanging branch, poked a wasp's nest with a stick — and ran. I remember how, sitting in pale sunlight on the front steps she once whispered, "You're not my *real* sister. You're *adopted*." And then, as I scrambled to my feet, she said softly, "It's no use asking Mama. Of course she'll pretend." What pain I caused her I shall never know. When I ask her now, "What went wrong between us? Why weren't we friends?" she says, "I don't remember you from those days. Not at all."

For the first dozen years of my life, I thoroughly enjoyed being clever. Intellectual achievement was overwhelmingly important in our family, and I was a good achiever. I came first in class, I wrote poetry, I acquired a considerable local reputation as an elocutionist. I won prizes. And — though I envied

Celia's flower-like charm — I never really doubted that my gifts were the ones that mattered. Until, that is, I turned thirteen and entered high school.

Celia had started two years before. What I knew of her career there inspired no envy: she had failed biology, and in algebra was assigned to a group ignominiously named "the awkward squad." From my first day at Gordon Bell, though, I sensed that in this new world my sister exercised mysterious power. When she walked to school, boys appeared to carry her books. In the halls between classes, she was surrounded. Evenings our telephone rang incessantly, a succession of young male voices — breathless, nervous, confident or shy — all brushing me aside with, "Is Celia there?" Once, I remember, the call was for me. Mama stood a few paces behind as I picked up the receiver. (Hadn't she always said it was a matter of time, boys would appreciate me when I was older?)

The voice was unfamiliar. "Fredelle? This is Aaron."

I couldn't offhand recollect any Aaron. Someone who had seen me at school, evidently. Maybe someone who knew I wrote poetry.

"Are you busy Friday night?"

"Oh, yes!" I said eagerly. "I mean, *no*. No, I'm free."

"Have you seen the new show at the Gaiety?"

Even if I'd seen it a dozen times, I'd have gone happily with Aaron. Probably he was a dark, brooding type like Heathcliff or Rhett Butler. The boy who sat next to me in assembly, the one who asked if I was saving the seat — *that* must be Aaron. He looked interesting. Certainly Jewish. "No," I said. I remembered Celia's graceful condescension on such occasions. "I'd love to see it."

"Well — in that case —" Aaron coughed, chuckled, shouted before the bang. "*Why don't you go see it on Friday?*"

The fact that I was not a brilliant social success in high

school came as no surprise. Boys had always teased and
tormented me when I was younger. But those were country
boys (hicks) and gentiles (barbarians). They were immature,
too insensitive to value my 100s in spelling. I had always
assumed — hoped, anyway — that things would be different
later on. Now here I was in Winnipeg, Jewish boys all around,
and failing miserably. If no one ever asked me out, I would
never marry, never have children. My parents would be heart-
broken. ("I want I should dance at my grandchildren's weddings,
that's all I ask," Papa used to say.) I made up my mind to try
harder, and I began by studying my sister. What was her secret?

She was tall, to begin with. She had marvellous long legs, like
a *goyische* girl. Obviously I could do nothing about that. She
was fair-complexioned. Again a lost cause. She was certainly
pretty, but looks alone didn't explain her apparently irresist-
ible appeal. No, it was something more elusive — an assurance,
a pleasure in herself as a girl, a quietly gleaming poise that,
along with the subtle fragrance of sex, kept our telephone
ringing. I set out to make myself alluring.

Money was tight, so it was a big decision when I took my
thirteenth-birthday dollar to Woolworth's and invested it in
beauty. I can still remember carrying home that brown bag of
treasures and laying out the contents on my bed. A card of
metal curlers, perforated rollers with spring clips — enough to
make three horizontal rows of curls. A lipstick, Passion Fire. A
round little cake of rouge. Nail polish, an orange stick to push
down my cuticle (fingernail moons were important) and some
white cream to put under the nail tips as a sort of border. A bar
of Camay, because Camay was the soap of beautiful brides. The
radio advertisement said just ten days' use made a difference.
And a blue-glass vial of Evening in Paris. No perfume I have
bought in the years since has seemed to me so exquisite, so full
of promise, as that purchase. It was bottled seduction, the kind

that led not to sinful dalliance but to those grandchildren with whom, on some impossibly remote occasion, my father might proudly dance.

Though I placed great faith in my cosmetics arsenal, I didn't neglect the intellectual approach. The *Woman's Home Companion* offered a booklet called "How to Rate Another Date": I sent away for my copy — fifteen cents plus a self-addressed envelope — and studied its contents eagerly. How strange its advice seemed — and how difficult! The popular girl must listen, not talk — yet she must also flatter. ("I think you're simply swell!" was one recommended formula.) Agreement with male opinions was essential. "When a young man expresses a view," the guide directed, "you should either repeat what he has said — 'Yes, I do think the League of Nations is a failure' — ask a question, or say, 'You are certainly right.' This is not dishonesty. This is tact." There was a chapter on "Ten Sure Ways to Please" that began with making goo-goo eyes and ended with the paralysing prescription, "Be amusing." After I read that, I borrowed from the public library a collection of jokes, copied out all that seemed possibly useful, indexed them by catchword and committed them to memory. To this day I can still recall those pitiful ploys. On *men*: "I can't get along with them — or without them." On *lovelight* (a most unlikely conversational cue): "Oh yes, I know about the lovelight that lies in your eyes — and lies, and lies, and *lies*." To the best of my recollection, I only once found occasion to show how amusing I could be. At a hockey game, someone remarked that the team's best player had been suspended for keeping alcohol in his locker. Now *alcohol* was one of the key words on my joke list. I fixed the speaker with a glassy goo-goo eye and ventured, "Well, you can preserve anything in alcohol — except dignity!" The boy stared. He did not ask me for a date.

I never once, in high school, had a real date. Sometimes I

attended class parties where I ended up making the popcorn or serving punch. But for the most part my social life was limited to all-girl affairs. In groups of three or four, we walked down-town Saturday afternoons and then, clutching bags of toffee or Spanish peanuts, sat through a complete double feature at the Capitol. Afterwards, we clustered around a table at Moore's Restaurant, and talked about boys. No one in my crowd had a boy-friend. We took turns, Friday night, giving "hen parties." On those occasions, we waltzed together, slow dances that conjured up visions of happier worlds, and played Monopoly. We also ate a lot. We exchanged jokes, the latest additions to a current cycle. One month the rage would be stories about a cretinous character called Little Alice; the next month Alice was out and the Little Moron was in. We speculated about sex but did not tell sex jokes; I suppose we were too nervous — or too ignorant. If we were feeling particularly bold we entertained ourselves making phone calls. Some of the girls knew fellows they could call just to kibitz, fool around with. That was exciting. My specialty was phoning tobacco stores to ask, "Have you got Prince Albert in the tin?" and then, in response to an affirmative, registering dismay. "Well, why don't you let him out?"

From all such kid stuff my sister Celia held herself serenely aloof. *She* spent Saturday afternoons shopping — not buying anything, but looking and pricing. She dressed carefully for these expeditions. I can still see her in the three-piece costume my mother sewed for her, a black and white checked suit worn with a red-lined cape. Swinging her red patent-leather bag, she clicked off to Eaton's French Room to inspect the latest imports and discuss possible orders. Often she came home with samples, scraps of fabric and lace. "Look," she would say, "I could have this georgette made up, with a shawl collar and flare skirt, for just under a hundred dollars. Oh, and they'll make a matching turban for ten." "On a hundred dollars," Mama would say, "I feed all of us for four months. I should only have a hundred dollars." Celia's elegant deceptions both shocked and thrilled me. To think that the French Room ladies took her seriously! But of course she looked right. Perhaps she was persuaded by her own fantasy.

Certainly Celia's experience with boys gave her reason to believe that anything was possible. Rich boys, poor boys, dullards and intellectuals pursued her. Sometimes she would ask me to brief her before a date with a literary suitor. "He's crazy about somebody called Shelley," she would say. "Give me the names of some poems." Or, "Do you know a good quotation?" Though she didn't go on to the university (Papa wept when he told her he hadn't the fifty dollars for first-year tuition) she never missed a university dance. During big party periods, like Christmas vacation, she often made two and three dates for one evening. "Well, I'm going out at eight," she would murmur into the receiver. "But I could have dinner with you." Or, "I should be back by midnight. If you park outside and wait, we could go for a spin." She kept a scrapbook, fascinating to me and my friends, in which each of her admirers occupied a double spread. There were photographs of the boy, as a rule passionately inscribed; invitations or dance programs of affairs he'd taken her to; notations as to what she'd worn on each occasion ("flocked net over red taffeta, really gorgeous") and — butterflies impaled on a pin — a few sample letters. Almost all were ardent. "You are the only one I could ever love," a young law student wrote. "You are my last thought at night, my first thought in the morning, and when I think of losing you the bottom drops out of everything."

Watching my sister leave, evenings, on the arm of yet another slave, I was overcome with sick jealousy. Oh, to be sought after. To *be loved*. I tried one crash diet after another, but no magical transformation occurred. By my last year of high school, I was resigned to not being "popular." I took it for granted, though, that I would attend the graduation dance. Didn't everyone? I remembered the progressive dinner party my sister's crowd had held on graduation night — bunches of girls like spring flowers rustling petals in our small bedroom, their voices rising in a litany of praise and self-deprecation. "You look fabulous!" "I look awful! But that green — I love that green on you!" Girls straightening the seams of silk stockings, girls dabbing perfume behind ears, girls arching proudly toward the mirror, licking a spit curl so it lay flat against a flushed cheek. And, just outside, the boys, with gleaming hair slicked back or waved in high full pompadours, slapping each other on the back and exchanging manly jokes. After the first course (we served fruit cocktail, strawberries in a melon basket topped with whipped cream) the whole group piled into cars and drove gaily off to the next house. I had a last glimpse of Celia in the rumble seat between two boys, chin lifted, eyes bright.

Progressive dinner parties were no longer the rage by 1938. That year the big thing was treasure hunts. As early as April, I heard whispers of graduation parties being arranged. In May, the school put up a Who's-Going-With-Who poster. I hurried past it mornings on my way to class, but after four, when no one was around, I'd study the list. The best girls — and boys — were taken early. Naturally. Some Jewish boys had invited gentile girls. How unfair. There weren't enough Jewish boys to go around in any event. I wondered if Mama would let me go with a gentile. By the end of May Sarah and Ruth, my best friends, had been invited. There were still — well, quite a few boys left. I didn't protest when Mama said it was time to start thinking what I would wear. Buying a dress had the quality of a magical act: if I had the gown, I would go to the ball.

We shopped for my first evening dress not at a retail store

but at a wholesale garment factory. There was no proper try-on room; I held the gown against my navy-serge school tunic, squinting into a narrow mirror while an impatient stockman said things like, "A size 12 is definitely too small. You need a 14." I had hoped for a touch of wickedness — Celia had gowns with low-cut sweetheart necklines and one with a back slit — but Mama chose pink chiffon trimmed with palest blue. "This one, with the puff sleeve jacket," she said, "is your type. So modest."

I had good reason to be modest. Two weeks before the dance, I still hadn't been asked. Our household continued as usual. No one seemed aware of my desperate circumstances. I tried talking to Celia. She was applying scarlet fingernail polish that day, painting each nail with long sure strokes, then holding out her hand, fingers spread, to study the effect. "No problem," she said. "There's a list of boys who've already asked somebody, right? So you take out your yearbook, you cross out those names, pick who you want from the ones that are left. And you vamp that one."

"How do I do it? I mean, vamp somebody?"

She blew delicately on her nails. "You can drive a fellow crazy just by looking. Wink at him — you know, just a flutter. Cross your legs high, above the knee, like this, and swing one ankle. Open your mouth wide when you laugh." (Celia's teeth were perfect Chiclets.) "Boys like a girl who's cute and snappy." She looked over her shoulder at an imagined admirer, demonstrating. "See you later, alligator. See you Samoa."

Though I hadn't wanted to worry Mama — she had enough on her mind with business worries — I had at last to confide in her. If she had any misgivings, she didn't show them. "You ask somebody," she said. "Somebody not from your school." She thought a minute. "I know. Rose's boy, Marty — a university student, a *mensch*, not one of these high-school kids don't know what's good for them."

"I hardly know Marty Simons," I ventured.

"Don't know him? Didn't you play together at the beach before you could walk almost? His sister isn't on your bowling team? I know Rose since she's a girl. Marty is *perfect*."

So I phoned Marty Simons. Remembering Celia's advice, I made a try at cuteness. "Marty? Guess who this is." Once he began guessing — Clara, Susan, Annette, Frema, Lucy — I realized my mistake. "Wrong again," I said at last. "It's Fredelle." "Fredelle *Bruser*?" There was no mistaking his astonishment. "Just a minute," he said. "I'll call my sister." "No, no, don't do that. I mean — you're the one I wanted to talk to. I thought — I've been wondering…well, would you like to come to my graduation dance? With me, I mean?"

"No," Marty said. "I wouldn't."

The reply came so quickly, so naturally and absolutely, that I was stunned. Maybe he was too. An instant later he recovered himself. "Look," he said. "I'm sorry. I haven't got a suit."

I suppose I must have said ThankyouverymuchI'msorryto havebotheredyou. I ran upstairs, took out my schoolbag and hurled myself at my English. We had a poem to memorize — "Sailing to Byzantium." It made no sense at all. "The young in one another's arms, birds in the trees — Those dying genera-tions — at their song…." Why should the happy young be described as *dying*? Celia was playing the radio much too loud. "Oh the music goes round and round, Oh Oh, Oh Oh, Oh Oh and it comes out *HERE*." My head ached. Mama called, "Telephone." It was Marty. "I'll take you," he said in a throttled voice. "My mother is buying me a suit."

All that week my friends and I talked graduation. What are you wearing? Has he said anything about *after* the dance? And flowers — what have you decided on? Sarah was getting a wristlet of red roses, Ruth wanted a corsage. "I think I'll ask for one white gardenia to pin in my hair," I said. "But I'm not sure. Marty hasn't called about flowers yet." "Oh, you're a lucky cheese," Ruth said. "A *university* student. Our dates will look like babies."

Marty phoned again the day before graduation. "Listen," he said. "I've been thinking. Your dance is at the Royal Alex. I live just two blocks from there, and you're at the other end of town. So it really doesn't make sense for me to go all the way down Portage and pick you up." He spoke rapidly. I got the feeling he had rehearsed this speech — also that his mother, my mother's good friend Rose, was out of earshot. "So I'm getting someone who lives near you to pick you up. I'll meet you at the dance."

I knew the suggestion was outrageous. No self-respecting girl....I thought of Mama, happy in the success of her plan — and of the way I'd implied, at school, that Marty had invited *me*. ("Yes, with Marty Simons. Oh, it's an old thing. He's been in the picture, but I wasn't too keen....") I scarcely hesitated. "O.K.," I said. "Fine. Who did you say is picking me up?"

I don't know whether it was malice that made Marty choose Phil Bokofsky. Probably not. Phil lived near me, he would obviously not have a date for the dance, and he was in no position to turn down a chance to earn, say, fifty cents. Phil's social standing was worse, even, than mine. His father was a junk dealer, he had terrible acne, he was a math brain mute on all subjects not connected with higher calculus. In short, he was universally regarded as a *schmo*. To be seen getting out of a taxi with Phil Bokofsky!

"That's Marty, I can tell. You're blushing," Mama said as I hung up.

"Mmmm," I said. "Last-minute arrangements."

Next day our whole household buzzed with activity. Mama

pressed my gown and petticoat for the third time, and took a snapshot of me standing by the fireplace. I barely managed to slip out during the afternoon to buy my gardenia. Even Celia, usually so lofty, took an interest. "Your first real date," she said. "And just think, this is only the *beginning*." For the new life, she styled my hair, combing it with sugar syrup and then pasting it on top of my head in fat little curls. "Put a drop of perfume between your bosoms," she told me. "Hum something romantic in his ear in the cab coming home. Don't let him kiss you the first time. Keep him guessing." When I told her I was meeting Marty on the street to save his coming up to our apartment, Celia moaned, "Gosh, how *klutzy!*" but Mama said, "Very sensible. Otherwise the taxi meter goes the whole time for nothing."

Phil Bokofsky appeared right on time. He wore a baseball cap and a windbreaker. "Well," he said, "I guess we want the North Main streetcar." I walked a few steps ahead of him, holding up my pink chiffon skirt and saying "Transfer, please" to the trolley conductor as if ordering a coach to Buckingham Palace. Phil made a few small attempts at conversation; I froze him out. Having someone to reject, maybe hurt, was oddly pleasurable. "Please sit," I said as the car swung past the Royal Alex. "I don't need your help getting off."

It had occurred to me more than once that Marty might not show but he was there, outside the hotel, waiting. As we entered the ballroom an usher handed me a dance program, white crinkly vellum with silver fan decorations and a silver tassel. There were lines for twelve dance partners — six before intermission, six after. Marty took the program and signed twice — No. 1, No. 12. "I'll be around," he said as he moved off into the crowd. "Have to see a man about a dog."

I never filled those ten blanks on my program, not one. Early in the evening girls rushed up with their escorts and then, when they saw no exchange of partners was possible, rushed off again. I spent a lot of time in the ladies' room, pinning up my shellacked curls and applying more rouge — occasionally adding another generous dab of Evening in Paris. Mostly I sat in one of the straight-backed chairs that lined the ballroom, watching the dancers with what I hoped was an appropriately casual air. Managing smiles was tricky. Every time a boy appeared to be heading in my direction I focused my smile ever so slightly, as if turning a flashlight on high beam; then, when I realized my mistake (it was the girl next to me he wanted), letting the smile melt at the edges again, growing soft and fuzzy and general to embrace the whole whirling room. My first dance with Marty was almost completely silent. Once he said, "*I'm* supposed to lead. You *follow*." But when he came to collect me for dance number twelve he was distinctly more cheerful. "Hey," he said, "we're invited to a party and it sounds like fun. Gladys Albert's. Know her?"

Know her? Everybody at Gordon Bell knew Gladys Albert — a pert, skinny, sexy blonde *shiksa* who wore her gym tunic pulled tightly in at the waist and was said to be fast. It was even rumoured that Gladdie had gone the limit. A party at her house would be something to tell the girls about. Maybe Marty and I would get along better there.

But in the car after the dance, Marty sat up front with Gladys. I was squeezed into the back with a group of noisy strangers who smelled of something stronger than graduation punch. The party itself was utterly unlike the few mixed parties I'd attended, sedate affairs where boys and girls played guessing games or a titillating round of Spin the Bottle. Gladys's parents were nowhere in evidence. Beer had been set out in the kitchen, and someone said there was "hard stuff" in the icebox. The Victrola played at top volume, songs you couldn't possibly waltz or polka to. Most of the kids were jitterbugging; I didn't know how. At one point Gladdie lifted her skirts so high you could see her rolled garters and thin white thighs and did a comic song-and-dance routine to "Down In The Meadow In An Iddy Biddy Poo, There Were Three Little Fiddies And A Momma Fiddie *Too*." No one paid the slightest attention to me. After the lights went out in the living-room people drifted off. I retreated to the brightly lit kitchen and read the *Free Press Cooking School Cookbook*, the only reading matter around. Eventually Marty would have to collect me and take me home. But at half past midnight there was no sign of him − and the North Main streetcars stopped running at one. I moved through the dark rooms, stumbling and bumping into couples.

Marty was in the porch hammock with Gladys. At first he didn't hear me. I had to touch his shoulder. "Marty," I said, "I'm afraid I really have to go home now." He sighed heavily − or was that Gladys? Then, half sitting up in the hammock, he pushed back his hair and said, "Oh, well. So long." "Thank you for taking me," I said. "I had a nice time." I ran down the steps and called into the darkness. "See you later, alligator. See you Samoa."

The streetcars had stopped running, which meant a four-mile walk. I didn't mind. The warm June night was sweet with lilac and honeysuckle. A little rain had fallen earlier in the evening; each upturned leaf sparkled with drops like diamonds, and the lilac heads hung heavy as grapes. I pulled off my gardenia − its petals browned now, the scent sickly, rotted, poisonous − and tossed it into a gutter. I ran my fingers through my hair and released the rigid curls. I took off my shoes and stockings too. The streets were deserted. There was no-one to wonder at a sixteen-year old girl walking barefoot down Portage Avenue in her graduation gown. By the time I reached home, I was over being furious with Marty. "The salmon-falls, the mackerel-crowded seas...." I knew what that meant, all right.

The light was still on in our living room. Celia and a new young man sprang apart as I entered. "Oh — *Delsie!*" Celia said. (That year she called herself Cele and me Del.) "This is my kid sister. She's been out on a big date. Marty's a frat man, isn't he, Del?" She rose — "Let me just make with the lipstick" — and the boy turned to me. "Well," he said, "I'd never take you two for sisters."

"So I've been told," I said. "We're totally different."

"Oh, I wouldn't say that." He looked past me, down the hall after Celia. "I'll bet you're going to turn into a heartbreaker like your big sister."

"I'm never going to be like her," I said. "It would be silly to try."

Months after my high-school graduation, Celia moved to Toronto, where she worked a few years in the *Star*'s classified ads department. It was her job to review records of deaths occurring within the previous decade, then telephone survivors to solicit ads for memorial verses. Since she was fluent on the phone and not easily embarrassed she did well at this. In her central social interest she proved less successful. Meeting men in a strange city proved difficult, and the men she met were often not serious (meaning, not ready to propose marriage). I, meanwhile, was realizing the family dream. In the fall of 1938, just turned sixteen, I entered the University of Manitoba with a full scholarship and hopes of glory.

A
Perfectly
Beautiful
Devastation

⋄—◇—⋄

I remember the footsteps — rapid, brisk, emphatic. Someone in the English Department office, where I stood talking to professors at the beginning of my last academic year in Winnipeg, said, "Maynard. Typical small man's walk," and before I had time to reflect on the tone of that comment, Max Maynard strode into my life. Neither then nor afterwards did he strike me as a small man. Short, yes. Compact and neat of build, moving with a muscular grace. Bones and eyes. High cheekbones, a formidable square jaw, cleft chin, jug ears. English blue eyes, deep set, exophthalmic. Straw-coloured hair, slightly receding from a high forehead. Upper lip so thin as to be almost invisible, lower lip sensuously full. His smile — closed mouth, to hide bad teeth — seemed guarded and faintly ironic. His dress, superficially conservative, had a faintly theatrical air. On that crisp fall day, when sensible Manitobans buttoned up their overcoats, he wore a raincoat of pale parachute silk; he had

turned down the brim of his hat all the way round. ("To catch
bird droppings," he said when I once asked him why.) In a
world of professorial three-piece suits, he wore loose heathery
tweeds (the pant legs unpressed, stove pipes) with cable-knit
sweater-vests and argyle socks. In my elementary world view,
he fitted no obvious category. Country, city? Sophisticated,
naïve? Athletic, intellectual? When he spoke, I recognized him.
This was an *artist*.

One man in his time plays many parts. Max had perfected
certain well-developed roles. There was the Englishman who
carried a walking stick, spoke with exquisite clarity and modu-
lation, and claimed kinship with the noble Shrewsburys. There
was the cowboy, a role based on the summer spent, during his
early twenties, on an Alberta ranch. There was the Bloomsbury
Group devotee; he read those incestuous biographies (Harold
Nicolson, Lytton Strachey, Virginia and Leonard Woolf, Clive
Bell) as avidly as more pedestrian spirits follow the exploits of
movie actors and sports heroes. There was the ex-Communist,
a small but dramatic part played for special audiences, on the
basis of what appears to have been attendance at a single party
meeting. (Sometimes, when carried away, he claimed to have
been part of a Communist cell, and so in a strong position to
expose Soviet iniquities.) There was the professor, an autocrat
who tolerated no latecomers to class, and who carried to The
Great Unread the doctrines of Dante, Bertrand Russell and
Alexander Pope. There was the lover. This was a major role,
played with a cast of hundreds, featuring naked exploits on a
bearskin rug before a blazing fire, and assorted cavortings in
daisy fields.

All these were aspects of the man. *Artist* was the core and,
though elaborated often with dramatic flourishes, absolutely
authentic. He had an educated ear, an infallible eye. Never
without a well-sharpened pencil, he sketched constantly, with

absorption, on the three-by-five cards he carried in his breast pocket, and at the end of his life, in a nursing home, on paper placemats. While colleagues droned on at English Department meetings, debating course calendars and curricula, Max drew dream landscapes and strange imaginary figures. On country walks, he would stop with a kind of ecstasy before a prospect where I saw only tree stumps or an abandoned privy. Once in Winnipeg, he hurried me outside in subzero weather — "Come and see, quick!" When I looked about, puzzled, he pointed to the telephone wires. "In this light…those angles…And do you hear the *thrum*? My God!"

His feeling about Art — unabashed capital — had a religious quality. In our courting days, fascinated by his skill, I often asked him to draw. Draw a grain elevator, a kitten with a ball, an Indian church, a unicorn. One day, with a kind of virginal prurience, I proposed that he draw a man and woman making love. He produced a quick explicit sketch. Then he stared at his work, appalled, and ripped the paper to pieces. "I have *never* done such a thing before," he said. It was as if a priest were to confess that for supper he had eaten communion wafers with butter and jam, washed down with a draught of sacramental wine.

When, at twenty, I met Max Maynard, I had been waiting for about fifteen years to fall in love. If that seems an exaggeration — well, I came from a world in which many concerns were exaggerated. Marrying well — finding, not a rich or successful man, but an intelligent *good* one — had always occupied an important place in family talk. I can never remember a time when I didn't fear that in this crucial area I might disappoint. "If no-one ever marries me — And I don't see why they should…" I studied the illustration for that poem in our *Book of Knowledge*, wondering whether the little girl shown was even less marketable than I. About my own marriage appeal I entertained profound doubts. Watching my mother bent nights over embroidery for my hope chest, I contemplated the mortifying possibility that hopes might fade as linens accumulated. Would I be left, at the end, that most pitiable of creatures, an old maid, alone with my towels and tablecloths? I saw my pretty sister pursued by boys. I studied photos of my mother in the days when she was the toast of Winnipeg. Most inflaming of all, I read and reread my father's love letters, written over a seven-year period during which my mother danced in the city while, from a Saskatchewan village, he pressed his suit. (The old-fashioned phrase seems right.) "I just got your letter, my sweet beloved girl, and my heart is beating wildly. Oh you dear soul, you are so precious, so lovely. You are a wonder, I owe you my very life." Sunday afternoons, throughout my childhood, I would take out the chocolate boxes, ribbon-bound, which held my father's letters. Though I came to know their contents well — the reflections on jealousy, family ties, Jewishness, marriage, loneliness — familiarity never dulled the impact of pure passionate emotion. Seventy years after its composition, I read a letter and hold my father's heart. "I miss your so-dear-to-me presence. I think of you and my heart is pressing more and more, there is a choking ticklish feeling in my throat and tears, hot tears, way down my cheeks are rolling. Please, my precious Ronachka, don't laugh at me. I can't help it, I love you so…." If I wept over those letters as a child, that was not just reliving my father's agony. It was fear — the fear that no one would ever love *me* with such passion, purity and style.

At university, I went alone to dances where I smiled with desperate gaiety at the whirling couples. My social calendar was filled mostly with all-girl events or meetings with boys who wanted to copy my English noteş. And then Max Maynard appeared. Had I set out to invent an ideal lover, a man of my dreams, I could hardly have done better. A university professor, handsome but in an unconventional way. He was dramatic, vital, sophisticated, charming, knowledgeable, witty, magically eloquent and, like my father, a painter. That he was much older than I seemed not initially a problem. I never got on well with boys my age. As for his being gentile — that gave me pause, to be sure. In my family, mixed marriage was the fate worse than death. Also, for that reason, exciting.

Our strange romance began with a professional arrangement. Max had come from British Columbia to the University of Manitoba English Department as a last-minute replacement, not formally qualified but known to the department head as a talented man. Knowing something of his history with women, the head took pains to provide, as assistant essay-reader, a student surely impervious to seduction. That's how I became Max Maynard's reader. How I laboured over that first batch of essays! Correcting, elaborating, commenting in the margins, I made of every marked paper a message to the instructor: *Look at me*. A few days after I'd turned in the papers, Professor Maynard stopped me in the corridor. "You're a splendid reader, Miss Bruser. But I'm afraid you've spent far too much time on these essays. You mustn't trouble yourself with tracing plagiarisms." "I didn't *trace* them," I said. "I *recognized* sources." "But you couldn't, without consulting texts, know that a paragraph had been taken from page 232 of Legouis and Cazamian." I explained that I had a freak ability to visualize pages. "My god, what a treasure you are," Max said. "I've been waiting for someone like you all my life. Look — why don't you have dinner with me this evening, and I'll give you the next batch of papers then?"

Over roast beef at the Fort Garry Hotel, he talked about a world to me incredibly rich and exotic: missionary parents, a childhood in India and then in Tunbridge Wells, adolescent adventures in the wilds of the Okanagan, a strange conflicted friendship-apprenticeship with the painter Emily Carr. There were amused, self-deprecating references to love affairs. When I asked his age, he said, "Actually, I don't know. I've no birth certificate, and my parents could never agree on the year of my birth." Coming from a small close Jewish family, I found this too exotic. Imagine a family so large, and parents so remote, so other-directed, that they couldn't be sure of their child's age. I walked back to the university with him in a trance. On his office desk, a blue porcelain plate held a mysterious fruit and a note: "A persimmon for Fredelka." He fed me the ripe fruit with a silver spoon, wiped the juice that ran down my chin with a linen handkerchief — then turned out the lights and embraced me.

I had kissed before, on doorsteps at the end of decorous evenings, the kiss preceded by a request for permission and followed by a brisk, "Thank you, I had a very nice time." This was different. Amazed, alarmed, ecstatic, aroused, hopeful, already terrified at the possibility of loss, now I understood my father. "Dear soul," he had written, sick with love, "how could I ever get along without you? You are so dear to me, I feel my heart expand every time I think of you. I ache, I feel like dancing. I am beyond the ability of expressing all I think and feel, my thoughts are one big entanglement, no start and no end to it."

And so we began. On one level, my life continued as before: library, classes, studying, writing papers. I scarcely broke stride in my pursuit of academic success. But with Max beside me, everything changed. He took me for walks in deep blue snow and showed me a city I had never seen, exulting in the black dawns of prairie winter, the champagne cold. He introduced me to French impressionists, to the Group of Seven. He strode through the Winnipeg Art Gallery, devastating the fake

Rembrandts and raging against the absence of Canadian paint-
ers. He played Mozart's horn concertos on an ancient phonograph. He took me to parties where the guests drank Manhattans
and spoke French. He read aloud from the mystical *Cloud of
Unknowing*, his own copy, transcribed by hand. He invited me
to his lectures, where students accustomed to aged academics
reading lives of the poets from yellowed notes sat dazzled by
his eloquence and iconoclasm, his brilliant blackboard drawings. (I remember him facing the class and describing on the
board behind him, with casual hand, an absolutely perfect
circle.) He sang, in a lovely rich baritone, songs of love.

> Here am I, here am I, and I'll stay here till I die,
> I've come for you, I'll get you too.
> Here am I, here am I, and you'll know the reason why,
> I've come for you, I'll get you too.
> Your father shakes his heavy stick at me, I don't know why.

He composed light verse for all occasions. On Valentine's Day,
when more prosaic lovers offered cards or chocolates, he brought
me a poem:

> *Not all the loveliest words will go*
> *In rhyme with "dear Fredelle,"*
> *But all the fondest thoughts I know*
> *Are subject to that spell.*
> *Like honey dripping from the comb*
> *In streams of amorous sweet they come*
> *As you can read below.*
>
> *My angel cake, my keg of rum,*
> *My quince, my pear, my sugar plum,*
> *My lollipop, my macaroon,*
> *My silver sky, my tender moon,*

My lily flower, my luscious peach,
My pretty octopus, my leech,
My swordfish whose sharp pointed dart
Runs precious panic through my heart,
My biblio-vandal whose least look
Rips all the pages of my book,
My dazzling jewel by whose glare
The very sun is in despair,
My arching sky, my curving earth,
My death, my life, my second birth,
My sun-warmed field, my shady tree,
My time and my eternity.
My brown-eyed squirrel, my sweet dove,
My dearest dear, my honey love,
My cigarette, my nicotine,
My coffee, tea and whole cuisine,
My loaf of bread, my jug of wine —

All this and more, sweet valentine.

Sometimes, out of the blue, no occasion and no reason, there would be a telegram, a single line, perhaps, from Synge's *Playboy of the Western World*: "I've seen none the likes of you all the long years I've been walking the world. There's the light of seven heavens in your eyes alone."

Years later, one of our daughters, in a black moment, asked, "How *could* you have married him?" I said, "How could I not?" My children never knew the man I married. He wrote once, recalling our beginnings: "What a time that was! Neither of us caring about anything except the strange delight of it all, yet knowing at the back of our minds that sooner or later we would have to face a regiment of fantastic difficulties. I would follow the same course again even if I knew it would end in grief. And you? Oh, I think you would too!"

Almost from the start it was understood between us that we wished to be together for life. Three months after we met, Max asked me to marry him, commemorating the occasion of the proposal in a pencil portrait. Looking at that portrait now — "Vlassie's Grill, November 25, 1942" — I am struck by the gravity of the young girl who, chin in hand, refuses to say yes or no and contemplates…the cup of coffee? the prospect of telling her parents she loved a *goy*? I had grown up with tales of pogroms, the dangers and barbarism of the non-Jewish world. One of the few "popular" books in my father's library was *I Married a Gentile*, the horror story of a husband who drinks, gambles and spits at his wife the dread epithet, *dirty Jew*. I had heard of Jewish women cast out for marrying *goyim*; their families sat *shiva* in mourning for a daughter lost. My own parents, I knew, would never abandon me. But how could I cause them such grief and disappointment? Would the shock of a mixed match kill my mother? Attempts to tell my parents how I felt about Max inevitably ended in frenzy and hysteria, and in my wretched promises to try and find a Nice Jewish Boy.

At twenty, I had still not truly separated from my parents. It was Max who first obliged me to confront the extent of my inappropriate dependence. When I expressed the fear that even half a century of married happiness would not convince my mother and father to accept a gentile son-in-law, he said, "Darling, they won't live for fifty years. It seems to me sometimes that you think of them as if you were still a little girl. If you are going to develop, it simply has to be out and away from the old roots." That I was able in any degree to cut those roots is evidence of his persuasiveness and power. Because *gentile* was not, it emerged, the only difficulty. "Maynard says he's *thirty-*

six?" a fellow student scoffed. "Forty if he's a day. Look at the skin on his hands." The worst blow descended when I told a friend I was going to marry Max Maynard. "He has a wife already," she said. I denied this fiercely. She shrugged. "Ask anybody who's been around him when he gets potted. Her name is Evelyn."

I ran to Max. "Darling," he said, "I didn't want to worry you with this. It's true I'm legally married — but I've been separated for years. I'm getting a divorce." The marriage? A kind of accident: he'd been seeing this pleasant young woman — nothing serious — when one day she burst into tears. "I've done a terrible thing. I've told Daddy we're engaged." What could he do? A man of honour, and she so pathetic....So they married, and Daddy (who owned a railroad) bought them a house, a car, a summer cottage....Well, naturally he hated being a kept man, he began to have affairs and the whole thing fell apart.

This account, curiously enough, I found reassuring. I was too inexperienced to know that once a man falls out of love he has trouble remembering the original passion. And though I doubted many things, most of all the possibility of our marrying and living happily ever after, I never doubted that I was truly, deeply loved.

Max and I had just ten months in the same city — my final year at the University of Manitoba. Though I have always said we knew each other for six years before we married, the reality was different and more complicated. At the end of our first year, I left Winnipeg to take up a scholarship at the University of Toronto. This had, before Max, been part of my plan for pursuing a Ph.D.; now I had the additional impetus of a promise to my parents that I would try to find an acceptable suitor. Max professed to honour this last commitment, but in fact his continuing long-distance pursuit made any new alliance unlikely. He wrote almost daily. In the Christmas and Easter holidays he

joined me, first in Toronto and then in Cambridge, Massachusetts. Over the entire course of our long courtship, we probably
didn't spend the equivalent of three months together, and
certainly we never lived together. The daily realities of his life I
didn't know and didn't think about. I loved a fantasy figure, my
creation as much as his — a composite of extravagant gestures,
apt quotation, artistry, differentness and rare eloquence. At
university during the academic year, and when I was home
with my parents every summer, he followed me with protestations of undying devotion. "What spells have you cast over me,
Fredelka, that I'm so enslaved?" he wrote. "Did anyone ever
love before, I ask myself? I want you more than I've ever wanted
anything in the world. I love the look of you, the feel of you, the
scent of your hair, the way you walk…I love to distraction the
sweet playful pilgrim soul of you." If, occasionally, alarmed by
such worship, I reminded him of my faults, he responded with
an acceptance so total that I felt, in the midst of danger, safe.
"I don't want a prim little border of forget-me-nots and daisies.
I *like* the prickly Fredelkian thistles that grow up around the
rose bushes. I want *you* — dominating, selfish, vain, whatever.
My malady is quite incurable. If ever I lose you, I hope one part
of me will still be able to bless God for having provided me
with such a perfectly beautiful devastation. Whatever happens
I could never regret having loved you. There could never be
anything like it again."

I was no less enslaved than he. Not, I think, that my head
was turned, though the extravagance of Max's courtship would
have unsettled soberer heads than mine. He turned my *heart*,
by giving me that rarest of all gifts, a vision of my best, my
possible self. I was used to being admired as a top student, a
clever girl; like any prizewinner, I feared I might be valued for
my ability to win prizes. This was the first man to make me feel
lovable in myself. "You have been too inclined to credit your

elegant memory with things that really belong to your perfectly
splendid understanding," he wrote. "You say I idealize you. Not
at all. I merely see what's there…I might discover things in you
I don't like at all. But the total effect — I love that so much that
life without you seems no life at all. I shall always love the kind
of human being that you are, and are likely to become." I
thought myself plain, overweight; he wrote, "to me you seem
ineffably beautiful." I saw my Jewishness as an obstacle, he
celebrated it as an enrichment of our relationship. When I
agonized over possible confusion and misery in the offspring of
mixed marriages, he fantasized about the remarkable progeny
we might expect, "with three thousand years of good Old
Testament rootage on one side and an exciting vein of New
Testament-Aryan-barbarian unpredictableness on the other." I
had grown up with absolute, unexamined beliefs about Truth,
Duty, Filial Devotion, Achievement. Max excited me with visions
of complexity. "The truth," he used to say, "is for those who
deserve it." Duty? "Seems to me we have to be self-willed to be
anything at all." On family ties he was uncompromising. "You
should recognize that growing up, developing, inevitably means
losing one's parents." He celebrated nonconformity and shook
my reverence for the academic world. "Christ, what a dull lot!
A conspicuous absence of anything breezy and spontaneous.
No solecisms, no 'unsound' opinions." Most astonishing of all,
he questioned the pursuit of academic glory. "We hear too
much about achievement and not enough about overstrained
ambition," he wrote when I was studying for final exams.
"You've never known failure, so you think it must be the end. I
suggest that you try to get rid of your fear by substituting
another ambition — a better and more human one — and that
is an ideal of composure based upon a purer concept of values."
I poured out in letters my fears, my anxieties, my difficulties
personal and scholastic. He responded — the French an

additional grace: "*Il faut se promener dans le monde avec humeur et calme.*"

When, after our first year together, I told my parents I loved Max Maynard, my father said, "Can you love a stranger?" How could I explain that all other men, gentiles and Jews, had been strangers to me? Only this man knew the country of my imagination. I understand now that there are many ways of loving, many bonds. What held me to Max went beyond physical attraction and compatibility, and certainly beyond the fact that he was such *fun*. He was my teacher. He found me a naïve young girl, bright and eager but essentially ignorant, with a limited, conventional world view. Like Annie Sullivan with the young Helen Keller, blind and deaf, he took my hand and spelled into it. Max projected a vision of art and beauty and the splendour of human possibility. That he located me at the centre of that vision seemed to me an incredible, an unlooked-for benediction.

We were, to be sure, an odd pair, Max and I, sufficiently unlike to give credence to the Platonic fantasy of love as two incompletes combining to make a whole. A much-loved child who had reined in all vagrant impulse to ensure the continuance of love, I was fascinated by Max's wildness. Bad boy, good girl. My mother had trained me to please, to accommodate, to keep promises and repress or deny anger. Along came this wilful, self-centred, feckless, raging spirit, a man who accepted no limits. I suppose Max expressed for me aspects of my nature (anyone's nature) which I had never dared reveal. Imagine saying to a fellow painter at the opening of his show: "Frankly, I feel something close to disgust. This is all frothy confection — and so vulgarly self-assured, pretentious, vain!" Imagine throwing a glass at a dinner party and then stalking out into the night. Imagine spending hundreds of dollars on a ticket from Winnipeg to Victoria and returning after one day. ("I found the place oppressive.") Imagine, imagine, a university professor, weary of marking student themes, pitching the whole bundle into the trash. Max was my fantasy life. When I try to imagine what I represented to him, I come up with an unflattering conclusion. Though he may have written eloquently of my beauty and charm, what really fascinated him, I think, was my discipline and doggedness. The fact that I studied eighteen hours a day at the university and committed an entire novel, *Silas Marner*, to memory for a final exam — these dubious accomplishments thrilled him. (After thirty years, Max would still introduce me as the prize student who won all the medals, one hundred in every subject.) He didn't deliberately choose me to keep him on track; he was without calculation. But instinct must have told him that he needed my severity almost as much as he feared it.

Attracted initially by the electricity of opposites, Max and I were held together by more complex forces. On the surface were certain straightforward exchanges. I offered intellectual companionship, a strong practical sense which presumably would enable me to run a household, easy gaiety. He, much older, would provide the benefit of his greater experience and knowledge; he was socially adept in ways that I was not; he would bring grace and freedom to my rigidly disciplined life. He did not wish to teach but conceded that, as head of a family, he would need a source of income more reliable than painting. These things we talked about.

Beneath this open agreement, what family therapists call the secret contract exerted its gravitational pull. The first level of our secret contract, not verbalized but conscious, involved private fantasies. Though I scarcely admitted it to myself, I saw Max as magically conferring upon me two qualities I had always coveted: original artistic gifts and Anglo-Saxon accepta-bility. He, aware of his own volatile nature, his reluctance to pursue difficult tasks, must have felt my scholarly diligence and persistence would be useful to him. If he could marry a Ph.D., he did not need to earn one.

So far, at least, the contract might have worked. For a while it did. Max could not make me an artist, but he both taught and inspired. He could not make me an Englishwoman, but he gave me his name and his impeccable WASP credentials. I in turn provided a solid base for what had been a recklessly bohemian existence. Beneath these tidy exchanges moved darker forces.

What we ultimately wanted of each other, I now see, was most fearfully complicated, unacknowledged and therefore, dangerous. Unsure of my appeal as a woman, I sought the confirmation of Max's sexual attractiveness. Unsure of myself as a person, I sought support. Both needs contained built-in contradictions. As evidence that I had won a desirable man, I at first enjoyed Max's flirtations; later, I was infuriated by them. The vision of Max as someone to lean on dissipated swiftly; he could scarcely support himself. In any case, nothing in my family experience had prepared me for a leaning role. My mother — steel hand in velvet glove — dominated my father; without knowing, I looked for a man I could dominate.

Max's deepest, unconscious needs were no doubt as convoluted as mine. He had grown up in the brooding presence of a powerful mother who alternately indulged and punished him. So what he learned, in the family which is every human's first learning place, was how to evoke from a woman these two antithetical responses. I think he was drawn to me in part by memories of the all-giving, all-devouring mother. By his behaviour, charm alternating with drunken furies, he trained me to play the part.

The story of Max's family emerged gradually in the years after we met; it was, in fact, part of his stock in trade as raconteur.

Whether these tales were embroidered or spun out of whole cloth doesn't much matter; they powerfully projected his vision of himself.

Tunbridge Wells, where three maiden aunts presided over the tea trolley, and British India, where his parents laboured in the Lord's vineyard — these became his reality. The scenes of this private drama were mostly static, inhabited by one-dimensional characters. Aunt Nell, Aunt Marian and Aunt Ann sat, composed and genteel, among the antimacassars and hand-painted china. Across the water, separately at first, Thomas Henry Maynard and Eliza Teague set out under the Salvation Army banner to save souls. In a climax as stirring as Sir Philip Sidney at Zutphen or Sydney Carton ascending the guillotine, Thomas Henry finds Eliza dying (malaria? cholera? the affliction changed from story to story), nurses her back to health, marries her and founds a mission station in the remote hills around Solipurnam. They rescue hundreds of famine orphans and convert them to the faith. (By now they have abandoned the Army to embrace a more rigorous and primitive Christianity.) The children are born: Theodore, a philosopher; Frank, the family's active spirit, later to die in combat during World War I; Grace, a gentle beauty; Norman, steady and practical; Basil, a spirit of angelic sweetness; Max; and Joyce, a tough, independent, feisty diabetic destined for death at an early age. Thomas Henry moves his family to Victoria, British Columbia, then returns to India. Periodically he reappears to oversee the brood's spiritual welfare; on one such visit, he adopts the three orphaned children of a church member, leaving his wife to care for them.

Max's family stories had mostly a curious preserved-in-amber quality. Listening, I used to feel that something had happened, all right, years ago, something that powerfully affected a small boy. But precisely because the event was so laden with emotion, he had worked it over, made it manageable by shaping it into an agreeable fiction. From the mostly theatrical episodes, two stand out. One is a memory of his sister Joyce, at eight or nine, running and falling on soft grass. She struggles to her feet and holds up one hand in a gesture of appeal: she has impaled herself on a slender steel crochet hook, its point now embedded in the palm's soft flesh. "Pull it out, laddie, pull it out!" He makes a few frantic, terrified tries; each attempt drives the hook in deeper. "Not that way!" Joyce screams. "I'll do it myself." As the boy watches, she pushes the hook *through* her hand.

The other memory is of his first paintbox, at the age of ten. He had known for years that he wanted to paint, but had never before dared ask for materials. The brushes and colours obsessed him to the point of recklessness. He painted, he read. And so he forgot or ignored a primary household rule, the sacredness of the Sabbath. Someone — he thought his brother Norman — saw him with Ruskin's *Stones of Venice* on a Sunday and reported. Thomas Henry was in residence that year. He summoned the boy to his study. "Max," he said, "I am told that you have been reading secular material on the Lord's day. Can this be true?" True. "Bring me your paints, Max." Not quite comprehending what his father had in mind, he complied. Mr Maynard put the box in his desk drawer and slammed it shut. "For one whole year, Max, you will not paint."

Other, later stories of parental blindness or harshness trace the progress of his defection from the family faith. The Plymouth Brethren forbade virtually all activities not specifically directed towards worship. Defying the proscription against theatre, Max took part in high-school plays. His mother maintained stony silence on the subject of this transgression; after her death, he found among her papers a box of press clippings reporting his triumph as Brutus in *Julius Caesar*.

What did Max feel for this austere, controlling mother? To the end of his life, Max spoke of her — of both parents — with awe. "My parents gave me a sense of what a really high reach meant in life," he told me. "They were moved by intense religious conviction; my reach has been different, but equally intense. They gave me too a powerful sense of the contradictions of human nature, of man's incorrigible imperfection, the vast disparity between the ideal and the actual. I saw my parents as almost sublime in their vision of what they wished to be and tragic in their inability to achieve the goal." The sense of parental fallibility in no way diminished his sense of failure and guilt. A remembered moment from his early twenties captures the tension between mother and son. Coming upon him smoking — another vice — she contemplated the sinner as, appalled, he butted out the cigarette and thrust it into his shirt pocket. "So you smoke, Max," she said at last. "*What else do you do?*"

Almost everything Max did alienated him from his family: his inability to pursue a business career; his first marriage to a worldly woman and, even worse, his divorce; his singularly flagrant love affairs. When I met him, both parents were dead; he had long been out of communication with surviving members of the family.

Only Max's youngest sister reached out to him. Refusing to be discouraged by his silence, Joyce pursued him with her letters and her generous brisk affection. "Max, my lad, do write. I long for news of you." "I hate to lose touch with you. I worry about you, lad, a great deal." Gravely ill with the illness of which she died, she wrote still with eager interest ("How are you — inner and outer man?"), appreciation ("I like your saying that the most important thing is to keep a vision of excellence") and, when appropriate, a mild sisterly reproof. "I heard you reading on radio last Sunday," she writes. "Very good, I thought. Your enunciation is excellent. By way of criticism: consciously or unconsciously, you have acquired a Sedgwickian intonation which I would say is a distinct disadvantage, though I like it in Sedgwick." (Garnet Sedgwick had taught both Maynards at Victoria College.)

Sometimes, when Max saw Joyce's characteristic pale-blue envelopes, he would leave the letter unopened for days. Here too he had failed: he should have written more often, sent money. Joyce never complained of his neglect. "I remember the little lad who used to run and hide when Mother called us," she wrote. "I know you, Max. Do not hide from me."

Though for most of his life Max hid from his family, he carried with him its peculiar pressures and constraints. These I came to understand more fully when, years later, I begged Max's adoptive brother, Fred Brand, to tell me about the Maynards. "Mr Maynard," he said, "was a noble man, cheerful and humorous. Mrs Maynard — we called her 'bossy M.' — was a troubled spirit. Both were totally committed to 'the will of the Lord,' a service based on rigid belief. So activities which might have contributed to generous humane development were suspect. Art was irrelevant — Max's gift here was neglected and partly savaged — even education ultimately did not matter. There was strength in this vision — we were taught the reality of the transcendental — but also threat. The price of disobedience was nothing less than the fires of hell. An error — divorce, say — became an existential fault, and gnawed at the roots of conscience. Under this severe heaven-or-hell upbringing the most trifling aberrations were enlarged, inflamed into an absolute kind of guilt that brought into question man's whole being and fate."

I think I first understood this world view, felt it on my pulses, when I saw the Maynard family album. Five young men — three Maynards, two Brands — are on their way to church. They wear identical black suits and black hats, strike identical poses, Bibles clasped to narrow chests. The attitudes of piety and religious awe, too, seem identical — except for Max, whose face is shadowed. Alone of the five, he rebelled early and violently against the family code of conduct, but those rebellions cost him dear. The reckless early love affairs, the failed first marriage — to the end of his life he suffered agonies of conscience over these and other derelictions. He was perennially tormented by his fall from grace. He believed with Socrates that the unexamined life is not worth living — and when he examined his own life he despaired. Everyone who encountered him was struck by the contradictions of his nature: gentleness and ferocity, insight and obtuseness, compassion and cruelty, formality and demonic wildness. Only those who knew him well realized how much pain the formal manner concealed. Surely that pain helps explain his drinking.

I don't know when Max became an alcoholic. I have asked everyone who knew him in his early years. Did he drink a lot? Usually the answer is, "No more than anybody else." Artists drank, university professors drank, students drank. Of course Max drank, and occasionally got drunk. Nothing notable in that. Coming as I did from a temperate family, I was not likely to spot a problem. Now, reading old letters, I am struck by recurrent references to alcohol. "To cheer you, I stood in line for an hour and a half today at the liquor store and came home triumphantly with a bottle of wine." (To cheer *me*?) "Company drab, but warmed up as the drinks began to flow." "Am feeling very sober and contrite today after a riotous party to which I allowed myself to be inveigled against my better judgment." Of a meeting in Toronto with Northrop Frye and Earle Birney ("drinks of course"), he reports, "behaved myself, I think" — but I note that after this well-behaved encounter he missed his train. As, later, Max and I talked in code about being "careful," so in these early days *not behaving*, a child's phrase, becomes a synonym for *drunk*. Childlike too, the sinner needs to confess and receive absolution. Though I was thousands of miles away and need never hear of his transgressions, Max reports on what was obviously a disastrous evening with friends. "I was in a state of black depression, hadn't slept the night before nor eaten all day, and as a result I behaved very badly and didn't like myself the next day *at all.* So you see I amn't the man you thought I was."

"I'm balancing paper on my knee," he writes to Cambridge, "so if the lines waver somewhat you are to know that it is *not* inebriation" — a possibility that would never have occurred to me. To be sure, I had observed that sometimes Max behaved strangely, but with a strangeness that bore no resemblance to my stereotyped notions of drunkenness. He was never loud or false-cheerful. Drinking, he might turn cold and formal, lofty. He could be rude, but with a precision of insult that appeared to rule out simple intoxication. (It took me years to spot the slightly glazed eye, the loosened mouth, that meant he had truly taken leave of his senses and next day would remember nothing.) Once, the year we met, he appeared at a university gala which I attended with an "acceptable" (i.e., Jewish) boy. He strode onto the dance floor, tapped my escort on the shoulder, presented me with a large bottle of perfume and walked away. Ten years later I would have said, "He's drunk." Then I thought the episode romantic, young Lochinvar come out of the west, claiming a bride while her mother did fret and her father did fume and the bridegroom stood dangling his bonnet and plume. In the same era, speaking to me on the telephone, he fell silent and I heard the phone drop. Later he explained, "I passed out." To me that meant *fainted.*

Only once, before we married, did I see a full-scale display of ugly drunkenness. I had been studying at the University of Toronto; for his Christmas visit I had arranged, with the eagerness and unwisdom of young love, a restaurant dinner with the teacher I most admired, Northrop Frye. Max arrived in mid-afternoon of a bitter December day. He had sat up all night on the train — and he had been drinking. "Three fingers of whisky and I could sleep on a barbed-wire fence," he said once of travelling without a berth. This time he'd had a lot more fingers than that. His speech was slurred, he lurched badly even when I held his arm. At his hotel, I plied him with coffee, one anxious eye on the clock. Six o'clock, six-thirty. I phoned the restaurant: "We'll be a bit late." We arrived two hours after the appointed time, in an atmosphere of considerable strain. Frye was polite, Max struggling for control and so more emphatic, more belligerent than usual.

Dinner passed without clear disaster. Walking home, Max turned on me. "You have sold out completely," he raged. "I thought I could make something of you, in spite of your provincialism and the clannish Jewish world you're so attached to. But you've crawled into the academic straitjacket, put on the blinkers. You've surrendered to a world of conventionalized vision and bamboozled perceptions. You and your professors! Annotators to books written by honest-to-goodness artists who know that *being* is worth ten of *knowing* any day." He held my arm as we walked, not tenderly but like a jailer. "You're dropping cigarette ash on my shoulder," I protested. "Am I? Am I just? How crude. How…*gentile*. Let me show you just how crude I can be." He spun me around to face him and then, very deliberately, held the cigarette to my blouse, over one breast. I watched as the fabric browned and burned, a jagged O. When I broke away and ran crying down Yonge Street, Max called after me. "You're not a scholar. You're nothing but a vulgar little egotist."

I might have realized, that night, that I'd learned something about Max. Instead, I thought he'd learned something about me, a nasty truth which ended the dream of our life together.

So I was astonished when he phoned next morning, affectionate and blithe. "Let's go to the Art Gallery. There's a new Milne
show." He waved away protests, anxiety, questions. "Last night
was nothing. I was simply exhausted — the rush of getting
away, not sleeping — and I got squiffed. Darling, I'm only
human. Forgive me. I love you to distraction. I long for you
with a positively biblical, Keatsian, Shakespearean passion.
Now will you come to the Art Gallery?"

Of course I went. There was no question of "forgiving"; I
blotted out the whole incident. And so we created together the
pattern which was to persist for more than a quarter-century:
affection, gaiety, strain, drunkenness, recrimination, rage, grief,
penitence and back to affection again.

Part of Max's nature — connected with the drinking, whether
as consequence or cause — was a deep vein of melancholy. A
strong sense of this life as a vale of tears lay just below the
humour and apparent cheerfulness; the family, and the Plymouth
Brethren, had marked him. I used to sigh over Max's habit of
beginning sentences with "I hate to tell you, my dear...." The
mournful news might be nothing — clock had stopped, supply
of paper towels had run out — but the little black cloud hung
on. The problem went beyond forms of speech. Always he saw
the skull beneath the skin. He experienced cyclical depressions (Christmas a particularly black period) and depressions
at odd times, inexplicable. Always he suffered from hypochondria. Max would have struck the most casual observer as a
vigorous man. He had — to use a fine old-fashioned phrase — a
splendid carriage. He strode hard, with confidence and spring.
In spite of what appeared to be superb health, however, he
worried constantly about joints, digestion, bowels, blood. He
did a lot of doctoring. He liked examinations, tests, medicine,
physicians and, most particularly, hospitals. In his courting
days he often sent me the results of his latest clinical adventures.

("X-ray, stomach acids, blood, everything. They tell me I have nothing wrong with me, nor ever had, and that I'll probably live to ninety-nine.") I thought this information intended to calm my anxieties about the difference in our ages — and indeed, the report on his century-long life expectancy ended with a lover's flourish: "gratifying, because I *do* wish to know what you will be like as an old lady of eighty-four."

Along with the family hypochondria, Max had acquired the family's curiously offhand attitude to money. "The parents' profession," Fred Brand recalled, "was to live by faith in the strict primitive sense, 'without purse.' That pretension failed, but remained a doctrine which they tried to instil into their children: 'Trust in the Lord.' The lesson actually learned was irresponsibility — unconcern with money, letting others pay one's way. Hence Max's drunken-sailor way with money." Max lent and borrowed with equal nonchalance. Since he seldom had anything to lend, it was borrowing that became a way of life. From our first days together, he would find himself without funds in restaurants and bookstores. "My dear, could you possibly…?" There was no calculation here, rather a kind of innocent trust that the Lord would provide. These amounts were modest and easily forgotten. About large sums, too, he could be disconcertingly jaunty. Five years after our meeting, with his divorce no nearer and seemingly impossible in Canada, Max decided that Florida courts offered the most promising route to freedom. He would see a St Petersburg lawyer — if only he had the fare. On a chunk of the scholarship money I'd just received from Harvard, Max travelled to Florida. He met all sorts of charming people there. The lawyer, alas, had been out of town.

With the 20-20 vision of hindsight, I can see that everything that became a problem between Max and me was manifest from the beginning. I chose not to see the irresponsibility, the depression. Also I chose not to see one further, self-destructive trait, which appears to have been initially the creation of Max's mother, fierce Liza Teague. It was she who first pronounced the judgment that became her youngest son's life script. Contemplating a wobbly table he had made for her, with the explanation that it needed just a bit more glue, she said, "Max, you never finish anything."

Even if this was not true at the time, it became so. Life plans were boldly formulated and quietly abandoned. He would take a Ph.D. in English at Harvard, in Art and Archeology at Chicago. He would get a painting scholarship at the Boston Museum of Fine Arts, return to graduate work at the University of Southern California. (He had gone to USC on a scholarship one year, but dropped out when his amorous adventures became complicated.) He planned to spend the summer "swotting away" at German and Italian in preparation for doctoral studies. (One would have to know Max to understand how unlikely such a summer seemed.) He was "committed to Cornell."

All the years I knew Max, he described himself as at work on a book. Not the same book, to be sure. The first venture was illustrating Paul Hiebert's comic tale of Sarah Binks, Sweet Songstress of Saskatchewan. Max loved Sarah, used to quote delightedly her translation of "*Du bist wie eine Blume*": "You are like one flower, So swell, so good and clean, I look at you and longing Slinks me the heart between...." A blizzard of early letters chronicles the success of his drawings: "Hiebert thinks we're both on the threshold of fame"; "Have them worked out roughly. Finishing will be easy." There followed, in due course, brief bulletins ("work not going well at all") capped by an impatient "I can't imagine Cézanne illustrating anything." Next thing I heard, he was writing a novel, *Welcome Proud Lady*, the story of his most flamboyant love affair. It would be a work of art, of course, but it might just make his fortune too. He had the characters, the events, was already roughing out key scenes. From Winnipeg, he reported the work's progress – "some pages not bad at all", "a terrific climax" – along with recurrent bouts of discouragement. "But oh, the sick feeling and weariness that comes over me when I think of the labour still involved."

Accepting as I did the necessity, the naturalness of labour, I had no idea then of Max's distaste for hard slogging. ("He had not been taught to buckle down to work and do it," Fred Brand says of Liza Teague's erratic mothering. "His showmanship was too much encouraged, so that his gifts grew into riotous short-lived bloom, with no root. There is a deeply laid weakness here, the result of early neglect.") It took me years to realize that Max's need for an audience drove him to settle for quick effects. Perhaps early frustrations led him to choose applause, admiration, rather than the satisfaction of mastering a task independently of other people's interest. Serious myself about projects undertaken, I imagined that Max must be serious too. I would inquire regularly about *Welcome Proud Lady*, and as regularly receive assurances. He was busy marking papers. He was writing a new opening. The novel was almost finished. "Am working now to get 15,000 words and an outline of the whole to send it to Dodd Mead by the end of March." A year later: "Hope to have enough done by March to submit it for the $2,000 Macmillan prize."

When Max moved from Winnipeg to New Hampshire with his possessions, I asked to see his manuscript. "I left it in storage," he said. Next summer he returned from a Winnipeg visit with news: Security Storage, claiming to have received no payments ("I'm sure I sent cheques"), had disposed of all his goods. The novel was gone. Never mind. He was writing a critical work on Sir Joshua Reynolds and the theory of the Sublime. The book would relate both visual and literary work to eighteenth-century aesthetic theories and – "well, it may just prove to be a landmark study." Of course he would need to do research in the Huntingdon Library. In another few months, he was "hard at work on a time-saving repository of interpretive information" on fifty poems designed for college courses. When I next heard of Max's book, it had been transformed into a commentary on Boswell and Johnson's journey to the Hebrides. After that, there was a new interpretation of Matthew Arnold, a little book on Blake, a collection of biographical essays to be used as a university text (this too a money-maker), personal reflections called *An Artist's Notebook*. When he died, he was writing the history of his family — and still finding audiences fascinated by reports of work in progress.

Conceiving a project, Max was confident, original. Execution bored or wearied him. On the brink of finishing a coffee table or a painting he would draw back, lose heart or interest, start again. Some paintings remained years "in process." He would remove a picture from its frame, lug it up to the studio to try new effects with paint or pasted-on coloured paper. In the hall of the house he loved, in Durham, New Hampshire, there hangs a lyrical celebration called "April Morning." The spring hills explode with young green, the clouds are blown cotton candy. And the birds, a rapturous swallow flight....Well, the birds are construction paper, held in place with Scotch tape. He never got it quite right.

For six years, between 1942 and 1948, Max and I alternately planned and despaired of a future together. My firm resolve to marry him would be undone by a pleading, desperate letter from home. Or, when we'd settled on a wedding date, Max would discover new difficulties in the way of his divorce. Mostly these were mechanical — the cumbersomeness of a Canadian divorce, the difficulties of qualifying as a Florida resident. But occasionally I glimpsed more ominous concerns. The day his divorce petition arrived in the mail, he said, "I don't see how I can do this to Evelyn." That I was able to ignore such revelations, that he constantly missed connections with lawyers, suggests how deeply mired we were, already, in denial and self-deception.

At last, in March 1948, we married in Durham, the small college town where he had taken a job to be near me. I wore a dress I had purchased for three dollars in Filene's Bargain Basement; the ring I had bought myself (another ten dollars) to forestall extravagance on Max's part. The ceremony seemed totally unreal: a Jewish girl married by a Protestant chaplain, my parents' darling "given away" by a virtual stranger, the head of the University of New Hampshire English department. As we stood on the railway-station platform after the wedding, awaiting a train to Boston, the station agent called out, "Mr Maynard, there's a telegram for you." Max took the envelope, glanced at it and thrust it into his coat pocket. "What is it?" I asked. "Good wishes," Max said. "No one you know." "Well, I assume they're for *us*," I said. "Can I see?" He didn't answer. Eager to assert my bridal prerogatives, and curious, I made a note of which pocket. What the telegram contained was not exactly good wishes. It was an ultimatum from the Personal Finance Company. *Payments seriously overdue. Send check immediately or legal action will follow.*

Our brief honeymoon in Cambridge, where I still lived — I was teaching at Wellesley College — was something less than euphoric. I had not told my parents I was being married; I sent a special delivery letter after the wedding. For three days we waited tensely for the reaction. Then my mother wrote — controlled (after what despair I can imagine), affectionate, reassuring. She and my father believed that after all this time I must have reached a decision that was right for me. They were eager to know my husband. (My father had never met Max, my mother only occasionally and warily.) They were sure that they would come to love him as I did and of course, they hoped to welcome us both at term's end.

This response should have lifted the gloom that attended our sober little wedding, but Max remained oddly quiet and withdrawn. In the months before, I had noticed a new tentativeness and unease, the once confident lover now inclined to self-deprecation. "I ain't of course nearly as good a person as you think I am," he had written. "It's quite likely that I'm not worth the struggle." Newly married, he struck an elegiac note, as though our sought-after union were already at risk. "If ever we were to part, the loss would be more mine than yours." I put this down to a natural fear of anticlimax. Six years of extravagance and protestation: a man might well worry about living up to such promises. I comforted myself with the old assurances: "If only we were together permanently, everything else would fall into place quite naturally."

We had agreed to spend part of our honeymoon — Easter vacation, between terms — in Durham, where Max had the use of a comfortable house. (Theoretically, he rented one room. But the absent owner had given him *carte blanche*.) Here he showed me to a pink-and-white-dimity room with a single narrow bed. "This is the bridal chamber?" I asked. He looked embarrassed. "Oh, I oughtn't to sleep here. I'm only paying for the third-floor bedroom." Half teasing but truly puzzled, I said, "I must see your hideaway." He blocked my path. "It's a mess." When he went out for cigarettes, I mounted the stairs to the third floor, and for the first time saw how my lover lived. I had known him as a man elegant almost to foppishness. The lunatic disarray of his bedroom took me by the throat: the Mad Hatter's Tea Party, only played in clothes, not teacups. Socks and shirts and shorts and ties and pants had been dropped and heaped and crumpled and flung. Fans of student papers, jaggedly red-pencilled, lay strewn about the floor. A small table sagged under the weight of what appeared to be several years' accumulation of loose change. The closet door stood open: a few suits, and more vodka bottles than I had ever seen in one place.

Tiptoeing back down the stairs, I told myself this must be how bachelors lived. I thought of Bluebeard's wife, given freedom of the castle on condition that she carry an egg wherever she went — and that she never enter one particular room. Of course she couldn't resist. Like that wretched wife, I crossed the forbidden threshold, and the egg turned blue.

Weeks passed. Committed to teach at Wellesley until June, I commuted between Cambridge and Durham, carrying my secret. When I came for weekends, Max would meet me at the station, formal as if I were an old student come to visit. He talked a lot about classes, committees, meetings, new books. Always he complained of being tired, short on sleep. I heard no more about how he started when he caught sight of a dark head bent over books in the library, or when he imagined hearing my footsteps. One day, wistful, I said, "Remember when you wrote, 'If love could be focused and made visible in a beam, you would walk always in golden light?'" He didn't answer, and I saw that he was weeping silently, whether for himself or me I did not know.

We never spoke of that upstairs room, where he spent so much time and, mostly, slept. I would hear him moving about long after I'd gone to bed, turning up the record player, Handel and Vivaldi crashing in the night. Then he would go downstairs to make tea and write letters which were never sent. They lay about the table for days, before he crumpled them into a wastebasket. Addressed to old friends, estranged family members, they asked forgiveness for injuries real or imagined. The voice of those letters was one I had never heard — unguarded, desperate.

One morning I found the previous night's letter laid beside my breakfast plate. At first I thought it meant for me, the salutation so familiar from the long courtship correspondence: "Dear my love...." But the name in the letter was Evelyn, Max's first wife, the woman he had claimed never to have loved. "The pain in my mind is an agony," he had written. "I think of you with grief and longing. What have I done?" I know now what Othello felt when he had murdered Desdemona. I am one whose hand, like the base Indian, cast a pearl away richer than all his tribe.

"And here I am with this clever little Jewish girl."

The Sunlight on the Garden Hardens and Turns Cold

Every union contains two marriages, his and hers. For many years, living with Max and, after the break, looking back, I saw only mine. Mine was hemlock: disappointment, frustration, bewilderment, bitterness, resentment and rage. What had I done to deserve this fate? Was I not devoted, considerate, loyal, kind, hard-working, conscientious, responsible, *good*? How had I been so deceived? Sometimes, during the twenty-five-year struggle, I thought of a drawing Max had sent me at a crisis in the love affair when he feared I might succumb to family pressure and marry someone of whom my parents would approve. The swift pen sketch shows a familiar fairy-tale land-scape: a beanstalk, rising from rocky ground, coils into the sky towards a gleaming cloud-castle. At its top a female figure, crowned, waves blithely. Birds and musical notes surround her. Far below, separated from even the plant roots by a deep chasm, stands a tiny figure. "And then Jack waved his handkerchief," the legend reads. "Goodbye, Cinderelka, goodbye Cinderelka! And even when he was a very old man he could still hear Cinderelka's voice and see Cinderelka's face as she stepped lightly into the golden cloud-castle where she belonged."

Moved as I was by the immediate impact of this vision, I did not until long after observe a curious distortion. Jack, of course, does not belong in the shimmering Cinderella romance with glass slippers and a fairy coach. (The only women in "Jack and the Beanstalk" are the giant's wife and Jack's mother, a grim repressive figure who sees only her son's ruinous impracticality, trading a milk cow for a handful of seeds.) Jack's spirit is all individual aspiration; he is artist, not lover, seeking the golden harp. So it was not at all likely that Jack and Cinderelka should, in their golden cloud-castle, have lived happily ever after.

As for me, I felt myself, after the marriage, an adored princess inexplicably reduced to cinders. Was I the divine creature of the letters — or a clever little Jewish girl? I gave no thought to the prince's situation, glamorous suitor dwindled into husband. I think of it now. What comes to me — strongly, sadly — is the understanding that for the six years of courtship Max played a role for which he was ideally suited. He had always needed an object of desire, someone on whom he could project his fantasies and to whom he could direct his imaginative energies. He used to quote D.H. Lawrence on the need to have, always, a woman at one's side, to inspire. But his dream of women was without Lawrence's naked sexual passion. In the hundreds of letters he wrote me — I see it clearly now — there is no shadow of physical lust. Friends marvelled that a sexually experienced man could accept for years a young girl's timid virginity. For him the situation was not only easy, it was ideal. I was his Beatrice, his Laura, his Heloise, his Lily Maid of Astolat — even, startlingly, the Virgin Mary. "In single pointedness I can match my mother," he wrote. "Her thoughts were fixed upon God as manifest in Christ, mine upon divinity in the opposite sex, meaning you." Max had loved other women before me. If he loved — read *idealized* — me more, it must have been because I fitted his deep needs so well. I was young, with no experience of men beyond awkward teenage grapplings — and no expectations. My head was full of English poets and the romantic yearnings they inspired. I appeared to him exotic, a Hebrew maiden, Ruth amid the alien corn. I was quick-witted and funny, a good conversational match, with a retentive memory and a dedication to the scholarship he admired but had no stomach for. "Fredelka gets the glory and I gets Fredelka," he once said playfully, commenting on some new academic triumph. He was like Shakespeare's playboy Prince Hal, responding to a father's reproof — *Look at Percy, the battles won* — with "Percy is but my factor, good my lord." A simple B.A., had he not won a Harvard Ph.D.? My credentials became his.

Above all — I did not realize, initially, the importance of this — I was blithe. The black moods to which Max had all his life been subject only occasionally shadow his courtship letters. What does appear there frequently is delight in my gaiety. "I need some lessons in chirpiness," he confesses on a grey day, burdened with papers and class preparation. *"How to preserve a smiling morning face by Fredelle Bruser."* Another day, another anxiety, he quotes, with a characteristic mixture of playful and serious, an obscure Browning poem about the cricket who compensates with exquisitely timed chirping for the missing string of a poet's lyre.

> So that when (ah joy!) our singer
>   For his truant string
> Feels with disconcerted finger,
>   What does cricket else but fling
> Fiery heart forth, sound the note
> Wanted by the throbbing throat?

That was my role, and I played it well — so long as I knew
only the poet in his singing robes. Then he was a true magi-
cian, a memorable storyteller, a rarely cultivated social being —
a matter not just of beautiful manners, but of grace and style.
For six years he showed me his ideal self: responding to that
vision, I created mine. And then we were married. A man who
disliked sharing a bed with a woman found himself with a
passionate bride. A man who craved drink lived with a wife
who despised drunkenness. A turbulent spirit was expected to
be orderly, an artist to take out the trash. Once, urging me to
defy convention, he warned me that compromise kills the soul.
"People who accept it are held together by things *outside*
themselves. The pressure of these things brings bitterness and
a sense of being alone and caged." Yet, alone and caged, he felt
as a convention-defier. Max surely longed for closeness, but
he feared it too; his deepest need was for freedom and privacy.
So the achievement of his dream, the end of the quest, must
have come as a clanging of prison gates. This he both knew and
did not know from the beginning. Months after we met, he
quoted Blake:

> He that bends to himself a Joy
> Doth the winged life destroy;
> But he who kisses the Joy as it flies
> Lives in Eternity's sunrise.

That my given name, Freidele, means *joy*, is an incidental irony.
He singed my wings. Over the years, I came very close to
destroying him with my rage, revulsion and contempt. I think
it was true, what he said in one anguished letter: "I should like
you to remember me as a man who loved you more than
anything in the world — more than any person he had ever
known or ever will know. Darling, darling Fredelka." Yet the

marriage must have been hell for him. After the wedding, he never called me Fredelka again.

In the autumn after our marriage, Max and I set up housekeeping in Durham, a picture-postcard town sixty miles from Boston. Like my mother when she married and moved to a Saskatchewan village, I assumed this would be just for a few years. My teaching position at the University of New Hampshire offered an acceptable beginning, a stopgap while Max upgraded his professional qualifications. Once he had a Ph.D., we could move on to some more prestigious institution. Meanwhile, we would start our family. That Max was decidedly hesitant both about having children and about pursuing graduate work I knew; I chose to see this reluctance as a passing phase. (When he saw how lovable babies were, how easy advanced study would be for someone of his intellectual power....)

The vision of a new life — high-powered career *and* children — began to dissolve almost immediately. When I became pregnant, the Dean of Liberal Arts announced that my teaching contract would not be renewed; the university did not employ pregnant women, or mothers of young children. Max, reminded about graduate-school applications, said he didn't see how he could handle a Ph.D. program in addition to his teaching load. Living with him, I grew increasingly alarmed by his moodiness and hot temper. Trouble signs accumulated. That brown-paper bag with a vodka bottle in the car's glove compartment? "A student must have hidden it." What happened to the jug of wine? "The workmen probably drank it when they came to fix the furnace."

In the tense atmosphere of post-marriage shock, my pregnancy created an additional strain. Max was deeply embarrassed by what he always referred to as my *condition*. ("In your condition, my dear, you shouldn't wear anything that attracts attention.") He did not wish to be seen with me on the street, objected to my swimming, maternity-suited, in the town pool. When I went into labour, he left me at the hospital door and drove off at high speed, clearly anxious to put as much distance as possible between himself and the mysterious, obscene rites about to occur. I had entertained fantasies of his pacing the waiting room, kneeling tenderly by my bed to rejoice in the newborn babe. In actual fact, he got very drunk at home and, from all reports, telephoned dozens of friends — some more than once. The bedside reunion occurred late and formally, in the unmistakable atmosphere of a morning after. I felt abandoned. The child was *mine*. (Throughout the marriage I spoke of *my* daughters.) Though I would always have said I wanted Max to love his children, I made closeness unlikely. Within days of Rona's birth I was diverting friends with accounts of Max-the-bumbling-father, describing how he carried the baby from the hospital like a stiffly held bouquet, laid her down on the car's back seat and then set on the window ledge, poised just over her head, a large chrysanthemum plant sent by a well-wisher.

Though I was the one who had wanted a baby, I was probably, in the first chaotic months, as shaken as Max. Yes, I loved my child. I was also frightened, nervous, depressed, irritable, exhausted by this totally dependent little person who constantly *needed*. I remember once when Rona, probably picking up tension and worn out by my desperate ministrations, screamed and screamed and would not be comforted. On a last furious trip to the crib, I lifted her out and laid her once again on the dressing table. Diaper dry. No pins sticking into her. Fed and burped just minutes ago. "What is the matter with you?" I screamed over her screams. "You've had *everything*. Go to sleep!"

Then I swung up the spindly legs and smacked her — a three-month old baby — on the bottom.

Afterward, holding my daughter and weeping with her, I groped for the sources of my rage and fear. My child's neediness was not the problem. That was normal, a part of mothering. What was not normal, at least not what I had expected, was my husband's strangeness and my own ineptitude in coping with a new life situation. When I married at twenty-six, I had a long history of academic triumphs, from always first in Saskatchewan classrooms to an accumulation of university awards. It might almost be said that I was a professional student: in my last years of graduate study, I received more in grants and prizes than I was ever to earn as a teacher. I had published in learned journals, presented papers at academic meetings. All signs pointed to a brilliant future. After a few months of marriage, I found myself in a New England village with no employment and no prospects. Dwindled to a housewife, I found I was not even a *good* housewife. I had neither training nor experience. My mother, herself a model housekeeper, kept me from mundane tasks. "Go and study," she would say if I half-heartedly reached for a dish towel. "Go write a poem." So I entered marriage totally unprepared, the world of floor wax and detergent foreign as the far side of the moon.

Even before my first child was born, I couldn't keep up with what seemed an endless accumulation of dreary chores. The arrival of a baby compounded my difficulties: sink always full of dirty dishes, kitchen linoleum gritty-sticky, fluffs of dust under the beds....How did other women manage? I couldn't master the timetable of meal preparation — vegetables boiling away to tasteless pallor before the meat was ready. When our paediatrician told me to add egg yolk to the baby's diet, I remember wailing, "I don't have time!" I spent my days in loose floppy garments called, appropriately, dusters, usually with sour-smelling infant spittle on the shoulder burping area. Living in a housing development, I had plenty of opportunity to observe and marvel at other women. How did they achieve those magazine-cover kitchens, every surface ashine? What was the secret of their rosy fragrant babes, their unimpeachable laundry? It seemed to me that my own infant looked a little dusty. As for laundry — diapers swiftly took on discolourations so shocking I draped rather than stretched them on the clotheslines in hopes no one would observe this additional evidence of my incompetence. Looking at my house, my image in the streaked bathroom mirror, I wondered, "What ever happened to Fredelle Bruser, superstudent? Who is this drudge?"

Within months of my forced retirement from university teaching, I began looking for work — something that would use my head and my skills, and could be done on a part-time basis. Rural New Hampshire proved unpromising territory. From time to time I'd pick up a tutoring job, rescuing a high-school student from imminent failure or prepping a candidate for college entrance exams. I had always loved working with bright students — or, indeed, the not-so-bright eager to learn. Now I taught mostly reluctant teenagers signed up by their parents, kids whose one interest was in passing, getting a grade. I took whatever employment was available. I did consumer surveys door to door, the seventeenth-century scholar asking householders what brand of toilet paper they used, and why they chose it. Once I sold children's encyclopaedias, an activity that might have been acceptable had it not required an utterly false and misleading sales pitch devised by the company. The technique was to interest a client in the books, then, when he was hooked, to show an ad listing an inflated purchase price, $500. At this point in the scenario, client's face falls. He cannot possibly afford that. Salesperson thinks hard (show of furrowed brow), comes up with happy solution. "I think I can help you. You look like just the sort of person we want in our encyclopaedia family. If you'd be willing to let your name be used — discreetly of course…maybe answer a few telephone queries from potential customers — I think we could let you have the set at a special discount, $199." Few prospects could resist this bargain. In actual fact, the come-on $500 ad had never run anywhere. The standard price for the set was $199. Sometimes, making a sale ($50 in my pocket) I thought of my grandfather who, sent to promote my father's photography business, also door-to-door, would observe a prospect's humble circumstances and say, "Listen, friend. Pictures you don't need." I felt rotten if I sold encyclopaedias, and rotten if I didn't.

Social life as a married woman reinforced my sense of loss. Durham is a university town: the first question asked of female newcomers was always. "What department is your husband?" No-one ever asked what I did or had done — though I recall one faculty wife murmuring. "Let me see…you were your husband's secretary, weren't you?" At parties I wore name tags (with or without the odious HI!) that said *Mrs. Max Maynard.* Though I was never invited to join the really exclusive old-family clubs, I was expected to sign up for Faculty Wives and Merry Mothers. ("It's important," Max said, "to participate in community life.") At Merry Mothers we exchanged baby clothes and childbirth experiences, mostly un-merry ("I was in agony for twenty-four hours!") and learned to make Christmas wreaths out of wire coat hangers and acorns.

Then there were the kaffee klatsches, also important for community life. Almost every morning around ten o'clock, until I had demonstrated my unsuitability, the telephone would ring and a bright neighbourly voice sang out, "Come on over. I've just put on the coffee!" I would bundle up the baby — uneasy backward glance at breakfast dishes, shirts waiting to be ironed — and set out for neighbourhood sociability. Mostly on these occasions we talked child matters. "Isn't it terrible, the price of Little Yankee shoes?" "I just love the way you're doing Nancy's hair" (three tufts, held aloft by a pink ribbon). "Is Rona dry at night yet?" (When I said "no," the questioner smiled complacently. "My Sheila has always been a very *clean* little girl.") And then there were the recipes, new ways to get more for less. I have forgotten the trick for making pork liver taste like *paté de foie gras*; I believe it involved soaking in hot milk. But two gourmet delights from these meetings have stayed with me through the years. One was Chicken Necks and Backs en Casserole. The other, more imaginative, Mock Steaks. To make these, you poured melted bacon fat into a bowl of stale bread crumbs, then moulded the fatted crumbs into steak shapes. ("You can make T-bone, sirloin, any style.") Once formed, the steaks were fried deliciously crisp in — what else? — bacon fat.

After a few years, I stopped going to morning coffees (or was no longer invited. I'm not sure which came first). In 1953 Joyce, my second child, was born. I began to make a life with my children, taking part-time work when I could get it.

I would have worked even if we hadn't needed money, but in those days getting paid mattered. With only one salary, we were hard pressed. Max had come to the University of New Hampshire in 1947 at $2,800 a year, rock bottom even for that era. Five years later, known as an exciting and original teacher, he was still getting $2,800. When he protested to the department head, the response was firm. "Max, we all know how valuable you are. But you don't even have an M.A. How can I put you up for promotion or a raise? Christ, you're lucky to be teaching in a university at all." A proud man, Max never asked again. Younger men with new Ph.D.s were regularly promoted over his head, with handsome salaries described as "competitive"; Max, not qualified for this competition, retired in 1973 after twenty-six years with an annual income of $13,000. By then, janitors were paid almost twice that amount.

How much the sheer humiliation of this cost our marriage is impossible to calculate. Certainly financial pressure took its toll. Max taught nights and summers — times he hoped to reserve for painting — whenever extra work was available. Even so, we rarely got through a year without a bank loan taken in June, when salaries ended for that term, and paid off, with difficulty, over the next twelve months. Skimp, cut, save was the household rule. A product of depression frugality, I took quite easily to this life, perhaps even enjoyed finding new ways to make ends meet. Max loathed counting pennies. His extravagance drove me to clutch the purse strings tighter, and between us there raged a subterranean battle over spending. Asked to buy a bottle of milk, Max would come home with a jar of champagne jelly, a tin of anchovies. I would then treat him to a lecture on what these luxuries represented in real terms. For what that jelly cost, we could have bought twenty pounds of potatoes. Sometimes, chastened or coldly silent, he would return his purchase to the grocery store. I ran to sales, often stocking up on bargains in fresh vegetables which deteriorated and then had to be thrown out. Max believed that *reduced price* meant defective or poor-quality merchandise. When I sent to Macy's for low-cost razor blades, he refused to use them. At that price, he said, these must be old used blades, from God knows what cheeks and chins, recycled. I was no less preposterous in my ostentatious economizing. I saved string and old wrapping paper, re-used envelopes, complained if Max threw away paper towels after a single wipe. No piece of bread was ever thrown away; dried and crushed, it would be added to a bread-crumb supply sufficient to gratify all of Durham with mock steaks.

It is hard to know at what point saving ceases to be a reasonable response to need and becomes pathological. Somewhere along the way I passed that point, saving to punish Max and, more complicated still, to punish myself. Buying Max, my peacock, a $25 suit in Filene's basement was one thing. Wearing my sister's hand-me-downs, including her shoes, triple A width for my D foot, was another order of madness. My sister was taller and slimmer than I, her dresses heavy on rhinestones and frills. I wore these unsuitable garments as a kind of hair shirt long after I began to earn money and could have paid for my own clothes. What happened, I think, was that after Max's fundamental rejection of me as a woman, I began to believe I did not deserve anything better than cast-offs. Though I had grown up in a household where good cooking meant eggs, cream, mushrooms, nuts and butter, I now worked at making cheap ingredients palatable. All through the fifties, my standard party fare was a famous Depression casserole: canned tuna, canned corn, canned mushroom soup and noodles, made elegant by a mince of green pepper. Not long after World War II, I read about a low-cost high-protein product, MPF (Multi-Purpose Food), being used in refugee camps. I sent for a case of the stuff. It turned out to be a noxious-tasting powder, so definite in flavour that it ruined any dish. My determined experiments with MPF (stirred into soups, used as topping) ended only when Max absolutely refused to taste any concoction with the distinctive high-protein aroma. I buried the last tins of MPF in our vegetable garden, comforting myself with the assurance that it would vastly enrich the soil.

Max and I seldom quarrelled about money. Rather, we made, each on our own, challenging gestures. If, for the university president's annual reception, I made a gown out of old curtains, he would respond by giving the cab driver a huge tip. I made a point of taking a sandwich when I went to Boston for the day; he, returning from a similar jaunt, would report that he had hired a taxi for sightseeing — and left it outside the Fine Arts Museum, meter ticking, while he contemplated the masterpieces within.

Open quarrels, rare, generally involved the children. At first we struggled over peripheral irritations. Max: "Why does our house smell of diapers all the time?" Me: "Because a baby lives here, that's why." Responsibility became a recurring issue. I would ask Max to look after Rona for a few hours, he would say he had papers to mark. The head of the English Department, he informed me, did not take care of babies. His colleagues did not take care of babies. Sooner or later we got to *I didn't ask to have this baby. It was your idea.*

As the girls grew, arguments took on a more philosophical cast. I cited authorities on child development, he waved them aside as irrelevant. Our children were not *ordinary* children. For Rona's second birthday, he brought home a spelling and counting board. At about the same time, and with considerably more success, he set about introducing her to painting. By the time she was three, her favourite book was *The Last Flowering of the Middle Ages*, illustrated with colour reproductions of Van Eyck, Memling, Brueghel. Sitting on her father's knee, she would peer delightedly into the depths of a Brueghel panorama as he pointed out tiny background figures. The French impressionists were introduced a few years later. In itself, all this seemed fine. Disputes arose when Max took to showing Rona off at the university Art Department, where she dazzled his colleagues with swift identifications. "That's Cézanne…Picasso…Chagall …Monet — no, Manet." Having been a performing child myself, I knew the strain of such exhibitions and the need to go on shining, pleasing parents. To my "Please don't ask her to do tricks" Max responded with "They're not tricks. She loves it."

For a few years, we could tell each other what the children

loved. "Rona loves the library," I would say, to which Max replied, "She spends far too much time indoors with books. She loves going for walks with me." Max claimed Rona disliked being dressed up (frilly hand-me-downs from my sister's children). "She loves it," I said. Once our daughters were old enough to declare their own preferences, Max and I regularly took opposite sides. He supported the girls' expressed desire to attend church, the way other kids did. "I'm Jewish," I said. "I don't want my children singing 'Jesus loves me.'" We argued over school assignments, in particular Max's impulse to turn Joyce's projects into a collaborative effort (Max running to the library, phoning colleagues). I encouraged Rona's passion for ballet; Max said grimly, "That girl needs to live in the real world. She should learn to skate, swim."

Differences over the children, passionately disputed, were partly, I suppose, a kind of shadow-boxing. The real issues between us were too dangerous to discuss. The word *drunk*, lighted match to a kerosene can, was not used in our house. Max drank, that was all, and his nerves were bad and his metabolism delicate and so sometimes, under pressure, he got *squiffy*. For years I held to this official version of our…problem. Having grown up in a household where wine appeared at Passover and Chanukah, and a single bottle of brandy served medicinal purposes, I knew nothing of alcoholism as a disease. Alcoholics were Bowery bums, derelicts who slept in the streets clutching bottles in brown-paper bags. They were not, could not possibly be, college professors. I came to understanding only very gradually. The first year of my marriage, when I began finding bottles behind books and under mattresses, I concluded that my husband was troubled. Later, I thought *weak*, and later still, *morally delinquent*. I never saw him as a sick man.

The alcoholic's family is always a nest of secrets and deceptions. Ours was perhaps worse than most in the extent to which we pretended not to notice the unspeakable, maintaining always a surface of civilized cool. In all the years I knew him, Max never missed a class through late-night carousing. His daytime manner was dignified and correct to stiffness. When things were going reasonably well, he would come home from the university in late afternoon, have one (public) glass of sherry, change and head for the third-floor studio to paint. If dinner was served promptly by six, he would appear more or less sober. If dinner was delayed − or if Max was caught up in a personal or professional crisis − he would take his place at the table like a cornered fighter awaiting an opening. The dinner menu ("You know I can't digest pork"), the girls' table manners − anything was pretext for attack. Sometimes he sobered up in the course of a meal. Other times he would upset his coffee and move unsteadily for the stairs. Shut into his study until we went to bed, he would emerge later to turn on all the lights, play Mozart and Beethoven (record jackets strewn over the living-room floor), make pot after pot of tea. If at some point he collapsed totally, I would come down in the morning to find the stove burner still going and the kettle reduced to a small flat stainless-steel coin.

Drink became Max's armour against fate. He got drunk when his sister Joyce died, when his children were born. On the few occasions when I was too ill to look after the household, he drank himself into oblivion. He drank when my parents visited. "Max has a migraine attack," I would say to explain his strange behaviour. He got drunk at parties, other people's and his own, savagely analysing a guest's character and capacities. I was always terrified lest the university community learn about Max's drinking. What if he lost his job? The truth is, virtually everyone except me knew that Max Maynard wasn't just a poor drinker: he was an alcoholic.

Not knowing — or not understanding — I saw Max's drunken-ness as a catastrophic, inexplicable failure of will. "I realize that once you *start* drinking you're lost," I would rage after occasions when, left in charge of the children, he got blind drunk. "But what about the moment when cold sober, you go to the liquor store?" I didn't realize that for someone with Max's malady sober is not necessarily *cold*. Sober may be hot, wild, desperate, insatiable. When the girls were seven and eleven, I became a consultant for the Educational Testing Service. The job — my first professional opportunity in years — required twice-yearly trips out of town. Preparing to leave for a few days, I would say, obliquely, "Max, you *will* be careful?" And he would respond, matching indirection with indirection, "Of course." I would leave casseroles, instructions about household tasks, phone numbers. The girls never telephoned me. I would call, hear the tension and fear in their voices. Had they had dinner? No. (Eight o'clock.) Was Daddy home? Well...yes. Everything all right? Long silence to this false question. "Mummy, when are you coming home?"

Drinking was not the only, or the deepest, unmentionable in our life of secrets. The ultimate off-limits subject was the disaster of our sexual life. I was not yet thirty when Max announced, "Sex is for the young and beautiful." I did not know whether this was a usual assumption, or evidence of my own undesirability. I did not dare make inquiries — and indeed, where would I have inquired? Magazines of the 1940s and 1950s draped "marital love" in veils of impenetrable delicacy. I found other women unwilling to discuss intimate matters. Therapy and counselling were not yet household notions. I accepted a largely non-sexual relationship as one more mystery in the larger mystery of my strange, sad marriage — one more truth to hide.

Ironically, most women found Max sexy. He was handsome

in a startling, off-beat, faintly demonic style. But the sexiness was not just looks. It was an impression of energy and vitality, along with humour and playfulness and intensity — a suggestion of turbulence barely controlled. His voice was Antony's, "propertied As all the tuned spheres, and that to friends: But when he meant to quail, and shake the Orb, He was as rattling thunder." That voice, with its extraordinary richness and range, had years ago in Winnipeg, got him a job on radio reading poetry to a daytime, mostly female audience. As John Gregory — John for earthiness, Gregory for style — he charmed prairie women with readings of "My soul, there is a country afar beyond the stars" and "Tyger, Tyger, burning bright In the forests of the night." He sang, too, in a lovely resonant baritone, old Scottish ballads ("He's taen three locks o' her yellow hair And wi' them strung his harp sae fair") and modern French love songs: "Auprès de ma blonde, il fait bon dormir." He played the flute, he recited and composed poetry, and he painted. What woman could resist this arsenal of charm when she felt it directed at her? Max used his charm consciously and confidently, always affecting surprise at the effect it produced. His letters, when I was in Toronto and he in Winnipeg, describe a succession of ripe exotic Jewish beauties whose passion for him he professed not to understand. ("I found Razelle waiting in my room…Sima calls daily…Corinne wants to pose for me. This is all quite baffling, because I certainly don't encourage them.") To the end of his life, Max attached enormous importance to his reputation as a lover of women. And this is sad, perhaps tragic, for Max did not love women. I think he loved men, but could not, for reasons aesthetic and moral, accept the vision of himself as homoerotic. So his sexuality was agonized, distorted, perverse. He played the libertine, but remained at core puritanical about sex. In twenty-five years of marriage, I never saw Max naked. Even on paper, he was modest. An early letter, written during a heat wave, describes him as sitting, not *naked*, but "clothesless." When, in early letters, he strains for aphrodisiac effect, the result is embarrassing: a hideous drawing of lovers kissing with wooden arms and huge lips; the man, a Max-caricature, appears braced for a death sting.

Had I been less an innocent when I met Max, I might have picked up clues to his sexual ambiguity. Wooing me at a distance and looking forward to reunion, he writes, "Really, I don't care what we do so long as I can look at you and hear you laugh." And when we are married, "We'd better resolve now, I think, that we will sleep a little o'nights and not talk the sun round." *Talk* — all night. I have never doubted that Max loved me in his fashion. What he really wanted, had the world and women been better suited to his needs, was to have me always in his life as companion, supporter, admirer, confidante, best friend. He would have made the ideal Platonic lover. "I'm not aching for a wife *in the abstract*," he wrote soon after meeting me. "I ache to be with you." But I was a sensual woman who wanted marriage and children and physical love — all burdens for a man of his complexion. He tried. And then he would get terribly drunk and lie on the narrow couch in his study where I would find him next morning, ravaged and bleak. "Max, what is the matter? What do you want?" I would ask in the early days. And he would turn his face to the wall. "My dear, I have defrauded you. I should have been a monk."

Many bad marriages survive, I suspect, because the couple enjoys the support of a coherent community — church, clubs, organizations of fellow workers or fellow hobbyists. The problems of our marriage were surely aggravated by our anomalous position in the community, an isolation partly self-chosen and partly imposed. The New England university town as I have experienced it is a closed and stratified world, in its own way as class-conscious as any English town. The élite were old families, some dating back to pre-revolutionary times. They lived in grand old houses furnished with colonial pine: their heavy engraved silver bore the marks of famous New England silversmiths. They had old money, but did not flaunt it. They sailed summers and partied in winter, always with "their own," and their children married mostly within the charmed circle. University administration constituted another, more miscellaneous élite: deans, heads of departments and presidents were important, but not as special as Old Blood. Faculty was of two kinds, clearly distinguishable: those who were staying, committed to the town and active in its affairs, and transients. Stayers were much respected: they could be counted on to attend town meetings, serve on committees and solicit funds for the Red Cross. Transients, even if tenured, did not matter. "People like that just use us," a UNH professor said of a colleague leaving for a more prestigious position at higher pay.

Max and I fitted no category. Clearly staying, since a professor with a B.A. had no professional mobility, we were also obviously not committed to the local creed's first tenet: that New Hampshire was the best of all possible states, and Durham the best of all possible towns. Max had taken out American citizenship in a fit of impatience, when he found it would take longer to renew a Canadian passport than to get an American one. But no one could have missed his pro-British, anti-American stance. In speech, style and attitudes, he remained an English gentleman. I remember a neighbour at a cocktail party planting himself in front of Max and, inhibitions loosened, asking, "Tell me, Maynard, do you have trouble with your legs? Why do you carry that God-damned walking stick?" My Harvard degree and the fact that I belonged to no local organizations marked me as a snob; my intransigent Canadianism was seen as rude rejection of the country that offered me a good life, liberty and the pursuit of happiness. Every year, as I picked up my alien registration form, the postmaster would say, "When are you going to join us?" A typical incident occurred at a school meeting on proposed changes in the teaching of reading. During the discussion period, I rose to argue the case for phonics as against flash cards. I had scarcely done speaking when a fellow townsman seized the mike to alert the audience. "Mrs Maynard is *not even an American citizen.*" It is no wonder that our younger daughter once asked, "Why is the world divided into Us and Them?"

It was not only the outside world that was divided into Us and Them. Beneath and beyond all particular areas of disagreement lay the primary tug of war, between Max's Anglo-Saxon Protestant world view and my European Jewish heritage. My attitude to gentiles was distinctly ambivalent. I had grown up in schoolrooms presided over by our gracious king, our lovely queen. I knew that Britannia ruled the waves. I regarded the English as models of breeding and style, and English culture as the finest flower of Western intellectual development. I had also grown up with alarming stereotypes of the non-Jewish world. *Shiker is a goy,* a gentile is a drunkard. *Every gentile is a barbarian at heart. Never trust the goyim.* Of course I thought Max an exception. We married — and the first cautionary stereotype proved true. He never called me *dirty Jew,* but he made references equally wounding. Drunk or angry, he revealed what I saw as a barbarian strain. So one effect of my marriage was to increase my suspicion of the non-Jew.

As for Max: in our courting days, he had professed to admire the Jewish people. To be sure, he'd known obnoxious Jews, vulgar and ostentatious. But the Jewish community of Winnipeg — intellectual, artistic — was another story. Some of his best friends were Jews….In letters, he declares his eagerness "to become a Jew in effect if not in fact. I'd adopt the religion like a shot if it would do any good — become a legend for piety and theological erudition, a sort of Orpheus going back into the shades of dead things for his Eurydice." Even during this ecstatic period, however, Orpheus sometimes played on his lyre a different tune. "I simply cannot understand the central and simple motivating fact behind the Jewish people – their passionate determination to live *as Jews*. It seems to me so desperately pathetic." After our marriage, I heard no more of Max's wish to be himself a Jew. Rather, I sensed increasingly his unease with a Jewish wife. I remember, for instance, his reaction when, during my first year of university teaching, I initiated a class discussion of racial prejudice. We had been reading Shirley Jackson's story, "The Lottery," a parable of the scapegoat. Into the shocked silence that followed the story's violent climax, I dropped a question. "Why do we sometimes abuse people who are different from us?" Fear, someone said. Ignorance. At this, a blustery youngster protested. "It doesn't have to be either one. Now, I personally don't like Jews. I sure as hell am not afraid of them. And I'm not ignorant either. I've known plenty of them. They're queer. Christ, you should smell their cooking!" I suppose I might have tackled the question of cooking smells as an index of individual or group worth. But I laughed. "Tim," I said, "here and now I invite you to dinner at my house. I'd like to know if you think my cooking smells or tastes queer." Max was clearly displeased by the report of this encounter. "There was no need to humiliate that boy," he said. Did he mean, "There was no need to reveal yourself as Jewish?"

Except on rare occasions – like the girls' brief interest in churchgoing – Max and I seldom referred to my Jewishness. We spoke in code. "This food is too rich" (from my husband) meant "You know I don't like Jewish cooking." "I'm uncomfortable with those people" (from me) translated as "They're anti-Semites." Shortly after we arrived in Durham, we were asked to chaperon a fraternity dance. Max had his dark suit cleaned, inquired several times what I planned to wear. "I think, if I were you, I wouldn't wear one of those *flagrant* costumes." More code. The day before the event, I learned that the fraternity excluded Jews. I telephoned the president to say that, as a Jew, I felt obliged to decline. Max was annoyed when I told him. "Chaperoning is part of our community obligation." When I said I felt no obligation to a group that discriminated against Jews, he said, "The members of a private organization have the right to choose what kind of people they're going to associate with."

I have thought a lot, over the years, about the difficulties of intermarriage. It seems to me that the most explosive areas involve style rather than belief. I was not attached to the Jewish religion; my husband was not a believing Christian. But my world view, what I found funny or sad, my tastes in food and dress, my feeling about family, my attitudes towards sex and sports and celebration were all profoundly Jewish. My natural style was earthy, extravagant; Max's was formal-cool. And these are things you cannot change — or change only at great cost. I attempted, at various times, to subdue my excesses, adopt protective colouration. I learned to serve tea on a cart, as the Tunbridge Wells aunts had done. But the effort was self-defeating.

I was often reminded, during my marriage, of Hans Christian Andersen's little mermaid, happy in her rich undersea world until, fatally, she rises to the surface of the water, sees a young prince walking a ship's deck, and falls in love. Her ancient grandmother explains the impossibility of such a match: the prince walks on human feet, she has only her fishy tail. Undaunted, the little maid swims through perilous waters to a witch's cave. There she makes a ferocious bargain. The witch will transform her tail into feet — but every step she takes will be as if she trod on sharp knives. And for the potion which brings about this change, she must surrender her best gift, her lovely singing voice. So the witch cuts out the sea maid's tongue; she swims to the prince's country and casts herself ashore. The prince finds her, loves her, his poor dumb foundling. But she has no language, and he cannot read the message in her eyes. In time he makes a suitable match, marries a princess. The mermaid, extinguished, melts into foam.

Though I was not extinguished in my marriage to a gentile, I made the inevitable discovery: that what you get, if you give up your real self, is not and cannot be love. Denying my essential nature, which I came to see was intimately involved with my Jewishness, meant destroying the most valuable thing I had to give — to my husband or anyone else. And I wonder, now, what Max gave up.

I was brought up to be happy — Freidele, Little Joy — and I worked hard at happiness during the early years of my marriage. There was, in fact, much to enjoy. Rona and Joyce were lovely lovable children. We lived in a beautiful house. (A widowed Englishwoman, who admired Max and wanted her house to remain in good hands, had offered it to us at a preposterously low figure.) I liked playing house — gardening, cooking, sewing, giving parties. The girls were constantly busy with projects. At one point, a whole room would be transformed into a town (called, after its mayor, Joyce Hickeldy) with its own charter, post office, its roads and vehicles and stuffed-animal inhabitants. Another time, the girls opened a store on the porch, printing money, producing magazines and hand-sewn articles to sell. They started a newspaper, laboriously typed, with hand-drawn illustrations of stories garnered by two energetic reporters. They wrote songs and plays and performed these in the living room, with tickets punched at the door and programs of the night's entertainment. We played charades and old-fashioned card games, we composed limericks and light verse. We celebrated holidays — not just Christmas and Chanukah and

Thanksgiving but May Day, Victoria Day, Guy Fawkes Day. And we *talked*. The outside world had come to seem hostile, even dangerous, but I loved my home.

Max's melancholy was not so easily dissipated. Maddeningly reasonable, I used to enumerate his reasons for sufficient happiness: work he liked and did well, a powerful talent, lovely children, a comfortable home. On reflection I came to see that though Max was often gay, he could never have been described as *happy*. Dark moods descended without warning, savagery flashed like a switchblade. He could not sit still. From absorbed conversation he would abruptly fling out the door: "I need cigarettes." (Years later, after he gave up smoking, this became "I need Scotch tape.") We would set out on a picnic, sandwiches and coffee and books in a basket, and halfway to the lake he would turn the car. "Do you mind very much, my dear? The sun seems to be clouding over — and I want a cup of tea." Before we married, he explained his melancholy in terms of a lover's natural fears. "How can I be happy so long as there's a chance I may lose you? Marry me, and I'll be happy forever."

We married. Still he could not be happy. He lost his temper over little things. ("Why are we always out of paper towels?") He drank too much. One day, as he brooded silent on the couch, I said, "Max, is there anything I can do?" He covered his eyes with his hand. "I don't know," he said. "I'm constantly distracted. I can't do my own work. I don't have the tools I need. My God, I don't even have a set of chains."

"*Chains?*"

"For the car. Another month, it'll be winter. You know what our car's like on snow and ice. I'm the only man I know who doesn't own chains."

I hadn't dreamed happiness — or unhappiness — was so simple. I juggled the budget, came up with the money for chains. The first time he drove off with them, he looked almost happy. Then it turned out the chains were more nuisance than we could possibly have imagined. They had to be removed by the garage whenever the snow melted and put back with each fresh snowfall. Links broke and had to be replaced. He tossed the chains into the trash can. What he *really* wanted was an *Encyclopaedia Britannica.* ("You'd be miserable too if you had to dash to the library every time you needed to look up something.") I bought the *Britannica* for his birthday. But it was the wrong edition, so of course he was not happy.

"My God!" he stormed one day, dressing for class. "I don't even own a blazer." A blazer. So that was it. Next time the College Shop announced its fall sale, I checked and sure enough, they had navy flannel blazers, brass buttons. Just Max's style. I hurried home with the news. He drove off and returned promptly with the happiness blazer. Weeks passed. He wore his old tweed jacket, his corduroy jacket....No sign of the blazer. His moods were cloudy still. "Why don't you wear your new blazer?" I asked at last.

"I haven't wanted to tell you," he said. "It doesn't fit."

"Doesn't fit? But you must have tried it on."

"Look," he said. "You found this sale. You are determined to buy things on sale, though you know I hate that kind of shopping. So I went and bought the damn thing. It's too tight."

When I cried, not so much because of the money as because the magic had failed again, he said, "I'll go back, I'll exchange it."

"After four months?"

"They know me at the shop." He went off, carrying the blazer still on its hanger, a thin dust line across the dark-blue shoulders. When he came home, he was carrying a small paper bag and he looked quite happy. "I traded it for a nylon shirt."

"Well," I said. "The blazer cost forty dollars."

"This," he said, "is a very fine nylon shirt."

He wore the shirt several times after that. Then it vanished.

"Don't you like your new shirt?" I asked. "I haven't wanted to tell you," he said. "But that weekend I went to Boston, I must have left my shirt in the rooming house. Don't worry. I'll get it back."

Weeks passed. The nylon shirt haunted me, a wraith of happiness almost grasped. Again he went to Boston — "Yes, I'll remember" — and when he returned he told me, "I got it." Oh, it had been touch and go. He knocked at the rooming-house door, and it was answered by a man wearing *his* shirt, "indescribably filthy." The fellow claimed to know nothing of a forgotten shirt, but when Max insisted, he disappeared briefly, came back wearing only his undershirt, and handed over the soiled garment.

"What luck!" I said. "Give it to me and I'll wash it right now."

"I didn't want to tell you, my dear," he said. "I seem to have left it on the bus."

"I Keep the Joy":
The Death of
Mary Ellen Cann

Finding myself in Durham with no teaching job and no prospects was more than a financial problem; it meant frustration of a lifetime goal. I have always been a teacher. As other little girls played house, I played school, lining up my dolls for their lessons or requiring my best friend and her baby brother to *sit still* while I explained the mysteries of reading and writing. (Arithmetic being pretty much a mystery to me, that subject was never included in the curriculum.) I loved chalk and blackboards. I loved — still love — explaining, seeing puzzlement change to the magical *aha!* like a light going on above the head of a cartoon character. No doubt many elements in the desire to teach are tainted with self-interest: pleasure in power, prestige, an audience. But beyond all such questionable lures, I was early drawn to the world of education by a vision of Truth, Beauty and Goodness — the three surely inseparable. Hardy's Jude the Obscure — his obsession with Christminster College in Oxford, his longing for that New Jerusalem — has always been absolutely comprehensible to me. Reading the novel at eleven or twelve, I was baffled by the hero's dallyings with vulgar Arabella. But I identified instantly with his longing for the city of light. "The tree of knowledge grows there....It is a place that teachers of men spring from and go to....It is what you may call a castle, manned by scholarship and religion....It would just suit me."

Long before I married and settled in New Hampshire, I had realized that universities were not necessarily cities of light. At the University of Manitoba I encountered professors who endlessly read aloud from yellowed notes, and young instructors who quoted authorities but had no opinions of their own. I sat at the feet of an Oxford graduate who first devastated my term paper and then — as I later discovered — incorporated it entire, without acknowledgment, in his doctoral thesis. At the University of Toronto I found a department head, representative of Christian humanism, who curled his lip when referring to the "maiden meditations" of female scholars and spoke of Negroes with disgust. Even at Harvard I observed petty vanity in the great, like the distinguished professor who called me in to ask why his work was not included in the bibliography of an article I'd published. But I never wholly lost my illusions about citadels of learning until I moved to Durham.

The University of New Hampshire in 1948 was still, as it was affectionately called, a cow college — a land-grant institution begun as an agricultural school. It had a small student body, mostly in-state, and a somewhat miscellaneous, cheerfully unprofessional faculty. There were no published writers, no publishing scholars. The head of the writing department had not, as far as one knew, written anything; his *curriculum vitae*, printed in the brochure for the annual UNH Writers' Conference, included the information that he had "compiled lists."

Department members came from the ministry, the newspaper world, forestry and even the stage. Most, New Hampshire born and bred, had earned their bachelors' degrees from Keene or Plymouth, the state teachers' colleges. I had naïvely imagined that the department would welcome someone who had taught at Radcliffe and Wellesley, and published in scholarly journals. But it was precisely these qualifications that made me *persona non grata*. My colleagues, during the year I taught, treated me with wary politeness but no warmth. In this atmosphere of uneasy suspicion, I made mistakes. I remember one of the full professors showing me an article he proposed to submit to a leading scholarly journal — his discovery that a nineteenth-century poem on the joys of the simple life was directly influenced by an eighteenth-century poem on the same subject. "Oh, but this is a translation from Horace!" I said. "You know that famous ode that begins 'Beatus ille procul negotiis.' There must be hundreds of English versions." The professor retrieved his manuscript without a word. He would not, I think, have welcomed my presence in the office next door.

For the three decades that I lived in New Hampshire, I occupied, along with Max, a distinctly anomalous position. Known for a sharp eye and sharper tongue, I was respected — and feared. I didn't suffer fools gladly, and Max didn't suffer them at all. I was *Canadian*, a person who said "hoos" and "aboot" instead of "howse" and "abowt." I took my children to foreign films and to the opera. I did not attend town picnics. In short I was, along with my affected English husband, an outsider, a snob.

There is a melancholy irony in all this, because one driving force in my pursuit of education had been the desire to escape my outsiderness. That I should be forever alien in a Saskatchewan village — agricultural, Norwegian, Lutheran — seemed natural enough. But to be excluded from a university community — that I had never imagined. The chairman of the UNH English department was a kind man. He brought us tomatoes from his garden, knew just when our children were ready for a potty chair or a piano he no longer needed. Often he directed a small job my way: here's a widow who wants her husband's journal edited, here's a course you can teach for adult extension ($500 a semester). But real work, employment — that he never offered.

Eventually, with both children in school full time, I made formal application to the English department. For a chance to teach, I would forgo promotion and tenure, indeed any regular rank, and simply work on a year-by-year basis. *Only let me return to the classroom.* Faced with this direct embarrassment, the chairman came to see me. After all these years, I remember exactly what he said. "Fredelle, no-one questions your qualifications. But the fact of the matter is, we can easily get a *man* to teach in your field — Renaissance, seventeenth century. How could I make a case for you? Now, the area where we have trouble getting people is Anglo-Saxon and Middle English."

"I'm not an Anglo-Saxon scholar," I said. "All I've had is the basic Ph.D. courses in early English."

"What I'm proposing," the chairman said, "is that you go back to Harvard. Spend a couple of years working on the early stuff, publish some papers. After that — well, I think I might persuade the Dean to let you teach."

Probably I should be grateful for what seemed at the time a miserable and mean-spirited response. The writing was on the wall in letters ten feet high: THOU SHALT NOT PASS. So I turned my back on Christminster, the city of light. I would teach wherever I could find work: that meant, probably, the public school system. I applied for substitute teaching in junior high and high schools. That year I was wakened often at 6 A.M. by a frantic principal. Could I teach history at Portsmouth

High? Algebra in Exeter? Biology in Somersworth? Over coffee and toast I'd attempt a quick review — "Arma virumque cano, Troiae qui primus ab oris...." "In the production of passive immunization, an antitoxin already elaborated in another creature is injected...." — then off to any one of a number of small towns where students were no doubt astonished by a substitute's determination to do more than just keep order.

For me, that year, a small miracle occurred. I discovered that high-school teaching was not a comedown from university work. In some ways, it was a come-*up* — up to the curiosity and enthusiasm of the young. At the university I had taught mostly middle-class students from families who valued education and could afford to pay for it. The towns where I taught high school had their comfortable and affluent families too, of course. But mostly the students were children of factory workers and parents in low-pay service jobs. They came from homes where there were no books, no meals eaten as a family because parents worked shifts. Many had never travelled more than fifty miles from home. They knew nothing of the university world, had never considered how education — or the lack of it — might shape their lives. I think it is true to say that most had no expectations. They assumed they would marry, work and die in Somersworth or Newmarket and that their lives would be, like their parents', hard.

Into that world I came with my excitement about learning and my own instructive history: a small-town girl who made good. I spoke of opportunities available to any serious student — summer programs at New Hampshire's best preparatory schools, university scholarships. Whether I taught English or history, my message was the same: you can learn, you can make something of yourselves. I invited students to my house. We attended films together, shared reactions. (I saw my first Bergman films in the company of teenagers who knew better than I the landscape of desolation.) Halfway through my year of substituting, opportunity knocked. After I had substituted for a while at a nearby high school, the principal offered me a full-time job for the next year, teaching English.

I knew the state laws on teacher certification. "You realize," I said, "I've had no courses in Education."

The principal considered this. "I think, for someone with your qualifications, an exception would be made. Why don't you speak to the state officer in charge of certification?"

So, one bright spring day, I drove to Concord. I had no serious apprehensions. My academic record was exemplary; I had proven myself as a teacher; I had a job waiting. The certification officer, Miss Park, greeted me warmly. "So you want to teach English at the high-school level. Splendid. We always need English teachers." She opened a folder and took up her pen. "You do have a college degree, Mrs Maynard?"

"Oh, yes," I said. "I have a B.A. from the University of Manitoba — "

"Fine."

"And an M.A. from the University of Toronto — "

"Oh, really?" said Miss Park. She didn't look thrilled.

"And a Ph.D. from Radcliffe."

Miss Park was not thrilled. Not at all. She put down her pen and asked the question. "Tell me, Mrs Maynard, *how many credits have you in Education?*"

I smiled apologetically. "None, I'm afraid. But I've had a great deal of teaching experience."

Miss Park closed the folder. "Teaching in college is *not at all* like teaching in secondary school. For that you would need special preparation."

"But I *have* taught in high school — " I began.

"Daily substitute work? Oh, that hardly counts."

"No, no," I said. "I taught three months in Somersworth — "

"You taught *three months* in this state? Without any educational background? My office has no record of that."

"You can phone the principal and check," I said.

"Oh, I believe you. But do you realize it's illegal for any school to hire an unqualified teacher without express permission from this office?"

The vision of myself as an unqualified teacher was disconcerting. I tried to accept the realities of my situation. "May I ask what I would have to do to become qualified?"

"You need eighteen credits in Education."

Eighteen credits! I was prepared to consider six, or nine — but eighteen!

Miss Park's pen moved once more. "See, these are the courses you would need. History of Education, Psychology of the Pre-School Child — "

"Oh, but I'm interested in *secondary-school* teaching," I protested.

Miss Park smiled coldly. "And you think you could teach adolescents with *no* knowledge of the pre-school child?"

"Well, I have *some* knowledge. I've read a good deal on the subject — and I have two children. And they both attended the UNH nursery school, which serves as the laboratory for that course."

"You would have to take Psychology of the Pre-School Child," Miss Park continued smoothly, "and Educational Psychology and Psychology of Learning — "

I tried a direct appeal. "Miss Park," I said, "I want very much to continue teaching. I care deeply about my subject and my students. I know I'm a good teacher. But I simply am not willing to devote 270 class hours to Education courses."

Miss Park stood, a guardian at the gates. "I can understand," she said, "that a Radcliffe graduate might be a snob about professional training. But without those eighteen credits in

Education, you will never teach in the high schools of New Hampshire."

Back home, I reflected on what I knew of teacher-training courses. Some, no question, would be valuable to a beginner. Others, fashionable during the sixties, seemed irrelevant and absurd. (In one UNH education course, students were required to provide detailed analyses of their sexual experiences. In another, the term's work culminated in a "creative" project. One girl I knew got an A in creativity with a blouse made out of her old baby blanket.) Group activities and "life situations" were enthusiastically promoted as the surest way to reach young minds. ("How do you teach *The Scarlet Letter?*" I asked a high-school teacher who had spent far more time in methods courses than in her official subject, English. She beamed. "First of all we build a scale model of Hester Prynne's house....") Elevated to a sacred principle, Dewey's notion that "you teach the child, not the subject," had produced certification laws emphasizing technique above subject matter. In New Hampshire, for example, at a time when the state required eighteen credits in methods courses, a high-school teacher was considered qualified for any subject in which she had six credits. So anyone with a full year course in college physics could have taught high-school physics. Einstein and Robert Oppenheimer would not have qualified.

My own dilemma was solved by happy evasion: persuading a local superintendent to hire me part time, not as a regular teacher but as a "special expert" in creative writing. I taught for four years in Dover, New Hampshire. After that, I became an educational consultant for ETS, the body which sets and grades college entrance exams in the U.S., and for a venture grandly named the National Assessment of Educational Progress. At NAEP, huge sums were spent on a computer specialist's fantasy. Hundreds of thousands of handwritten student themes were printed up for the computer, which then produced (in two volumes) an alphabetical index of all words used in these themes. I asked what the index was *for*. "Well," said the expert, "say you're a teacher. You'd like to know how eighteen-year-olds use *over*, or how often *hopefully* appears in student writing. The index will guide you to *every single* use of those words." Seeing that I appeared sceptical about the value of this information, he went on. "In the process of tabulating, we've made significant discoveries. For instance, we found that the longest essays are generally the best, and the shortest the poorest. Of course, we can't necessarily conclude that all long essays are good, and all short ones poor."

I left the world of professional education in 1970, thoroughly disenchanted. Perhaps I knew from the start that a little learning is a dangerous thing. The most melancholy discovery, after three decades, was this: that even a lot of learning did not necessarily make men thoughtful, or wise, or humane, or fair, or good. I had dismaying encounters with college presidents, department heads, state officials, school boards, fellow teachers. The most sobering experience of all occurred not to me personally, but to a gifted young teacher, once my student, who ran afoul of small-town prejudice and the educational bureaucracy.

I don't know the whole story of Mary Ellen. Now that she is dead, no-one will ever know. Different people hold bits of the puzzle — the teachers she worked with, her students, her young husband, the friends who (for whatever reason) drove her down a perilous path, the doctor. My part in the drama was small but, like everyone else who touched her life, I am haunted by what happened. And, by odd chance, I was there at the beginning and the end.

I met Mary Ellen Cann the year she was fourteen. That was in 1956. I remember that when the call came I was decorating cupcakes for Joyce's third birthday. Suddenly, into a world of pink frosting, came a most unlikely request. Would I teach French and Latin at Somersworth High — starting at once? I tried to explain. I had two small daughters, my only experience was in tutoring and college teaching. Besides, I taught *English*. Yes, I'd studied French and Latin, but that was ages ago.

The superintendent persisted. "You've got a Harvard degree, you can handle it. These are mostly beginning courses. It's only for a couple of months. Look...our language teacher went into the hospital today for emergency surgery. If you can hold a Latin book, we want you." Considering how desperately I'd wanted some sort of professional employment, and how much we needed the money, I took the plunge. I found a friend to care for Joyce and pick Rona up after school; two days later I set off for Somersworth High.

The town of Somersworth was only ten miles from Durham, but in tone and general character it was light years away. Durham was a small New England college town with picture-postcard church, stores that sold Hathaway shirts and Vera scarves, large handsome houses overlooking well-groomed lawns — the kind of town where, when fourth-graders made up a Thanksgiving food basket, they couldn't find a needy family to give it to. Somersworth was dominated by mills. Shoes, textiles, electrical parts. Its shopping district was grimly practical, its houses ran to peeling tenement. The high-school building had a no-nonsense, you-are-not-here-to-enjoy-yourself air. Local taxpayers were not interested in fancy landscaping.

As soon as I walked into the school, I realized that the problem would not be my shaky language skills. Any reasonably well-educated adult can keep a jump ahead of a class if she works at it. But it takes a special kind of person to teach children who are in school only because they have to be — and clearly Somersworth had lots of those. "You've got an alarm buzzer connected right with my office," the principal told me. "Don't try to handle heavy trouble by yourself." As I made my way up a staircase crowded with blank-faced loungers, no-one moved to let me pass. I caught a whisper. "That's her. That's the substitute." Somebody had emptied a box of thumbtacks on the teacher's chair, then arranged them carefully, points up. I reached into a drawer for chalk and just missed the mousetrap. So I knew, even before the bell rang, what to expect.

All that day, classes stampeded through my room. I made every mistake possible. To the first group I said, "I've never taught high school before. I hope you'll help, tell me how your regular teacher does things." After that, I couldn't hear for the shouting. ("Mrs. O'Malley *always*...Mrs O'Malley *never*....") The next hour I tried firmness. "Sit in your seats and raise your hand if you want to speak." As if they'd rehearsed the performance, the class turned deaf and dumb. Advanced French told me they usually played Bingo ("to practice our numbers"); I passed out the dried beans, and within minutes was caught in a hailstorm of pellets flying so fast I couldn't point to a single offender. By lunch time I'd discovered two facts not mentioned by the superintendent. Somersworth was a *French-speaking* community. Most of my students were bilingual, children of French-Canadian immigrants. Their spoken French might be hybrid, but it was rapid. Mine was careful book-French, unpractised. Often I couldn't understand, let alone keep up. The other fact, even more alarming, concerned the special status of the teacher I'd replaced. Every high school, I guess, has at least one Character, the figure about whom legends develop. Mrs O'Malley was Somersworth's legend. Her off-colour stories, her practical jokes, her liberal extra-credit system, were famous. Some of my students had waited three years to get "the big dame" — and here they were, stuck with a substitute. Their reaction was a furiously resentful *We'll show you.*

I had pretty much decided, by my last class that day, to give up. The whole school was hostile. How could I teach in a storm? And then, in walked the little Latin class. I remember them that way, not only because the group was small — ten or twelve — but because, compared with the rebellious adolescents I'd been battling, these struck me as *children*. They were notably well groomed — boys in jackets, girls wearing nylons. I got the feeling that, in a school dominated by the "general" or vocational curriculum, these students consciously carried the college-bound standard. They entered quietly. If they'd already had the word about me, they gave no sign. The class mood came across as serious, a little worried. As the girls took their seats, I became aware of Mary Ellen Cann.

I have often wondered since, why Mary Ellen? At first, perhaps, I noticed her because she had two correctible physical defects that had not been corrected. She toed in — very slightly, but enough to give her walk a forward-pitching effect. Her eyes were crossed. Something else, though, set her off from the other fourteen-year-olds. She had the air of a girl intensely aware of everything around her, yet at the same time quite separate from it. As a performer selects one face to sing to, talk at, I selected Mary Ellen. If I could win her, I could win the class.

Not that this class braced itself against me. On the contrary. These children had no desire to push me over the precipice. If I fell, who would teach them Latin? Their suggestions were eager but deferential. Maybe we could start translating Caesar? Well, no, I wasn't ready for that. (Mary Ellen looked grave.) How about a grammar review? Fine. (Mary Ellen relaxed.) I started with verb conjugations, something I felt sure of. *Amo, amas, amat, amamus, amatis, amant.* This went briskly. Then, along about the third conjugation, I sensed trouble. Faces registered alarm. I searched my memory. To form the future tense, you add *bo, bis, bit* to the verb stem, right? "Ducebo, ducebis, ducebit…" I proceeded firmly. That was when Mary Ellen Cann caught my eye. (For a cross-eyed girl to send eye signals is a trick. She managed.) She was mouthing syllables. Of course. The rule changes for third conjugation, future. Not *bo-bis-bit* but different vowels. I made a quick recovery. "Excuse me. *Ducam, duces, ducet.*" Mary Ellen smiled.

On that unlikely ground − the future of Latin verbs − Mary Ellen and I became friends. It was never a cosy association. Other girls in the class, as weeks went by, gathered around my desk, books clutched to their chests, to ask about my family or tell me about theirs. Not Mary Ellen. The friendly-puppy eagerness of a "good" ninth-grader was as remote from her style as the cocky aggressiveness of the toughs. When we spoke, it was about homework, a sticky sentence in the *Gallic Wars*. And all that term she kept me straight on the third conjugation.

I stayed at Somersworth three months. There is no doubt in my mind that I lasted because of the little Latin class. I came to feel for them a kind of love, the special joy and affection that develops when young people are learning well and a teacher knows herself privileged to guide. The Latin class rescued me from humiliation, gave me back myself. By the time Mrs O'Malley was ready to return, I knew that even Advanced French would miss me a little. On my last day, a group of vocational boys gave me an incredible sweater, orange encrusted with pearl beads. The Latin class gave me a book (Rembrandt's drawings) and a letter I still keep. "When you first came," the letter began, "we were alarmed. But you have helped us with our Latin, and taught us other things we are grateful for. We shall remember you. Do not forget us." Even before one of the boys told me who wrote the letter, I guessed. It was Mary Ellen.

I have something else Mary Ellen wrote, as Caesar would say, in the fifteenth year of her age. I had given the class an assignment that had nothing to do with Latin: to write a short personal statement that would help me get to know them, as friends. "Think about the kind of activity that makes you feel most truly, completely *you* and write about that," I said. "For me, that would be teaching. What is it for you?" Most of the responses were predictable. *I am a skier. I am an actor. I am a scientist.* I thought Mary Ellen's would begin *I am a student.* I was wrong.

"I am a loner," she wrote, "and I don't like it. I wish that I could sense a bond with people; that I could share feelings, interests and experiences. But I can't. I seek a friend — one would do. I study people, hoping to see in them real honesty and goodness, but I have yet to find it. Until I do, if I ever do, I will be alone. I can take it." That was on one side of her paper. On the other, she had scribbled, "If you don't care for this, that's all right. I found it difficult to be honest. This exercise has shown me that no person can be typed under one specific heading. I *am* a loner, sure, but I am also a bookworm, a Josh White fan, and a TV addict. We are, all of us, individuals. And each man must be judged by the composite of his interests, not by one trait or fault. Thus, only by knowing the whole man can we measure his worth honestly. And even then, we might so easily misjudge."

I left Somersworth in 1953 and, though it was only minutes away from Durham, never returned until 1970. Some of my old students came by to visit, either shortly after my departure or when they appeared in our town as students at the state university. I never saw Mary Ellen, but from time to time I heard about her. She was doing outstanding work at the university; she had had an eye operation and "looked good"; she had graduated and married a Somersworth boy who worked in the mills; she was teaching English at Dover High School. The last bit of information pleased me. After my French-and-Latin experience at Somersworth, I'd spent five years at Dover as a teacher of Honours English. Mary Ellen would be a real addition to its faculty, I thought; she would like Dover's students, a lively mix of Greek, Armenian and French with traditional Yankee stock.

A teacher never wholly leaves any school where she has taught. (What is it Tennyson says? "I am a part of all that I have met.") I was always listening for word of Somersworth or Dover, still saw students from both places. So I couldn't help knowing that in the very first year of her teaching, Mary Ellen — now Mrs McCrillis — ran into trouble. No-one seemed to know why, but she didn't get along with the head of the English department. "She's trying to change things," one boy told me. "She wants more modern lit, independent projects. It'll never go at *that* school." Evidently it didn't. Word came along the grapevine that Dover's administration was leaning on Mary Ellen, trying to force her out — but that she was determined to stay. She lost all her Honours courses. One of the few teachers in her department with a Master's degree, she had been given vocational students only. When I heard that, I expressed indignation. "Oh, no, that's O.K. She doesn't mind," my informant told me. "She'd doing great things with those kids."

The next news was official. I picked up the local paper and a headline leapt at me. "DOVER TEACHER FIRED FOR INCOMPETENCE AND INSUBORDINATION." "That's outrageous," I said to Max. "Mary Ellen might be insubordinate. She's a stubborn girl. But she couldn't *possibly* be incompetent."

Max had a long history of battles with officialdom. "Please," he said. "Stay out of it."

I certainly intended to stay out. I couldn't even imagine that my help would be needed. Mary Ellen must have friends, colleagues, loyal students. Days passed. Newspaper reports accumulated, still the central events remained unclear. "Actions prejudicial to the best interests of the school": what did *that* mean? And then, one by one, a procession of young people appeared at my door. Most were former Dover students, members of my class and later Mary Ellen's. Some came from the university; they'd taken courses with Mary Ellen or met her on campus. One had been, years back, a member of the little Latin class. From them, I learned the story behind Dover's ugly headlines.

The root of the trouble, everyone agreed, was personal, a matter of temperament and belief. In a school deeply conservative, dedicated to traditional ways of doing things, Mary Ellen appeared a dangerous iconoclast. She threw out *Ivanhoe* and substituted *Demian*. To students paralysed by pencil and paper, she said, "Here's a camera. Write me an essay in pictures." She broke up the formal row-by-row classroom into little groups, each with its own project. And, in her personal life, she had taken the questionable step of filing for divorce. But teachers can't be fired for such reasons. "They were waiting," someone said, "and they got her." At last, after an accumulation of minor challenges, Mary Ellen gave them legal cause.

All her classes that year were vocational — shop boys, cosmetology girls, Home Ec girls, kids who would cry a little in the graduation march because for them the future was past. Though her assignment represented a demotion (only college prep classes confer status), Mary Ellen accepted it enthusiastically, "I thought I could do something important," she was to tell me later. "The school revolves around the bright kids and athletes, the ones who are going places. Vocies are treated like nothing, so they end up *feeling* they're nothing. I wanted — O God, I wanted them to see themselves as free, dignified human beings." One day she showed an all-male class a sex education film that featured an out-of-wedlock pregnancy. That was safe enough; the school had approved the film. Afterwards, she asked each boy to write his reaction. "That's just like it is," one wrote. "My parents hate my girl. They always think the worst and they tell me I can't see her or anything and so what happens when I do get to see her, all I want to do is fuck." Mary Ellen mimeographed a group of essays for class discussion, as she always did. She hesitated about including the paper with "The Word," then decided that, as a matter of fact, it might serve a useful purpose. Wouldn't it be good for the boys to consider whether easy obscenities expressed what they really wanted to say? She typed up the essays and had them reproduced in the school's printing department. The day after she discussed them in class, the principal called her into his office. She was suspended, as of that moment.

I suppose this is the kind of issue that would divide any community. I can understand that some administrators, some parents, would be shocked by class discussion of a four-letter word. Or alarmed by it. I have been a teacher much of my adult life; I take very seriously a teacher's responsibility to the community, but I think her primary responsibility is to the student. If Mary Ellen believed some valid educational objective was served by that paper, some gain in understanding or self-knowledge, then she was right to ignore possible repercussions. Frankly, I wouldn't myself have used it — but that was because my experiences had made me a bit careful about putting my head on the block. In any case, I'm sure no tender minds were damaged by classroom exposure to a word regularly heard in high-school corridors. As a former Dover teacher, I wrote to the school board defending not Mary Ellen personally but the educational principle involved in her action. "Mrs McCrillis may have committed an error in judgment," I wrote. "It is the sort of error any beginning teacher might make. But here is a young woman regarded at the university as unusually able and promising. She has earned the regard of students. I am sure you must share my concern about the awesome responsibility of any step that endangers her entire professional career."

The school board did not reply. I read in the newspaper that, at the dismissed teacher's request, a public hearing would be held. That surprised me. The girl I remembered — private, deeply reticent — would never have sought a public confrontation bound to be acrimonious if not downright ugly. "What can she possibly gain?" I asked. Kate, the college student who seemed to have appointed herself Mary Ellen's chief representative, flamed. "Don't you see? She owes it to the kids. She has to — well, like it's a whole rotten establishment at Dover. Mary Ellen's going to expose them all. We've got her a lawyer."

I wondered then, I wonder now, about Mary Ellen's supporters. Some were unquestionably moved by honourable motives; they cared about this young woman, they believed in her cause. Some, I'm afraid, were just excited. They liked the idea of a public sensation, especially one involving sex and obscenity. Others, campus activists, clearly saw an opportunity to "get into" the high school. In 1970, university campuses everywhere were boiling with revolt — against the "racist imperialist power structure," the Vietnam War, middle-class convention, "irrelevance" (any study not related to their concerns), American materialism and bureaucratic procedures in general. Radical students eager for provocation and confrontation found in a dismissed teacher a perfect symbol of the Berkeley slogan, "I am a person. Do not bend, spindle or mutilate." She would be their truth-telling martyr, her students converts to the cause. I remember I once said to Kate, "Mary Ellen's students obviously mean well, but that petition they're circulating — the one the newspaper printed....It's unfortunate. The tone will put people off." "Oh, *that*," Kate said. "The kids didn't write that. *We* did." So I never had any illusions about the hearing, never imagined it to be a clear-cut showdown between the good guys and the bad. On one side I saw a group of school administrators. I thought them misguided, inflexible, maybe self-interested. On the other side, a motley anti-administrative group. And in the middle, a courageous and independent young woman, a teacher who, if she lost this battle, would never teach again. How could I stand aside?

I sent Mary Ellen a note. Could I be of any help to her at the hearing? And if so, would she get in touch with me, let me know what the charges were? The reply came in a telephone call from Kate. "I'm bringing her over tonight."

At twenty-eight, Mary Ellen was quite a pretty young woman, though one got the feeling that prettiness didn't interest her. She looked tired and ill. Neither of us referred to the old days at Somersworth. She still behaved in the slightly formal, aloof manner, only the intensity was greater now. So was the control. One detail I remember as characteristic and absolutely right; she did not thank me for coming to her aid. She knew I was not "doing her a favour." Both defending a principle, we met as equals.

I asked to see the charges. "They're ridiculous," Kate said. She handed me a typed list. *Specifications of charges brought by Superintendent of Schools relative to the suspension and dismissal of Mary Ellen Cann.* (Mary Ellen was once again using her maiden name.) Nineteen separate counts. "They're not *all* ridiculous," I said. "This about the wallpaper being torn, and the radiator scratched — that *is* absurd. You can't be held responsible for damage to a classroom used by half a dozen teachers. But some of the claims about class discipline, walking out of meetings with the principal: they're serious."

"Look," Kate began. "Whose side are you on anyway?"

"Let me talk, please," Mary Ellen said quietly. "Let me tell you." Yes, she had walked out of a meeting with school authorities. She'd been called in about "curriculum policy" and handed an ultimatum: she must follow assigned reading lists in all courses. In particular, she was to abandon "that wild project" with her senior class, a production of O'Neill's play, *The Hairy Ape*. "But we're right in the middle," Mary Ellen had protested. "The boys are learning lines, building a set. You gave me per-mission — " The English department head smiled. "I had no idea it would take so long. You'll have to drop it." "I asked for just one more week," Mary Ellen told me. "So the kids wouldn't feel their work was wasted. She refused. I got up and said, 'I'll go back to the reading list — as soon as the boys have finished their play. Call it insubordination if you wish.' So yes, you could say I walked out of a meeting." In the matter of disci-pline, it was true she had failed to report a classroom fight. It had been a brief scuffle, resolved within minutes. But one of the boys got a black eye, and later that day a teacher quizzed him about it. "Sure, the rule book says teachers must report fights. Do you know what happens if a boy gets sent to the office for fighting? He's suspended. Then he goes home, tells his parents, and maybe he gets another beating. There are parents who'll say, 'O.K., you good-for-nothing bum. You make trouble at school, you go get yourself a real job, see how you like that.' Lots of times, when a vocational student gets suspended, that's the end."

Everything I know about Mary Ellen's teaching I learned as we reviewed the charges. I didn't agree with her on every point. I thought she was too casual about the mechanical details that keep a department running smoothly — getting exams in on time, preparing book lists. But in everything that really matters — concern for students, enthusiasm for her subject, preparing material and presenting it imaginatively — she was unmistakably superior, a dedicated and gifted teacher. I thought, if the school board hears this girl speak, they will have to reinstate her.

On the night of the public hearing, the case of Dover High vs Mary Ellen Cann, the defence witnesses met together for the

first time in the lawyer's office. There was a professor of education; he did not know Mary Ellen, but was prepared to discuss,
in principle, the validity of the main charges against her. There
was a sturdy, determined nun who taught at a nearby parochial
school; she'd heard about the supposedly offensive composition and wanted to speak her mind about that. There were two
Dover teachers, both in their final year at the school and so free
to oppose the administration. There was the father of a boy
Mary Ellen had taught. And me. We did not know one another.
We had no time to prepare a strategy. Innocents to the slaughter,
we went forward to confront opponents who must have
rehearsed their performance carefully, and to be judged by a
jury that could hardly be described as impartial, the Dover
school board.

The trial of a teacher is a rare, exciting event; the auditorium
was packed that night. On the stage where so many amateur
theatricals had taken place, we gathered for a real-life drama.
On one side sat the principal, the assistant principal, the
superintendent and the English department head – all, in
happier days, friends and colleagues of mine. On the other,
Mary Ellen's supporters. ("We're certainly a mixed bag," Sister
Teresa whispered as we took our seats.) And in the middle, the
seven-man school board, clearly uncomfortable in its quasi-
judicial role.

The administration spoke first. No question, they kept very
efficient records. They knew every time Mary Ellen had been
absent or late. They knew that on one occasion, between 1:30
and 2 P.M., she had left the school to pick up film for a class
showing. ("It is unthinkable," said the principal, "that anyone
would leave the building without permission.") They knew she
often put texts aside entirely so that students might produce a
play, make collages expressing their feelings about a poem – or
just talk. ("If the youngsters have not used books for three

days, a serious loss has occurred," said the department head.)
They were alarmed by the unorthodox appearance of Mary
Ellen's classes. ("I stopped in one day," the assistant principal
reported, "because I saw the paint on the door was peeling.
Students were split up into little groups. They were talking *and
laughing*.") Above all, they were dismayed by Mary Ellen's
casualness in submitting records. "*She has no seating plan*."
"She doesn't turn in a plan book every Monday. Plan books are
crucial in a regulated school society."

The case against Mary Ellen continued for two hours. The
curious, depressing thing about the charges was that almost
none of them concerned teaching or learning. One felt the
school was run not by educators, but by janitors and book-
keepers. Oh, yes, there had been classroom visits from time to
time. The principal's complete report of one such visit, read
into the hearing, stated: "Condition of the room, untidy. Teacher's
appearance, average. Teaching or audio-visual aids used, none.
Teacher's manner, unconcerned. Teacher was asked to keep the
chairs away from the walls and radiators to prevent tearing
wallpaper and scarring paint on radiators." No one connected
with administration seemed ever to have *listened* to one of
Mary Ellen's classes. As for the fact that she was "popular" —
we were reminded that "the very same thing that makes a
teacher popular would tend to make her incompetent."

No participant in a controversy can be an impartial judge. I
am not impartial. But the record of that hearing shows beyond
question that Mary Ellen's "side" concerned itself with what
most people think schools are for, student growth. We were
challenging, I suppose, the whole notion that a school is
wallpaper and radiators and plan books and seating charts.
Starting from the simple proposition that the business of a
teacher is to teach, we insisted that Mary Ellen must be judged
by her effectiveness in the classroom. "This teacher has had a

profound good influence on my son," said the parent who had come forward to protest her dismissal. "It's pretty hard to say that a boy has blossomed — but that's what he's done." As for records — well, we had all known brilliant teachers who kept poor plan books and poor teachers who made brilliant plans. The two teachers who had taught a course in conjunction with Mary Ellen spoke of her seriousness, her sensitivity to student needs, her originality and drive. Sister Teresa supported the discussion of an obscene word in "an atmosphere of mutual trust," adding, "I was amazed, when I met Mrs Crillis to find she was a *young* woman. The observations she's made were of such a depth and showed such a professional stance, I expected a middle-aged woman with at least twenty years' experience."

Then Mary Ellen spoke. I had guessed her inner strength, but never imagined she could use it in so public and painful a situation. Several times during the evening, I saw her whole body tremble and thought, "She'll break." But when she stood and faced her accusers, it was as if she had stepped out of that glass prison at last. Yes, she had disregarded the regulation about keeping up-to-date plan books. "How can a teacher communicate through the margins of a book all her hopes and plans for a course of study? To do that, I would have needed a very large book." And how, without a plan book, was the department head to evaluate her teaching? "She could have visited my classes." The prosecuting attorney leapt at that. "So, rather than following regulations, you demanded something of her?" "Yes," Mary Ellen said calmly. "I demanded something." Had she not departed from the official reading list, one she herself had prepared some time ago? She had. So it wasn't a worthwhile list? "I never said it was not. However, that was two years ago. I have been teaching for five and growing, I hope, during that time." Did she indeed believe — the prosecutor looked grim — that students shouldn't be obliged to read anything that didn't interest them? "I don't think," Mary Ellen said, "you can force anyone to read. You can try to stimulate him." It was true she had often used mimeographed material instead of official texts. "That way I can make use of new, exciting things I come across in my own reading and experience." It was true she had no seating chart. "I can tell whether everybody is there without a seating plan." For the most part her manner remained cool, offhand, with flashes of grim humour. I recognized the "unconcerned" demeanour noted in the principal's report.

But twice she blazed. The first time occurred in connection with her use of the "offensive" student paper. "You asked to have the copies returned to you after class," the prosecutor charged, "because you didn't want to get in trouble." Mary Ellen didn't bother to conceal her contempt. "If I'd been worried about trouble, I wouldn't have had that paper run off by the business office. I was not hiding it. I collected the copies because it was a private statement, not something to be passed around all over the school." Her most passionate outburst was prompted by a question from her own attorney. I suppose he was trying to justify her dangerous indiscretion on the grounds that she was dealing with difficult, low-calibre students (the kind of boys, perhaps, who could only be interested by sex and smut). "Would you," he prompted, "describe the type of student you get in vocational classes?" Mary Ellen refused the lifeline. "I find that impossible to answer," she said. "It goes against my grain to put my students in any category. I suppose vocational students are generally considered to be more difficult in terms of disciplinary problems. That's because they often have emotional and reading problems. But for me, after five years' experience, they have been very much like any other class — vital and rewarding to work with."

The hearing lasted six hours, so late that the board declined to make a decision that night. I took Mary Ellen's hand and said, "They'll have to clear you." She smiled, a student amused by her teacher's naïveté. "Not a chance. But you know, this hearing did one thing for me. It made me realize — I'd given up the idea — that I want to teach again."

A week later, the school board announced its decision. The dismissal of Mary Ellen Cann, without compensation, was confirmed and upheld. She responded in an open letter to the newspaper. "The board's decision in my case," she wrote, "demonstrates the need for an unbiased third-party procedure in cases of teacher dismissal. Harsh measures are uncalled for, when the evidence indicated no failure on my part to consider first and foremost the welfare of my students. It is sad indeed that the school's action sets a precedent for such a narrow definition of competence. In a field as vital and complex as teaching, competence should surely be assessed in terms of creativity, initiative and knowing one's subject rather than in terms of stultifying bookkeeping chores which actually prevent communication between students and teachers, between department heads and teachers, and between teachers and their fellow workers. More than any other institution, the school should make human approaches to human beings; learning demands this." A few days after the letter appeared, I got a telephone call from the principal of a nearby school. How could he get in touch with Miss Cann? "I attended that hearing," he said. "I'd like to have her at our school." I sat down to write her and was clattering away on the typewriter when I heard our dog barking at the newsboy and I ran down for the paper. That was when I learned that Mary Ellen was dead.

Of her death, I know only what I have read. On that last night, a local physician enlisted by the university's radical group telephoned two different hospitals. Would they admit a woman who had had a "miscarriage" and was haemorrhaging badly? The answer both times was No. It seems that hospitals — like

school administrators — have to be very careful. So Mary Ellen
was dispatched in an ambulance to a hospital sixty miles away.
State troopers questioned her as she lay bleeding to death. *Who
did it?* And — how thorough the law is — *Who was the father?*

A very small funeral was held in a very large new church.
Students appeared, looking frightened. There was a delegation
from the mill where Mr Cann worked; I saw two teachers from
the school. Candles were lighted, the organ played, and then a
pitiful little procession moved down the aisle. First, Mary Ellen's
parents, holding each other up. Behind them, wheeled like a
gun carriage or a bassinet, the coffin. I thought the pallbearers,
boys looking unnaturally old in their dark suits, must be all
from the high school. But someone told me, later, that one was
Mary Ellen's husband.

Not long afterward our newspaper carried the story of a Dover
senior who had just won a national English award. I read the
account of his honours, his high-school training. "Ninth grade
teacher: Mary Ellen Cann." And I remember, now, something
she said the night we couldn't save her. The prosecuting attorney had charged Mary Ellen with deliberately flouting regulations. "It was not *deliberate*," she said. "I just didn't think in
those terms. I took joy in the growth of my students. Whatever
happens, I keep the joy."

Writing
for Life

--◇--◇--◇--

I came to writing, I must confess, by accident. Child of a devoted, ambitious mother, I understood early that it was my life's mission to shine. But at what? My first thought, inspired by juvenile biographies of James Watt and Alexander Graham Bell, was that I might invent something. I thumbed hopefully through *The Book of Knowledge*, looking for suggestions. It turned out that all the best things had been invented already. I did make one stab at distinction through science. Observing, from the encyclopaedia article on carbon, that a pencil, a lump of coal and a diamond were basically all one substance, I set out to manufacture diamonds. The first step was easy. I took a few generous lumps of coal from the basement bin, buried them carefully in a coffee can filled with dirt, and sat down to wait. A day passed, two. The coal showed no signs of change. Hasty consultation of *The Book of Knowledge* revealed that pressure was involved in the happy metamorphosis. I added a stone; still no diamonds. At the end of the week I renounced science and embraced the arts.

Painting I ruled out from the start. I had no art materials other than my box of Crayolas, and anyway I couldn't draw. But words were my specialty. And judging from the examples in my school primer, poetry was easy. You took a word like *cat*, changed the initial letters and there was your poem. I gathered that poets lived rich romantic lives, died beautifully, and had attractive monuments reared over their funeral urns. Furthermore, there was a distinct shortage of women in the field. I would be a poet.

The next problem was subject matter. Armed with a freshly sharpened pencil, a clean scribbler and an apple, I sat down to think. Milton meditating on man's first disobedience and the fruit of that forbidden tree could not have been more dedicated than I. Possibilities rose and dissolved. Love? But my feelings for Sammy Barlow, a redhead in smelly corduroys, seemed hardly appropriate for verse. Death? Too gloomy. I must find a topic universal in appeal, rich in possibilities for rhyme, and happy to boot. Like Minerva from the head of Jove, the answer leapt shining forth. *Christmas*. I felt for Christmas the passion possible only to a Jewish child living in an otherwise gentile community. Christmas was magic and starlight, the gift-wrapped package at the end of the rainbow. It was ideally suited to the *toy-joy-boy* routine. Loud and clear the muses sang. They also whispered that the alphabet might provide an ideal framework on which to hang my notions. In my best Parker Penmanship script I wrote flourishingly: "'The Christmas Alphabet.' By Freidele Bruser, Age 5 Birch Hills, Saskatchewan, Canada, North America, The World."

The first couplet came easily:
A is for Apples we eat Xmas night
To celebrate Santa all jolly and bright.

The second, featuring Santa's Bag, was a natural, as was C for Christmas. ("It comes once a year And gives all folks a jolly good cheer.") I began to wonder why more people didn't write poetry. E gave me a bit of trouble, until I remembered that of course on the return journey Santa, all jolly and bright, would be toting Empty bags. F for Frost, G for Gate (surely he must pass one somewhere along the route), H for Hat...the verses flowed on, through U for the Underwear which Santa was wearing to the closing triumph of X for Xmas and Z for the Zillions of happy children on Xmas morn. My father, bursting with pride, copied out the poem in his elegant old-world script — "Certified original, B. Bruser, father" — and sent it to the *Saskatoon Star-Phoenix*.

This auspicious beginning — a published author at the age of five — launched me on a career involving unexpected, wholly delightful perks. Authors did not dust or wash dishes. Also (this I gathered from my reading), authors required *inspiration*. How, without appropriate stimulus, could I rise above humdrum daily concerns? When my mother — immortal longings in her — suggested that I write another poem, I stared thoughtfully into the middle distance. "I think I might be inspired," I murmured thoughtfully, "if I had some fudge."

Moved by regular infusions of chocolate, nuts and butter, I became a practising poet. My parents were not hard to please, and the editors of the *Star-Phoenix* Sunshine Page welcomed each ray of gladness. ("Meet things always with a smile, No doubt you'll find it worthwhile. In days to come you may be glad For being happy instead of sad.") I produced invocations to night, nature, the seasons, beauty and even the fruit of my mother's cooking. "Oh blintzes, my darlings, Oh won't you come to me? Oh, how I wish all blintzes Were growing on a tree." Uplifting fiction became a rewarding sideline.

But my parents reserved their highest enthusiasm for the

mother-poems that became my specialty. To Mother on Her Birthday, To Mother on Mother's Day, To Mother When She Got Back From Winnipeg and, simply, Mother Mine. "Though you could search the world for years And shed the largest pool of tears," runs a typical effusion, "I'm sure you couldn't find another Even half as nice as Mother. To me you are millions in silver and gold, Diamonds and rubies and riches untold." Unregenerate little atheist though I was, I composed prayers begging God's grace so that "never, never shall we part, For I love you, Mother mine."

My own favourite among these early works is a story which, like a Rorschach test, startlingly reveals the child I was. Janet, the story's heroine, is so unpopular that she's left out of all teenage parties. Never mind, she has her work. Laden with books, she trudges home, preoccupied with the upcoming examinations for which she must study. Classmates mock her industry and dedication: "You'd rather work than play, wouldn't you?" Ignoring their insults, she walks four miles to the family hovel, where she milks the cows, churns butter, cleans the barn and draws water from the well. After all this, she's tired — but not so tired as her frail old mother, who has been out washing clothes and is feeling awful. Mother collapses. The doctor, hastily summoned, says, "Typhoid fever. Three weeks' quarantine." Janet is devastated, because her exams are to be held in just *two* weeks. All that studying gone to waste....Reading the newspaper between chores, however, she spots the notice of a story competition, grand prize $700. She dashes off a story and dispatches it to the International Printing Company, the competition sponsor. A week later, the letter of congratulation arrives, with accompanying cheque. "Now, thought Janet, she could send her mother to the hospital. She'd be out of quarantine in time to take the exams." Two paragraphs later, her cup runneth over. Not only has she triumphed in the critical examinations, but academic success (aided perhaps by that $700) has transformed her life. As she walks proudly home, she hears classmates whisper, "Are you invited to Janet's party? She's such a popular girl!" Fading into the sunset of the last line, Janet smiles to herself.

In time I graduated from the Sunshine Page to the *Star-Phoenix* Young Author's Page, where my contributions elicited an enthusiasm now hard to understand. "We will meet her in the monthly magazines some day soon, and then we will be proud to have been privileged to encourage her." Illusions of glory dissipated swiftly, however, when I entered university and discovered that there was more to English poetry than Ella Wheeler Wilcox and Edgar Guest. At sixteen, I read Yeats and T.S. Eliot, and laid down my pen — I thought forever.

But after several years of marriage, worried by our lack of money, discouraged by my temporary teaching positions, depressed by a vision of myself as an incompetent wife and mother, I found myself embarked on the course charted by Janet, heroine of my early attempt at fiction: I determined to write my way out of quarantine.

Naturally the chosen territory must be one appropriate to my talents and training. *Harper's, The Atlantic, The New Yorker.* Without reading the magazine, I felt I understood *The New Yorker* formula. No plot, no snap ending. Urban characters and scene, a somewhat world-weary tone, events short on surprise and heavy on implication. Between baby feeds and changes, I produced something suitably cryptic and dispatched it to *The New Yorker.* Back it came with the speed of light — not even a rejection letter. *Write what you know,* the old composition course maxim, became in that moment revealed truth. And what I knew was most certainly not Manhattan cocktail-party chatter. It was diaper rash and burpings and cries in the night. I tore up the story and took for my theme — how easily it came! — "The

First Baby Is The Hardest." Humbled now in my aspirations, I sent the completed article to a magazine distributed free through infant-clothing departments. The editor of *Baby Talk* expressed delight at finding a mother who could spell and punctuate, and sent me $31.50 (payment at ½¢ a word). I was launched.

I wrote about babies for the next four or five years, watching my own children for Good Topics but already apprehensive as to what I would do when they left babydom. Then I discovered that kindergarteners were even more fascinating, provided more good topics, than toddlers. Having put toilet training behind me, I moved on to children's art, the meaning of play, early reading, school problems — interests that carried me into *Parents* magazine and to my first serious study of psychology. I had attended university at a time when — this seems curious now — psychology was not taken seriously as a subject for liberal-arts majors. Real thinkers read Hegel, not Freud. I was thirty when I discovered Freud — the writer, not the collection of popularized clichés having to do with sublimation and revealing slips of the tongue. Reading Freud, Jung, Karen Horney, Melanie Klein, proceeding through Piaget and Winnicott to the contributions of behaviourism and family therapy, I had a sense of having truly found my world. *Rediscovered* is perhaps more accurate. The great theorists confirmed what I had long ago intuited, from the tales of Grimm and Andersen, about sibling rivalry, parental ambivalence (ogre fathers, jealous stepmothers), childhood fears of rejection and abandonment, the child's powerful instinctive drive for autonomy and a kingdom of his own.

Human behaviour became a passion, pursued through reading and the opportunity, now, to talk with psychologists and psychiatrists. And that is how I became a journalist. I never set out to be a magazine writer — could not, in the beginning, have imagined one might earn a living that way. Like Jack in the old folk tale, I planted a few beans, not knowing they were magic.

When a vine sprouted and coiled skyward I climbed, for the pleasure of the journey and curiosity as to what I'd find at the top.

For the first ten or twelve years, my harp played domestic melodies only, simple tunes. I professed myself content with publication in *My Baby* and *Parents*. Of course every minor league player dreams of the majors; I dreamed and, occasionally, tried, dispatching large manila envelopes to national magazines. They all came back. In time I accumulated a drawerful of rejects — advice, humour, autobiography, comments on the contemporary scene — which my daughters read, as one child heartlessly said, "for laughs." It was 1963, a date to remember, when my older daughter, skimming one of these manuscripts, said, "This is actually not bad. You know, Mum, *Good Housekeeping* has a regular department for this sort of thing." This sort of thing was a personal story based on a family like ours but rather more ideal; the point, as I recall, had to do with living well on limited means. I sent it off, by a miracle of timing, at the very moment when the magazine's editors found themselves obliged to kill an article on Jackie Kennedy's extravagance, a subject unthinkable after the president's assassination. So there was a hole in the next issue — and here was this unoffending piece by a New Hampshire housewife. The features editor telephoned, barely concealing her surprise at my literacy. She offered to purchase the article at a price that came to roughly a hundred times what I was then earning as a writer. I allowed as how that would sit fine with me.

Good Housekeeping's eventual discovery that I was not a simple country maid rather spoiled what had become a favourite staff story. "We opened the envelope, and here was a publishable piece written by a totally uneducated person from rural New England." They had, however, found a willing drudge for "My Problem and How I Solved It," a long-running series designed, I always thought, less to advise or inform than to reassure. Women reading about *Good Housekeeping*'s melancholy procession of drug addicts, battered women, betrayed wives, mothers of monsters and menopausal wrecks, were bound to feel that, after all, they were pretty lucky. For several years, I regularly contributed invented problems with invented solutions, becoming in turn an alcoholic, an unfaithful wife, a helpless invalid, a victim of agoraphobia. Churning out such stuff proved easy, but inexpressibly dreary — until I got a chance to tackle a real-life reader Problem.

I had been lunching with the features editor — one of those by now regular occasions when we discussed possible features over the crab and martinis — and we had come back to her office to talk. Rather to my own surprise, I had become fond of Polly. She was totally unlike me and didn't understand me at all — and yet there had grown up between us a curious friendship. In the beginning, it was a practical arrangement. Polly was *Good Housekeeping*, was $1,500 per article. And to her, in the beginning, I was her New Hampshire find, a writing housewife picked out of the slush pile and put to work for Hearst. Over the series of lunches, though, our relationship acquired a new dimension. Polly saw me as a link with the world she left when she graduated from Vassar. And I? Well, I was touched by her feeling for me, and by occasional glimpses of the wreckage in her personal life: the disastrous first marriage ("He went *every* day to his analyst"), the psychotic episodes of her older daughter ("When she was just a kid, she used to cut her finger with a razor blade, hold the finger over the toilet, and then show me blood in her urine"). She talked smoothly about how good things were with Ralph, the second husband, but she was too strained and brittle. I never told her anything important about me, and certainly I never said what I thought about the way she edited my copy, underlining the obvious, converting ambiguities into commonplace. After all, it was her magazine; she knew who read it.

Now, in the after-lunch chit-chat, she pushed a paper across the desk to me. "Here's something rather interesting — letter from a woman in Tennessee, claims she got hooked on a diet pill. We're thinking of sending someone out to interview her. I thought of you, but you're too intellectual. You'd scare the pants off a simple little housewife." I was scanning the letter. Yes, it was intriguing. Here was a woman whose doctor started her on diet pills because she'd gained fifty pounds with her first pregnancy. Result: she got her weight down, became decidedly more energetic. So she went on refilling her prescription for five years until, on the verge of mental and physical collapse, she realized she was an amphetamine addict. The account was carefully written — vocabulary, syntax and punctuation decidedly above average. And though the writer claimed to be moved only by virtuous impulse ("I want other women to know how dangerous these drugs are"), there was evident calculation. "Oh, I don't think she's all that simple," I shrugged. *Jeopardize, lethargy, rationalize, dubious* — this was not backwoods Tennessee. "Anyway, you don't know how homey-folksy I can be."

Polly sharpened. "Want to take a trip?"

I wasn't sure, but I had learned, in the course of my strange career, to keep all the doors open just in case. I told her there was nothing about weight problems I didn't know, that as a matter of fact, I had taken diet pills myself. I left it there and we moved on to other matters, parting without further mention of Kay Berger, the pill-addicted housewife. But I wasn't surprised when, two weeks later, Polly telephoned from New York. "Wade wants you to do that diet-pill story as a problem piece. How soon can you leave?"

I had already packed my bags when a slight problem occurred

to me. Kay Berger was meeting me at the airport nearest to her home in Erwin — a sixty-mile drive. And she was arranging to have me meet her doctor and was seeing to hotel accommodations. She was, in short, putting herself out and, remembering the tone of that letter, I could be sure it wasn't just for thanks. Also, recalling other *Good Housekeeping* interviews, I knew that "Thanks" might be all Hearst had in mind. I put in a call to New York.

"Polly, I don't mean to pry, but I think I should know before I put this woman to a lot of trouble. Is Kay Berger being paid for the interview?"

Polly was offhand. "Well, naturally we pay something if a person *asks*."

"What I mean is....Look. She's picking me up at the airport and I'm sure she'll take me back next day. Do I do something about this, or have you taken care of it?"

Polly hesitated. "I guess offering to pay her gas wouldn't be the thing."

"No," I said firmly. "It would not."

"Hmm. We could do something like this. Tell her the magazine expects to pay for her time and ask her what she thinks her time is worth. Try to keep the figure down. A hundred, hundred and fifty is O.K."

I wasn't happy about being left in charge of financial negotiations — but a successful interview might well depend on Kay Berger's state of mind. She'd want to be very sure she was doing more than alerting other women to the dangers of amphetamines. As I boarded the plane for Bristol, I felt the weight of my role: half girl reporter, half Hearst hatchet man.

At Bristol airport, I scanned the scattered crowd. That woman with the little girl — no, Kay Berger had boys. I smiled back at a fancy hat and gloves, but she was waving at a hatted traveller behind me. Someone was watching, though: a smallish, windblown woman in baggy slacks and soiled yellow jersey. A cheap machine-embroidered sweater was thrown about her shoulders; her feet were bare in scuffed loafers. She was not fat, but she could have used a good brassiere.

"Mrs Berger?"

She nodded, and I was struck for the first time by the profound heaviness of her movements. When she lit a cigarette or opened a car door, you felt you were watching the action on a slow-motion film — the revolution of the wrist, the opening and closing of fingers. Looking closely, I saw that she had fine blonde hair and a pretty face, but few people would bother to look closely. She had the manner of a woman who simply shakes her hair out of her eyes mornings and applies lipstick in the dark.

"Car's over here." She moved toward the brown Chevrolet. Two little boys disentangled themselves from the shrubbery and tumbled after. "Oh, this here's Jon...Eddie. Hank we pick up near the school." She had made no arrangements to have the boys taken care of, then. Damn. I had counted on the afternoon for interviewing. I stared out the windows at the unfamiliar world — lots of rhododendron, evidently growing wild, a brilliant strange red bird, signs advertising scrapple, funny ramshackle tacked-together stalls and stores along the roadside. And mountains all around. "I didn't realize we were in mountain country."

Kay turned her head slightly, slowly. "Shut up, boys. Yes, this here's Appalachia. You're seeing the better part. But just maybe five miles from our place, at Bumpus Cove, you'd see things you wouldn't believe. People living in shacks, no doors, no windows. Lots of kids don't go to school 'cause they've got no shoes." Her voice was dark molasses. Though she told me she grew up in Massachusetts, her speech retained no hint of the East.

I exclaimed at an old woman sweeping her yard: she wore a hat like a popover. Oh, yes, Kay said, plenty of *those* on the old people. Come spring, you could buy sunbonnets in the stores anywhere in Unicoi county. A little farther on I saw something even more startling than the Kate Greenaway headgear. "Is that a *bottle tree*? Oh, could you stop a minute, please?"

The car squealed and ground to a halt, the two little boys fell forward and howled in unison. "Shut up, boys. Now, what did you say about a tree?"

I pointed. In the front yard of a mouldy-looking shack, a bare-limbed tree was hung with coloured bottles. The brilliant January sun flashed on blue and green and yellow; odd bits of yarn and ribbon fluttered in the wind. I had read about bottle trees — in Eudora Welty's "Livvie" an old black man keeps one to catch evil spirits. Kay Berger squinted and shrugged as I told her. "Yah, I guess I've seen 'em before. Never thought about it. Course this's a pretty backward area. You take Erwin, now. That's the town where they hanged the elephant."

I confessed ignorance; she was pleased to be able to tell me. "Thirty years or so back, a circus came to Erwin and the elephant went berserk, trampled a man to death. Townspeople were all up in arms. They rounded up the elephant, had a trial, and found him guilty. So they hung him."

"Hung *the elephant*?"

"Yep. From a big crane. Right up until a year or so ago, you could still buy photographs of the elephant hanging from the top of the crane. But then the town fathers got the idea that kind of thing gave the place a bad name."

When I asked her what people did for a living, she said, there was some industry, and "crops. Strawberries in spring, tomatoes, tobacco. And moonshine — *lots* of moonshine."

I began to feel part of a musical comedy, or a folk song. "That really goes on?"

"The woods're full of stills. Matter of fact, that's one of Chuck's problems. You know he's a ranger. Well, if he comes on a still, he's supposed to report it, and then, when the report's travelled all along the line, government comes along and blows the still sky-high. But you get known as a ranger who does that, you end up one dead ranger. So mostly Chuck is careful not to find stills. When he smells mash, he goes the other way."

I turned the conversation, discreetly. Cost of bootleg whisky ("white lightning"), average income....When she told me that teachers got around $2,600 a year and she sometimes substituted for $6 a day, I figured the time had come to strike a blow for Hearst. Polly Rand's speech ran trippingly from my tongue. "Naturally the magazine expects to pay for your time. What do you think your time is worth?"

Edge and concentration emerged from the sluggishness. Kay Berger's eyes were on the road, but I felt as if they were fixed on me. "What do *you* think it's worth?"

I shrugged. "Well, you know best what you might be doing if you weren't talking to me. Cleaning house, teaching — "

Kay was no fool. "Well," she said carefully, "I know *Redbook* pays $500 for a story."

I had expected calculation, but not *that* amount. What crust, I thought. "*Redbook*," I said firmly, "pays $500 for a finished, publishable manuscript. A letter is not a manuscript."

She sulked. "I could've written lots more. I told that editor so."

"Mmm. But our experience is — " (*Our*, indeed. What was I saying?) "Our experience is that very few women tell their own story in a form the magazine can use. So we prefer to have the material presented by a professional writer."

A small tight silence. She was in a box: I was already here, too late to bargain. "I'll think about it," she said. I assumed that meant she would consult her husband.

"Fine," I said. "Tell me" — looking out the window again — "why do they paint the trunks of the trees white?"

"Do they?" Her eyes followed mine. "Oh, yah. I haven't any idea."

"Some forester's wife you are."

"I'm just not that interested in trees. Not that I've got anything *against* 'em."

Erwin was a dowdy town. Store fronts and window displays were brown drab; people moved more slowly than on the streets of northern cities, dress was more conservative. I commented on the absence of blacks and Kay nodded, "Oh, you wouldn't find a Negro would *dare* come into Erwin. I saw one driving through once, but that was ages ago. Your hotel's down that street — see, with the pillars." I thought perhaps the moment had come to make firm plans. "Would you," I asked, "have time to start the interview this afternoon? I'll plan to eat dinner at the hotel, and then maybe this evening — " "Oh, well, if you want spaghetti with us, you're welcome." I tried not to look as if I'd counted on an invitation — but I needed all the time I could get. Besides, dinner at the Bergers' might provide all sorts of material. I accepted happily, asked if I might stop at the drugstore on the way to her house. While she double-parked, I bought a five-pound box of chocolates. When I gave the plain brown-paper bag to Kay, she glanced inside quickly and folded the bag tight shut so the little boys wouldn't see it. "Hey, wha'd the lady give you?" "It's aspirin," she said shortly. "The lady has a headache."

We picked up Hank and started for home. The Bergers' house was about five miles from town, a small cabin-like structure set squarely on its lot. No path, no ornamental planting of any kind.

The door led directly into a kitchen-dinette, and from here you could see almost the whole house. It was ugly. Not cheap ugly, just ugly ugly. Imitation braided rug (Colonial), pseudo-brocade sofa (Regency), a monstrous mosaic coffee table (do-it-yourself), an obviously expensive spinet marooned on a chenille-y carpet. There was an air of things having been very recently put in order, but with imperfect success. I detected, here and there, the precise path of mop and cloth through settled dust. A miscellaneous pile of toys, books, clothes was heaped behind a half-shut door.

Kay flopped into a chair by the oilcloth-covered table. "I get so *tired*, she sighed." "I never did have much get-up-and-go, but since this pill business, it's been murder." I abandoned, sadly, my visions of a good cup of coffee, and took out my notebook. How to get her started? I needed to find out why those diet pills had such a hold. Kay Berger's physical appearance confirmed my hunch that weight control was not the chief motive; this was not a woman to whom looks were all that important. "Suppose you start telling me about yourself," I suggested. "What kind of child were you? Have you always had a weight problem?" Jon appeared with a tray of plastic blocks, fussing because the red one wouldn't *do*. Kay smacked him impersonally, as one might swat a fly. "What were you saying? Weight problem? Well, I was always on the plump side, but solid, not bulgy. I never move less'n I have to. I guess that's got something to do with it. When other kids were out playing relevo or kick-the-can, I'd be curled up on the couch. I'm a real easy-going person. Nothing ever makes me mad. I'd have to be told what to get mad at, y' know? And I'm lazy. I never made a big effort for anything in my whole life." "Not even for Chuck?" I suggested.

She shrugged. "Nah. Actually, that's how I got him. I mean, all my sorority sisters chased him, and he was fed up with pushy women. Chuck was one of the best-looking fellows on the U. of Massachusetts campus. You wouldn't think it to see him now, but he was a real attractive high-living boy." Did she fall madly in love? A pale smile. "Christ, no. I'd just about written him off — he graduated before me, and left for a job in Texas — and then, about March of my senior year, he sent a ring and said he was coming back in June to marry me. Well, I usually do what people tell me to. Anyway, I was graduating and what else would I do? I certainly didn't want to go to *work*." Had the marriage worked out well? Yes — they fought about little things, but they were both interested in politics, and people, and music. It was a pretty good arrangement.

"Hard at the beginning, though. That first job of Chuck's was in Cleveland, Texas. What a dump. One paved street, and nothing to see when you looked up or down. If a horse leaned against the porch to scratch his back, the whole place shook. Inside, cockroaches ran around like mad. I'd pick up a broom and a baby water moccasin dropped out on the floor. And damp! You could sit and watch things mildew."

Kay had a teaching job in East Texas — "Chuck got it for me. I've never found a job for myself" — but she became pregnant almost at once. "I was hungry all the time, and I figured what the hell. Breakfasts, I took to eating three pieces of toast instead of one, and all three goppy with butter. I was gaining five, six pounds a month, but my doctor didn't fuss at me one bit. I weighed 180 when Hank was born. Quite a lot to carry if you're five foot four. I didn't worry, though. I figured I'd lose it all when the baby came."

There was a wild scream, then howls, shouts, sobbing, from the living room, where the boys were watching TV. Kay didn't move. She sighed. "That's the way it's been ever since. One thing after another."

"Mama!" Hank dashed in. "Mama, Eddie's dropping Caldonia head first into the Tinkertoy box, and Caldonia don't like it!"

"She do so like it!" Eddie was a very small three-year old, but full of fight as he appeared with a cardboard cylinder in one hand and a dusty kitten held by the neck. "Look!" He dropped Caldonia nose first. The tube was narrow; the kitten scrabbled and squealed. Kay shook her head. "You can see why Eddie's got those cat scratches on his face. Some day he'll be blinded, and that'll be that."

I asked how many animals they had. Four, no, five cats. (There seemed to be more. Cats raced across the kitchen counter and over the table as we talked.) They used to have a raccoon — Chuck found it in the woods — and she liked him fine. "He was smarter than the cats. Could open the door with his hands. He'd go out for a walk every morning, play around in the woods some. Round supper time, he'd turn the door knob and walk in. Almost like a person." What was his name? "Just *Raccoon*." I said I'd like to see this cultivated creature. "Oh, we left him in Lufkin, last place we lived." Did they give him away? She seemed surprised by the question. "We moved one afternoon while he was out moseying around." The same picture occurred to us both simultaneously. She looked sad a moment. "Yah. Sometimes I think about him coming home for supper and trying to turn that knob."

We returned to the story of Kay's weight problems. After Hank was born, she dropped to 165 pounds and there she stuck. "I wasn't exactly a Barbie-Doll figure before, but this was new. Size 18. I didn't have a thing that fitted, so I mostly flopped around in dusters feeling sorry for myself." She considered dieting, but felt she couldn't keep going on less food.

"Hank was colicky, a big healthy baby but rotten-acting. Cry, cry, cry. And then Chuck'd come home from work and chew me out because the dishes weren't done, or I hadn't put his shoes away like he likes them. Chuck isn't a mean man, but he's a bug on neatness. You should see his bureau drawers! His folks never had much, and he was brought up to take care of things. Besides, there were three women in his house — grandma, cousin *and* mother — so naturally he's used to everything being just so. Now my background was absolutely different. My mother was easy-going. *And* extravagant. She hated leftovers. Anything left from a meal — could be a T-bone steak — it went to the cat."

Mention of meals prompted me to suggest that maybe she'd like to start getting dinner ready. It was five o'clock, and for the last hour the little boys had been foraging in the cupboards. Kay didn't move. "No call to do anything till Chuck gets home. What was I saying? Oh, yes, Chuck and me. Like I say, he's a driver. I'm a floater. Maybe it's glands. I never had much energy. You know, the four years I went to college, I didn't once make my bed. Mother'd send me off with a pile of linens and a quilt. So I'd use the quilt for a bedspread, and every night I just rolled myself up in the quilt. I had a system with clothes too. Mother always packed these beautiful suitcases full of nice things. I used to take off the top skirt and sweater, then shove the suitcases under the bed for the rest of the year. That way, when I went home, I had my suitcases all packed."

The strain of the baby, her own extra weight, Chuck's impatience, were too much for Kay's limited energy. "I was sinking deeper and deeper. Then I got pregnant again and I thought, well, this is the end. I just cannot cope. But round about this time Chuck got transferred. I had a new doctor, and this one said right off, 'We've got to do something about your weight. I

want you to take one of these pills every morning and see if it
doesn't help get your mind off food.' "

"Well, the pills took my mind off food, but that wasn't the
half of it. About half an hour after I'd swallowed a pill, I went
off like a rocket. It was like I'd been given a shot. I wasn't
nervous, but excited inside. And energy! For the first time in
my life I felt zingy. I went right out and got a job, pregnant and
all, helping in a kindergarten. Every morning I'd fix breakfast,
take Hank to the baby-sitter, dash off to school, dash back at
lunch, pick up Hank, feed him and bed him down and then get
going on the house. I had no trouble with weight. Who wanted
to eat? A month after Jon was born, I weighed 130. Chuck was
real pleased."

She was still taking the diet pills then? "Oh yes. I mean, I was
planning to give them up, just as soon as I was on my feet
again. But you know how it is with a new baby and another
still in diapers. Run, run, run. I couldn't imagine getting through
the day without that extra lift. I'd say to myself, 'I won't take a
pill today,' and then I'd remember I had to go shopping or clean
house or **make** a cake. I always had a reason to take one."

There was a spatter of gravel against the side of the house,
and the little boys tumbled out of the living room. "Daddy!
Daddy's home!" Chuck Berger was a tall man, lean and light-
moving, with a serious, almost academic air. Kay performed
introductions. He nodded and moved to the refrigerator. "How
about a drink?" I accepted gratefully. I'd had nothing since
breakfast, and it was now almost seven o'clock. Chuck fixed
two Scotch and sodas; Kay moved with her glass of port to the
kitchen counter and opened a can of spaghetti. The rest of the
dinner was prepared with one hand. Kay emptied a package of
hamburger into the bowl, shook into it a large bagful of commercial bread stuffing. Then an egg. She kneaded the mass

dreamily with her right hand, sipping port and talking, her sentences punctuated by the occasional thud and sputter of a meatball hitting the hot grease. "Like I was saying, I kept up my pills right along. When Chuck got transferred — that was here to Erwin — I took my prescription. Had no trouble getting it filled. So until two months ago, I took a pill every day. I never missed one. If I was going to be away, even overnight, I carried my pills with me. When we went on holiday, I made sure I had plenty of pills. The only reason I didn't take two or three at a time was because they cost a lot. O.K., boys, supper's ready!"

We sat down at the oilcloth-covered table. Kay slapped down six white plastic plates, emptied into a white bowl the pan of coiled spaghetti and set out on a platter eighteen lumpy balls. Frying had shrunk the fat out of the hamburger, and now chunks of bread stuffing projected oddly from charred surfaces.

I occupied myself with the ice cubes in my drink, grateful for the distraction created by Eddie's sudden howl. "I asposed to get cake! It's my birfday!" Kay said "Oh, Eddie, it is *not*," and Chuck asked, "Haven't we got a bit of cake?" She rummaged in the breadbox, muttering. At last a pale rectangle of commercial sponge cake appeared, still stuck to its accordion-pleated wrapping. She shaved off five thin slices, and I was contemplating what might be my share when Chuck said, "Let's have coffee in the living room." We moved off, each clutching his mug. The boys shoved back their chairs and escaped. Out of the corner of my eye, I saw that Caldonia had got my meatball.

"Eddie must have been born in Erwin," I prompted. Kay nodded. "Mm. I got pregnant a month after Jon was born. That was some happy news. I didn't tell the new doctor I was on diet pills, because I'd made up my mind to stop as soon as the baby came. But that year the roof fell in on us. My mother died, and Dad came to live with us. He was pretty shook up, and the kids made him nervous. And it was forest-fire season. Sometimes

Chuck'd get three, four calls a day. He'd be out all night and come home at 8 A.M. wanting a steak — just when the kids were hollering for cereal and Dad pattered into the kitchen looking for a cup of tea. I was practically out of my mind."

"Didn't the pills make you *more* nervous?" I asked.

"Oh no. At least, not jittery-nervous. Later on, my nerves did go, but that was more a kind of depression."

Chuck interrupted for the first time. "You were different, Kay. I noticed that. You were blowing up at the kids quite some."

I scanned my notes. "You say the diet pills made you depressed."

"After a while, yes. I'd been on them — oh, maybe four years — when I read about a new law against refilling amphetamine prescriptions. Now, of course I didn't *know* whether my pills were amphetamine, but I had a kind of hunch. Specially when I started hearing about people getting hooked on pep pills. But after all, I was taking just one pill a day, and I didn't have any trouble getting my prescription filled at the drugstore. Everything *had* to be O.K., but I was worried. Moody, too."

"Moody is a mild word for it," Chuck grinned. "She was bloody hell to live with. One night I came home late from a fire, and here was a note propped on the kitchen table. Says she's leaving me. Just like that."

"What did you do?"

"Well, my first thought was to go and kick her out of bed. Then I thought again. 'Chuck,' I said to myself, 'whatever rut you choose now you'll be in for the next twenty, thirty years.' So I got me a can of beer and thought it over. Maybe I hadn't been helping as much as I should. Three boys is a lot of work. And losing so much weight might've hit Kay harder than I knew. I figured I'd sleep on it, talk things over next morning. But next morning, she'd forgotten all about the note."

Kay was leaning back now, eyes closed, one loafer barely

dangling from the foot slung over the couch edge. "Round about that time, I got so I thought I was losing my mind. I'd have these weird memory lapses — like forgetting the name of somebody I'd known for years. Or I'd be driving along in the car and realize I didn't know where I was supposed to go. People talked to me, and I couldn't concentrate. Sometimes I felt all shaken up inside, but then I'd ask Chuck, 'Is my hand steady?' and he'd say, 'Sure.' " Her voice trailed off, and I rose with a brisk "I mustn't tire you. We can finish off tomorrow. Perhaps your husband — "

Kay sat up. "Oh, I'll drive you to the hotel. Chuck can do the dishes and put the kids to bed." Heading back to town, she was briefly animated. "One good thing about this mess, I get a lot more help from Chuck. He's better with the boys than I am. I was never all that anxious to have kids. I like mine well enough, you understand. But the home and family bit really isn't my kind of thing."

In the comfortable darkness, I tried a direct question. "What *is* your kind of thing?"

She spoke for the first time with a suggestion of eagerness. "I love cities — people — theatre. I used to think I'd maybe go into backstage work. That was before I married a ranger."

"Did you have a hard time deciding to give up the theatre world?"

"Well, I didn't exactly *have* it to give up, you know. I was active in college dramatics, that's all. Everything considered, marrying Chuck has worked out pretty well. Only it's not what you'd call exciting."

"What times in your life do you think of as specially exciting?"

The car jerked to a stop at a red light, and Kay turned to me. "Oh, the plays — getting ready. Any crisis before a performance revved me up. Like the time I was on properties for *Teahouse of the August Moon*, and the director decided, twenty-four hours before opening, that he wanted forty pillows dyed orange. I had to do it all myself, on the double. That gave me a terrific lift." The light flashed green, she tapped the accelerator, and as we plunged onward through the night she said, with a kind of wondering, "You know, that's how the pills made me feel. As if I had to dye forty pillows orange, and go-go-go."

We never had time to visit Kay's doctor. Next morning, by arrangement, Kay picked me up after breakfast. (I was feeling deliciously sodden after what the drugstore counter girl described as a "little old honey bun," a marvel of spongy richness and sweetness coddled in sizzling butter.) We stopped by the post office, and she sorted eagerly through the mail. "You get lots of letters," I observed. "I write lots," she said. "That's mostly what I do, besides read. I write to magazines, newspapers, actors, manufacturers, radio programs....Like if I see a show I like, I write in; and when I see one I don't like, I write and say why. That's how I got involved with Peter Brown."

"Who's he?"

"An actor. He gets mostly small parts, but I have a feeling things'll break for him very soon now."

"You know him personally?"

"Well, not exactly. You see — oh, ages ago — I saw him on this TV show where he was really good, so I wrote in to tell him I used to think he was too pretty but now I'm changing my mind. And I got an answer from the president of his fan club. So now I correspond regularly with her — she sends me all the clippings — and I try to do what I can, writing around to producers and asking 'Why don't you get Peter Brown?' There's a big deal cooking right now....Maybe something in *Variety* —"

I noticed the rolled copy of *Variety* in her mail bundle. "That's a surprising paper to find in Tennessee," I observed.

"Mm. It's expensive — Chuck doesn't dream *how* expensive — but I need it, on account of Peter."

Back at the Bergers', we settled at the kitchen table once more. Kay shoved aside the breakfast dishes and got out her Peter Brown scrapbook; I riffled through two thick volumes of Browniana. Peter Brown in his first movie bit roles, Peter Brown with assorted starlets, Peter Brown with his first starlet wife (Cindi or Marti or Suzi or Candi), domestic joy, domestic trouble, rumours of rifts, separation, reconciliation, divorce, more starlets, second marriage (to Roni or Merri or Kathi or Luci), baby. Determinedly, I dragged the conversation back to diet pills. "According to my notes" (a professional frown) "you began to have trouble after you'd been on the pills five years."

"That's right. I started to get these terrible cramps in my arms and legs. I'd wake up as tired as if I'd already walked ten miles. An hour on my feet, and I couldn't take the pain. I'd have to lie down. Mornings it was all I could do to get the boys dressed and fed before I flopped on the couch again."

"You didn't consult a doctor?"

"I did, sure. But I didn't say a word about the pills, and he couldn't seem to make any sense out of my symptoms. I had headaches too, and one infection after another. Well, Josh — that's our doctor — took X-rays and gave me some B vitamins and calcium pills. But I went on feeling sick and awfully depressed."

"Had you made any connection in your own mind between the diet pills and your illness?"

"Sort of. But I didn't face up to it, not until last October. That was when I came down with gastro-enteritis. I called Josh — I had a temperature of 103 — and he said to stop by the hospital. Well, I thought it'd be just for a shot, so I didn't have so much as a pair of slippers — and, of course, no pills. Not that I thought about it at the time. I was so weak — dehydration, virus, green death, all at once — that I could hardly walk. That was a Saturday. For two days I was flat out with sedatives, but when I came off them I was fit for a straitjacket. Talk about drug addicts climbing the walls when they need a fix....Let me tell you, I know what that means. I couldn't sit or lie down or stop moving. I drove the nurses crazy, pacing the floor and shaking with nerves. My head felt like it was separated from my body, just floating. Tuesday morning, Chuck took me home. I went straight for my bottle, took a pill, and half an hour later I was 'normal' again. So I knew I was hooked all right. On a simple little diet pill."

The phone rang. "Mm," Kay said. "Yah, she is. Oh, I think you'd better not. I'll tell you all about it tomorrow, O.K.?" Hanging up, she shrugged. "That was my neighbour. She's dying to see what you look like. Of course, I haven't told but a few people about a magazine writing me up. It's got to be a secret, because in Chuck's job, you're not supposed to make the news. And I wouldn't want to get the druggist in trouble."

"I wonder if he realized that refilling your prescription was dangerous as well as illegal?"

"He realized, all right. That day, after I got home from the hospital, I phoned and asked, 'What's in those pills I've been taking?' He said, 'Dexadrene and compazine.' I said, 'Is that any kind of amphetamine? Because I've been on them for five years, and I think they're making me sick.' Well, I could see he was scared. He was slow answering and then he said, 'Dexadrene's a stimulant, one kind of amphetamine. You'd better stop right away.'"

"And you did stop?"

"I sure did. I went right to Josh's office and told him the whole story. He was wild."

"Had he ever had other cases like yours? Women becoming addicted to pep pills?"

"Matter of fact, he had. One patient — just a girl, a high-strung type — ended up with a nervous breakdown. And Josh's no country bumpkin. He's U. of Tennessee, a really sharp doctor. He'd read a lot about the subject. Like a study of amphetamine addicts in Japan, where droves of women had to be hospitalized, they were so shook up. Most of them were O.K. in six months, but some were in poor shape fifteen years later. Boy, that scared me."

"What did the doctor say about your case?"

"He doesn't commit himself. Just that it'll take time — and willpower — before I'm back to normal. I've got pills for withdrawal pains, but there isn't anything can help with the way I feel."

From the playroom, where the two younger boys were watching TV, came a terrific ruckus. Slaps, shrieks, cries of "It's mine!" alternating with "Is not, is not!" Kay lit another cigarette and shook her head wearily. "Stuff like that I could wear myself out with. Chuck goes in and cracks the whip when the kids act up, but I figure they've got to learn. Settle their own problems. I've got all I can handle just getting through the day."

"You're still feeling the effects of the pills, then?"

With her left index finger Kay traced a star design in the breakfast crumbs. "I'm tired all the time — and it's been months now since I went off the pills. And I get so depressed. Oh, I'll have a couple of good days, and then I'll get up one morning and I can tell right away, *This is it.* I get cold inside, so cold nothing warms me up, and weak. Days like that, I can get a crying jag over nothing. Eddie'll spill his milk, say, and that sends me off. Sometimes — I haven't even told Chuck this — I've thought of suicide. What's the use of living if *this* is life? But I'm not brave enough. And things are getting better. There's a longer stretch between the bad times — and the bad times don't last as long. I think my mind's clearing too. When I was on the pills, I got so I couldn't remember. I'd read a book, and when I was finished I hardly knew what it was all about. But the other day I gave myself a CBS news test, and I came out pretty well."

I glanced at my watch. Two hours to plane time. "Perhaps we can finish on the way to the airport."

Kay looked disappointed. "You know, I've got other stories too. Like my adopted brother who turned out psycho. And the time one of my father's friends tried to rape me in our basement − "

Gently, I rejected the offered wealth. "For the time being, I've got just about all I can handle. Now, I remember you were anxious not to be recognized in the magazine story. So I'll change a lot of facts − your husband's occupation, your state, the number and sex of your children...."

The look now was disappointment *and* dismay. "Good grief, if you change all that, it won't be *me*, will it? I'd like for you to keep Chuck a forester − and just make the place Appalachia, which is true enough. I think the three boys should be in it. You can change the names."

Driving back to Bristol, Kay was chatty. I could tell she was trying to get me back on the subject of fee, but − rather maliciously − I ignored the cues. Finally she took the direct line. "I've been thinking about what you asked − you know, what I'd expect to be paid. When I talked to that editor on the phone, she said there'd be a couple hundred dollars in this for me."

I shrugged non-committally. "She certainly couldn't have meant *more*."

"Well..." − eyes on the road, with an air of grudging condescension − "I guess two hundred will be all right."

We said no more about the money, and when we parted, it was with the air of good friends after a pleasant reunion. "Sure hope you'll come back!" she called as I boarded the plane. "I don't know when I've talked so much!"

I started writing up the interview on the Washington-Boston flight. As I wrote, the story shaped itself into something much more than fat-woman-hooked-on-diet-pills. Kay Berger would rather be thin than fat, but weight was not an obsession with her: she told me she'd gained twenty pounds in the four months since she gave up dexadrene, but that clearly bothered her less than the loss of energy. The real story was the tale of an almost pathologically lethargic woman who found a new personality in the amphetamine bottle. When Kay talked of her pills, she talked of pep, vitality, get-up-and-go. "For the first time in my life," she'd said, "I wasn't a party poop. And I'd do all kinds of motherly things, like whipping up a cookie mix instead of buying a box of graham crackers." The story wrote itself; I kept, as far as possible, to Kay's own idiom and the slow, circling rhythms of her speech. Rereading the finished account, I was pleased with its faithfulness. It was to go in the "My Problem And How I Solved It" series, but it didn't sound like the series. Most of the problem pieces were written by professionals and read, in fact, as if they'd all been written by the same professional — slick, reasonable, articulate. But the Berger account, written in the first person, sounded like Kay — a little blurred, disorderly, self-involved. I sent the manuscript off to New York, sure that Polly would find it a welcome change.

A week later, Polly phoned and there was trouble in her crisp cordiality. "Look, I hate to ask you to redo this piece, but my God!" She spared my feelings as much as possible, but clearly she was appalled. Everyone in the office was appalled. Wade said it sounded like *True Confessions*; Connie wondered who would read about a drip like that; Harry was sure the woman had glandular problems which should be explored. And Polly thought there was no clear story line. "You've confused the issue. All that stuff about her college bedspread, and forty orange pillows.... Look, this is a story about a fat girl who goes overboard on dieting, right? Keep to that, leave out the itsy details. And watch your style. This copy's loaded with clichés."

I tried to explain that the clichés were deliberate — they were the woman's voice, what she was like.

Polly was brisk. She wanted me to skip the realism and deliver a nice clean problem in my own prose by the weekend. The May issue was already moving into cast proof.

I was done well before the weekend. It was easy. I eliminated the interesting, simplified the complex pattern of impulse and motive, transformed Kay Berger into the Ideal Magazine Narrator. Polly phoned to congratulate me — "It's *really* good, they love it" — and the cheque followed. I hardly glanced at the May issue when it came, but a glance showed me there had been still further simplifications. I winced at the fake photo of a model, and the caption. What would Kay Berger feel when she opened the May issue of *Good Housekeeping* and saw "her" story? I know that I experienced, not just disappointment, but dismay and shame. Making up stories was one thing. I'd always done that. Converting real people into cartoon characters, truth into cheap fiction — that was a betrayal of my central self. I had never seen myself as a mute inglorious Milton (that one talent which is death to hide lodged with me useless). On the other hand, I had surely not studied the classics of the Western world in order to write about a fat girl who goes overboard on dieting or a man locked naked in a car trunk after the rape and murder of his girlfriend. It was the car trunk assignment that ended this phase of my career. "I can't do it," I told Polly. "I am not going to ask a man how he felt watching a thug strangle his fiancée with her own pantihose. And I can't see any possible justification for publishing such a story." "It has social value," Polly said. "That man went to prison for a crime he didn't commit. So you see...." I didn't see. Faced with an impasse, she produced an alternative. "O.K. We'll find you something else. How would you like to be Dr Joyce Brothers?"

In the 1960s, Dr Joyce Brothers was a household name. A man-in-the-street query would instantly have produced the answer, "Famous psychologist." Few people, however, knew how she had become famous — as a successful contestant in the wildly popular TV show, *The $64,000 Question* (and later, with inflation, *The $124,000 Question.*) The program's basic gimmick depended upon unlikely expertise. Though few viewers would have sat patiently through the interrogation of a Shakespeare expert on matters Shakespearean, hundreds of thousands watched transfixed as a cop on the beat demonstrated his familiarity with the Bard. Joyce Brothers — image a petite adorable blonde — appeared as a psychologist expert in, of all things, boxing. (A cynical friend of mine once commented, "You can find everything anyone would want to know in *The Encyclopaedia of Boxing*, which is not a big book. A smart person could master the field in a week.") The program featured an impressive array of devices designed to establish authenticity: a soundproof glass booth in which contestants were isolated (to prevent prompting from the studio audience); questions delivered on air, in locked boxes, by uniformed representatives of a well-known security firm. Under these trying conditions, the expert of the night searched his memory, agonized, rapped his forehead — and did or did not produce the magic words. "Leporello is a character in Mozart's opera *Don Giovanni*." "Robert Clive was a British soldier and statesman in the service of the East India Company." Then a disgruntled contestant exposed the program as a complete hoax. Attractive contestants, those who drew viewers, were fed questions in advance; when the whistle-blower's popularity declined, he was cut off from pre-program access to questions and flunked out. Other exposures and confessions followed. Almost alone among the motley crew of self-styled experts, Joyce Brothers emerged squeaky clean. So she moved on, a boxing authority become, in the way of American hype, an authority in matters psychological. She appeared on more talk shows, wrote books, promoted courses in popularity and marital joy, became a magazine columnist. Her bland, super-sweet, faintly rabbity smile now appeared everywhere over material best described as "Advice to Everybody about Everything."

I was surprised by *Good Housekeeping*'s suggestion that I might become Joyce Brothers. Wasn't there a real Dr Brothers? Polly explained. Dr Joyce, with all her wisdom, was not exactly a writer. Besides, she had many, many commitments. She needed…an assistant. Under the proposed arrangement, Dr Brothers would choose topics for her monthly column, "On Being A Woman." She would send me relevant research and her "point of view." I need only write it up, give insight the grace of art. I would be paid what sounded like perhaps one-tenth of the columnist's fee, but even that wasn't bad. Tempted by the prospect of a regular income – every freelancer's dream – still I hesitated. After all, I was not a psychologist. Polly smiled enigmatically. "Believe me," she said, "you know enough."

And so it proved. Every month I received – sometimes at the official last moment, more often late – a large package from Joyce Brothers. The envelope marked Research contained newspaper clippings (old advice-to-the-lovelorn columns, AP dispatches) and articles from *Reader's Digest, Cosmopolitan, Pageant, Psychology Today* (this last the heavy stuff). And then – glorious, unforgettable – Dr Brothers's personal thoughts on infidelity, alcoholism, mental illness, abortion, retirement. No problem was too complex, or too profound, to resist solution in a few crisp paragraphs. Has your husband lost interest in sex? Take out your hair rollers before bedtime. Oh, and be sure never to appear in a soiled nightie at the breakfast table. "Make yourself more interesting." "Work at it, because what he doesn't get at home, he'll surely find elsewhere." Along with problem-solving, Dr. Joyce offered maxims to live by. My favourite – I've forgotten the context: "A lithe young lover is better than a pot-bellied one."

Though my name was not to appear in connection with "On Being A Woman," I could not in conscience offer such material to trusting or anxious readers. Every month I filed away the research and point-of-view package and headed for the library. So it is true that Joyce Brothers, though not in the expected way, contributed to my education. I learned a lot, reading and interviewing. After five years as acting psychologist, quite enjoying my role, I came home one day to news from the cleaning lady. "Oh, by the way," she said, swirling her mop. "A Dr Brothers phoned. She said to tell you you're not doing the column any more." *Sic transit*; a new editor had come in, with his own stable of ghosts. I was out.

Like most setbacks in my life, this one proved, if not a blessing in disguise, at least a salutary shock. I would have found it hard, on my own, to give up that assured $500 a month. With the column suddenly, unceremoniously taken away, I was liberated from deadlines. I had *time*. I went back to the stories of Chekhov and Joyce, read more Hemingway, Faulkner, Mansfield. I discovered Isaac Babel and Isaac Bashevis Singer. And I began to feel that the short-story form provided the mould for my most important experiences. For the first time since my *Saskatoon Star-Phoenix* days, I longed to write.

I did not immediately act on this new vague stirring. As always, there were things to do. A few months after Joyce Brothers and I parted company, I made my twice-yearly trek to Atlantic City to grade essays for the College Entrance Examination Board, a job I got on the basis of a recommendation from a former student. It was Christmas, always for me a season of mixed emotions. (Should I hang a wreath on my door? Could I possibly join a carolling party and sing "Away In A Manger"?) Atlantic City, in that post-boom, pre-casino era, was a ghost town, ugly and bleak. The weather was grim, the work exhausting. I was homesick and miserable. One day, after eight consecutive hours reading and grading student themes, a fellow examiner told me what he thought was a funny story. He'd heard two top College Board officials discussing recent minority-group pressures for representation on the examining committee. "Well," said No. 1, "we've got our token black." "Oh?" said No. 2. "Who?" "Fredelle Maynard," said No. 1. And No. 2 said, "Fredelle Maynard's not our black. She's our Jew." After this good joke, I went back to my room and found a story unrolling in my head just as if I were reading it projected on a screen. "Christmas, when I was a child, was the season of bitterness...." And that is how I came to write a story called "Jewish Christmas," the title a deliberate paradox, about the anguish, the deep sense of exclusion, which I felt as the only Jewish child in a devoutly Lutheran community. After "Jewish Christmas," other memories crowded in. I wrote them down as they came to me — recollections of prairie schoolrooms, the autumn excitement of Eaton's catalogue, my careful friendships with little girls who sang in the church choir, the marvels of my father's general store. I never thought of myself as writing a book, only as recording the images and sensations that pressed themselves upon me. My father died, a wrenching of my foundations; I wrote about my father. Eventually I looked in my desk drawer and there was a book. I called it *Raisins and Almonds*, after the gentle hopeful lullaby my father sang to me through years of bedtimes.

And that is how I became a writer. I still write for magazines, and still about children, as well as education, women's health, personal and family relationships. When strangers ask, "How can someone with your training write for *Woman's Day?*" I tell them, truthfully, that I write almost as I breathe — all the time, compelled, because writing is the way I make sense of my experience. E. M. Forster put it well. "How do I know what I think till I see what I say?" Writing has become the way I satisfy my bottomless curiosity about everything from school curricula to changing social mores.

I am conscious of having two voices. One is cool, cheerful, practical, daily — in effect, response to an assignment, with rewards changing over the years (my parents' praise, a teacher's grade, a magazine's fee). This voice I have always summoned at will. The other is, I suppose, my singing voice. It is the gift of life — of my rich lonely childhood, a marriage which forced me to confront my deepest feelings, my suffering love for my children, my experiences of failure. That one I don't control: it comes and goes.

A Mother
and Two Daughters

When, at fifty, I published *Raisins and Almonds*, a memoir about my childhood in rural Saskatchewan, my mother was proud. Magazine articles were all very well — she kept mine always on the coffee table, ready for visitors to admire. But a real book — that was special, an Achievement. Happy to have pleased my mother, laid one more triumph at her feet, I did not at first reflect on a certain oddness in her response. Though the book dealt almost entirely with our family's life, she never discussed with me a single incident. Of the secret childhood griefs and anxieties I had for the first time revealed, she never said, "I didn't know you were so unhappy," or "That's not really the way things were." Far from correcting me, indeed — or questioning my version of events — my mother accepted instantly my occasional elaborations and inventions; I would hear her telling friends, as her own experience, something that never happened; she read it in *Raisins and Almonds*.

I think that was when I first confronted an uneasy truth about my family: that, with the possible exception of my father, we did a lot of play-acting. What appeared, to us and others, on the surface — the affection, gaiety, sweetness and moral vision — was authentic. Looking back now I partly see and largely guess how much churned beneath that surface, hidden even from ourselves. My mother wrote the script for our ideal family, and assigned the roles in accordance with her own needs. Although he hadn't painted anything in years, my father was the Artist, a role that rescued him from the country-storekeeper category and conferred on us all a certain distinction. My mother was The Competent One. "Mama can do *anything*," my father always said, and that was pretty much the case. She cooked, cleaned, baked, gardened, sewed, nursed, entertained, knitted and embroidered and crocheted, worked in my father's store, all with efficiency and even brilliance. What she needed most, a career outlet of her own, something more significant than painting on silk, more productive of power and regard — that she did not have. So I became my mother's bound delegate, the one to fulfil her dreams. I was The Clever One. And along with cleverness, I was assigned subsidiary functions necessary to its fruition: industry, obedience, cheerfulness, responsibility. "I can count on Freidele," my mother would say. "Freidele is always cheerful. Freidele is a perfect child." How, in the light of these thinly disguised directives, could I admit my fears? How could I acknowledge my own feelings when my mother *told* me what to feel? "I hate Celia!" I once screamed after a sibling squabble. "You don't hate her," my mother corrected. "She's your sister, and you love her."

Celia, my sister. What paragraph can contain her, how can I explain her tragedy? In the first book I wrote about our family, she scarcely appears. Casual friends asked, "Didn't you have a sister?" and I'd say, "We're not close." The truth was, I could not let that genie out of the bottle. When parts were handed round in our family, my sister Celia got The Pretty One. To understand the bleakness of that assignation, you would have to know that my mother set no store by prettiness, a commodity which, as she had good reason to know, got you nowhere. Pretty was frivolous, pretty was insignificant; it was weak and so, in practice, almost certain to prove *bad*. As I was expected to toe the line, Celia was expected, almost directed, to disappoint. "Let her have it," "Let her do it," my mother would say when my sister, four years older than I, behaved unreasonably. "Show her *you're* the big one." Like all young children, I watched for signs of parental favouritism. My father I saw as even-handed. "Ah, a *keppele*, what a head!" he would say of me, and of Celia, with affectionate understatement, "A sweetness! She'll pass in a crowd!" My mother tried to be fair, but her preference and prejudices were clear, even to a five-year old. I got the heart of the cabbage, the yolky "unborn eggs" in the chicken soup, and the icing spoon to lick. When my mother sold her hand-crocheted coverlet to buy the twenty-volume *Book of Knowledge*, she said, "Freidele needs it. For her future." When Celia was twelve, she was − incredibly − sent away from home to live in Winnipeg with a distant cousin because, my mother said, she couldn't be trusted around *goyishe* boys, gentiles. She rejoined our family when we moved to the city a year later. By then she had become the tall young beauty of "That Sensual Music." "All she thinks about," Mother said, "is *accessories*."

Many years after the event, I asked my sister how she had felt about that early exclusion from the family. "Nothing," she said. "It was fine." Very early she had learned a dangerous survival skill, not seeing what could not be borne. And the unbearable truth − it seems evident to me now − was that for mysterious and complicated reasons, my mother could not love her firstborn daughter. Was this in part because Celia was not her first child? Very early in her marriage, my mother had a son, a thirteen-pound baby, stillborn. The blow must have been terrible. Years after, my father still wept at the memory of Ephraim — "a beautiful boy, I held him in my arms." And my mother — using the blockout strategy she taught both her children — my mother *laughed*. "He was too fat," she said. "Papa made me drink cream all the time I was carrying, to make the baby strong. Anyway we're lucky we don't have him. Two children these days is plenty." My mother had chosen not to see the infant; his birth — and death — were not revealed to us until we were nine and thirteen, and then only by accident. When I pressed for details — Was there a funeral? Where was my brother buried? — Mother grew impatient and severe. "Buried? Funeral? *Michigas*, foolishness. I told you, he didn't live at all."

But she had carried him nine months, a young woman far from home, struggling to make a new life in a cruel climate. That she did not care is inconceivable. Did she bury all her grief and rage — and transfer it to the pretty baby born the next year? I speculate, yet feel I know. I study old photographs, my young mother with Celia, and am struck by stiffness and distance. The child is beautifully dressed — double-breasted white chinchilla coat, hand-knit leggings, a fluffy angora bonnet with huge taffeta rosettes — but always held out, away from the body. (Early photos of me show a nestling, pressed to the full bosom.)

Losing her son was not, to be sure, my mother's only trauma. By her own account, she had grown up despised and ignored by a fierce matriarch who valued only male children. The stories she told throughout my childhood were tales of affliction. Both my parents had a vast fund of family anecdotes. But where my father's were comic or morally uplifting, my mother's memories of her Russian childhood rivalled Grimm in their cruelty and pain. While her brothers played, she gathered firewood, carried grain for the horses and slop for the pigs, dug for potatoes with her bare hands. She picked wild strawberries but never tasted the jam. "Sometimes," she said, "I got a spoonful of the scum that came to the surface when it was cooking." A Russian Cinderella, she scrubbed floors and beat laundry by the stream while her brothers played. Years later, I cried when my mother told me her mother's ritual imprecation: "Out of my sight, *meiskite*, ugliness!" My mother was not crushed by this treatment; it seems, if anything, to have strengthened her resolve. An early photo, taken before the family emigrated to Canada, shows a blank-faced dark child leaning on her father's knee. She wears a curious flutter of rags, and looks crippled. My grandmother sits by her sons with fierce, implacable countenance, a centre of power. Ten years later, a similarly posed family photo reveals a shift. My grandmother looks ill, the boys sprawl indolent and foolish. In the back row, with a rose in her high-piled black hair, my mother blazes — a beauty, and she knows it. Also a power.

She learned survival early. When Cossacks swept through the village, she fled towards the Orthodox church and melted into a religious procession. ("I'll carry that cross for you," she said to a startled worshipper.) One day, picking beets in the garden — she was nine years old — she became aware of a soldier watching. "Come here, *krasavetsa*," he called. "I'll show you a game." She picked up her basket. He vaulted the gate and carried her, his pretty prize, to the summer house. "I knew what his game would be," she told me many years later. "You don't grow up on a farm for nothing." When I asked why she didn't fight or scream, she smiled at my innocence. "A grown man and a child? A Russian soldier, a Jewish girl? I wanted to live." So she sat, terrified but still, on his knee until it was over. Then she wiped away the blood with her torn undershirt and ran to tell her mother. She guessed, correctly, that she would be beaten. "I had to tell," she explained, "so my mother could take me to the rabbi for a certificate, to explain how I became a woman. Otherwise, who would marry me?"

My mother related these experiences in a matter-of-fact style not much unlike her usual brisk cheerfulness. If, on occasion, I expressed outrage at my grandmother's harshness, Mother responded with the ritual formulae of filial devotion. "I loved my mother," she would insist. "There is no day I don't think of her."

This last, allowing for some exaggeration, may well have been true. As a child, I wondered only how my mother could repay such unkindness with love. Older, I wondered why she told those shocking stories. Now, at last, I think I understand. My mother had no tolerance for ambiguity; with her, things were black and white, good and bad, never shades of grey. The idea of a *bad* mother being unacceptable to her, intolerable, she was obliged to see herself as mistreated by a *good* mother. Where then did the denied anger go, and the resentment, and the desire for revenge? I think it went underground, awaiting its target through all the years that my mother demonstrated abundantly her patience, sweetness and generosity. She married out of an affluent household and found herself in rural Saskatchewan — hard labour once again. She bore and lost a son. And then, when she was twenty-six, along came my sister, conceived just after my grandmother was found to have inoperable cancer and born a few days before my grandmother's death.

The story of my sister's birth was as familiar to me, growing up, as "Bluebeard" or "Snow White." "My mother was dying in Winnipeg," Mother would tell us. "I couldn't go to her because I was expecting. I cried all day. Every week I baked *sucherlach*, sweet rusks, for her. When my pains started, there was a big blizzard, forty below and snow to the windowsills. I made supper for six men, workers in our store. Then I crawled up the stairs. The baby came so green and sickly we thought she maybe wouldn't live. She didn't like my milk, she screamed night and day. One morning I dragged myself out of bed — 'I have to make *sucherlach*' — and Papa said, 'Rest. Yesterday your mother died.'"

Would my sister's fate have been different if she had been a robust and easy baby born, as I was, when the prairies exploded in summer bloom? If she had not, in my mother's mind, been linked with death? There's no telling. What I remember is that Mother gave my sister the best clothes — as a little girl, wide panama hats with velvet ribbons, a long white worsted cape (in Foam Lake!) and later, in her teens, exquisite handmade costumes of pure silk, Irish linen and crêpey wool. Celia was raised to take pride in her appearance — and then deprecated as superficial. She was, from my mother's point of view, a difficult child, stubborn and disobedient. Who is to say which came first, my sister's recalcitrance or my mother's rejection? A casual observer might have thought Mother favoured Celia because — to use a skipping image — the rope was held lower for her. She was not expected to come first in class, not required to shine. But of course, in our family lowered standards meant lower regard. Mother accepted from Celia behaviour she never would have countenanced in me — up to a point. On one memorably dreadful occasion, Celia, who was then nine or ten, pushed my mother past that point. Asked, then ordered, to perform some small household chore, she dug in her patent-leather heels and said, "I won't. You can't make me." My mother never raised her hand to us. Her punishments were more refined: silence, sarcasm, and — worst of all — suffering martyrdom. This time, however, Celia's defiance broke through her usual restraint.

"When Papa comes home," Mother said, "you are going to kneel on coals." I can't imagine where she had come upon this quaint literary notion. Certainly she didn't realize that *hot* coals were involved. When my father appeared, he was dispatched to the basement, emerging wretchedly with the coal scuttle. Celia howled, my father looked imploringly at my mother, she pointed to the corner. "There." So my father laid three or four bits of coal on the floor, then folded over them his linen handkerchief. We were all trembling now, even my mother. I suspect she felt the proceedings most un-Jewish, but it was too late to back out. "On your knees," Mother said. Celia lowered shaking knees, barely touched the hankie-covered coals — and screamed. My father snatched her up and comforted her, but the humiliation must have been complete, coals that glowed in the mind long after. It is no wonder that my sister tormented me, pinching and tattling, only to discover that her persecutions backfired, enhancing my golden reputation. "Freidele didn't wash," she would announce at the dinner table, displaying her own well-scrubbed fingernails. "That should only be the worst thing people could say about you," my mother said after one such report. "Better dirty hands than a cold heart."

When I think of my sister during her teenage days, pursued by admirers, the word that comes to me is not *cold* but *cool*. Though we shared a bedroom and a bed, I knew almost nothing about her. Whatever strong feelings she possessed lay buried fathoms deep. She showed no emotion when our father's business failed (again) or when Mother underwent critical surgery for a malignant tumour. She spoke flippantly of the suitors who sometimes wept in our parlour, desperate for her love. "His father's a janitor," she said, as if that obliterated the young scientist who begged her to marry him. She accepted without a struggle the announcement that there was no money to pay for her university tuition. (When my father wept, my mother said, "What for? She only wants it to join a sorority and go to dances. Dances she can go to without university.") At eighteen she was once more, in effect, sent away. My parents returned to the country, I went to live with a favourite aunt — and Celia moved into a rooming house. Though we both remained in Winnipeg, we met seldom. I would see her at a dance and she'd whisper, "Your hair's a mess," or "Wipe off those circles of rouge. You look like a clown." I found my own ways to cut, references to academic triumphs which I didn't greatly value but knew she would envy. I observed that she had gained a lot of weight and taken up smoking.

Winnipeg's Jewish world was small in those days, the late thirties. By the age of twenty, Celia had exhausted the city's marriage prospects — this one boring, that one not rich enough. She moved to Toronto, expecting to repeat her social success, and found herself in a big city with lots of good-looking girls. Her letters home — filled with descriptions of clothes and dates — now scarcely concealed an undertone of panic. Twenty-three, twenty-four — and no husband in sight.

At last came a letter with the good news — strangely reported. She had met a Jewish man, from a rich family — coloured telephones in every room. His mother had given her a mink coat, she was shopping for a diamond and would be married shortly. No need for any of us to attend. My mother, studying a photo of the bridegroom with Celia and the rich family, pronounced him a *schmo*. My father, withholding judgment as to character and intelligence, worried about something in the groom's manner. "Look how his hand hangs on her shoulder, like a dishrag," he said. "What kind of man holds a *zaftige maidele*, a ripe young girl, like that?" In the event, both parents proved right. A premarital clash produced startling revelations. The groom had only one good eye, the other having been knocked out by a brother during an argument. He had been married before; his first wife ended up in a mental institution.

All this, the stuff of melodrama, would have reduced most young women to helpless grief and fury. Not Celia. Her cool was astonishing. She did not telephone in the heat of crisis. Only much later, did we find out that her intended, in a fit of rage, had attacked her physically and been dragged off by employees of his father's firm. At the time, she sent the briefest possible note. "Dear Mum and Dad: This will come as a surprise but I've broken my engagement." No explanations, no agonies, just an assurance that she was feeling fine and keeping the coat and the ring. Though my sister had always seemed to me utterly unlike my mother, I recognized here a familiar stance. *We have no failures in our family. Everything's under control.*

Shortly after this débâcle, Celia married. "He carries hundred-dollar bills in his pocket," she wrote. "He showed me his account books. He is very rich." Mother sniffed. "As if she understands anything about books!" Soon she had an apartment and a new baby. We received bulletins regularly, all composed in language of such extravagance that the concrete reality of her life was rendered invisible. Her husband was fabulous, the baby gorgeous, the apartment a dream. She was fantastically busy shopping, so much to do. She just hoped that some day I too would have such a terrific husband and a terrific baby and a terrific life. Whom was she trying to convince?

Within a few years Celia was playing the lead in her own family drama: attractive young matron with two little girls in matched smocked dresses or frilly pinafores, custom-made. She struck me as a strange parent, obsessed with details of costume, toilet training and diet, but emotionally distant. Anything messy, likely to rumple or stain, she abhorred. So she didn't cuddle, discouraged play with mud or sand. Every summer she brought her little daughters to my parent's home in a small

Manitoba town. She must have hoped, through her children, to win what had so far eluded her − my mother's love and approval, at the very least her interest. That never happened. Towards Celia herself, my mother never softened. As for the children − a curious, fascinating, absolutely comprehensible phenomenon − she did what she had done all her life, she *split*. One of Celia's daughters she singled out for special favour, the other she virtually ignored.

With time, the subterranean struggle between my mother and my sister came closer to the surface. Celia complained. "I find it so hard to cope with *continual misconstrued interpretation*," she wrote me. My mother carped. Celia's house, with plastic covers on the couch and lamps, was uncomfortable, her provisions were niggardly. "A rich man's wife, she re-uses aluminum foil to heat up," Mother reported scornfully. "So the apple crisp tastes from hamburger." Often my mother's observations were correct. But she seemed to have no glimmer of understanding as to why this rich man's wife saved torn pantihose and never entertained. ("People come to gorge.")

After years of envying my sister, it wasn't until we were both middle-aged that I finally came to see in her often trivial and absurd economies, a withered spirit. How can you give if you feel you have not been given to? How can you love yourself if your own mother does not love you? In the course of her long marriage, Celia never once took a real trip − a trip, that is, other than to visit sick relations. There would be talk of a holiday − Acapulco perhaps − and then weary dismissal. "I just don't feel up to that. I don't have the energy to dash madly to my dressmaker, and all my clothes need lengthening or cleaning." Increasingly, too, she produced new reasons for her narrowly confined life − a host of psychosomatic problems with knee, foot, eyes, back. So she sat on her couch and hired decorators. Swedish modern, Chinese, French Regency, Art

Nouveau — the winds of change swept through her living room, certain artefacts frugally surviving each renovation. The lamp with a Dresden shepherdess at its base acquired serially a triangular shade, a Chinese parasol, ruffles and then curlicues of braid.

I don't know whether I ever loved my sister; my mother, all the while urging family harmony, fuelled my resentment and distaste. But certainly I grew concerned, as I watched her melancholy charade: the façade of brightness and the darkening cloud. Committed to happiness, unable to admit disappointment, she found an outlet in anger. Her rages against department-store clerks, false friends, cleaning ladies who failed to turn mattresses, were epic. Here, from a letter to our mother written in her fifties, is a typical fury, the object a young cousin who had borrowed our old bassinet. "I am still most annoyed with Naomi and her attitude, and also disappointed that *you* didn't take a *firm stand* and insist that if I wanted the crib at some future time I am certainly *entitled* to it. The fact that you said she could use it didn't mean it was hers *permanently*. She had no right to assume possession of something that was not rightfully hers to claim." The bitterness of the dispossessed reverberates through this strange tirade — underlinings, exclamation marks and furious repetitions. "You were at fault too, knowing how strongly I felt about that issue and have spoken about it to you on *many* occasions." On and on goes the rant; then, suddenly, a turn to civility and daughterliness. "I do hope you'll have a good holiday in San Francisco. Keep well and take care of yourself and let's hear from you soon. We all send our love."

For thirty years my sister sang, however unconvincingly, contentment and joy. I *am* happy, I *am* loved. Reporting "a real tragedy" (someone else's), she would lay claim to suffering compassion and then suddenly veer off into fashion. "Oh, by the way, if you see another pair of earrings like yours, sterling back and crescent-shaped disc drop in muted shades of blue, I'd be interested." Small anxieties, half confided, would be dismissed with a bizarre non sequitur. "Well, life can be beautiful." Only when our father, her protector, died, could she reveal her misery. Having now a reason, one unrelated to her carefully defended personal life, she let go at last. She wept hysterically, consulted doctors, took pills, wrote letters still mannered but expressing a genuine, bottomless despair. To our mother, responding to some fancied oversight regarding birthday wishes, she wrote: "I didn't call because I wanted to spare you my agony. I can't cope with the loss of my Dad. During the day I'm not too bad, I keep going at such a rate I don't have the strength to cry. But come evening I'm in a terrible state, I just can't control myself. How can I even begin to describe the love I felt for my Dad? Ever since I recall, as a very young child, I was so proud of my Dad and so fortunate to have my love returned so fully to me." Love returned, love not returned. Her life revolved on that axis. After my father died, she and my mother quarrelled more harshly and openly. She sank into a depression so engulfing that we hardly noticed when she slid over the edge. One day she tried to walk through the living-room wall; I dismissed that as a momentary abstraction. She had, it seemed, been sitting on the couch for years, declining to cook, refusing to go out. So when a neurologist said, "Alzheimer's disease," we were shocked.

My sister's illness progressed rapidly. A year after diagnosis she was moved to a nursing home. My mother saw her there just once. Visiting Toronto, she maintained at first that she couldn't meet Celia, wasn't up to it. I insisted. Together we entered the ward where my sister sat, drugged and stuporous, her hair cropped like a convict's. I took her hand. She said, querulous, without looking up: "What are all these people doing in my kitchen?" Mother approached — timid, almost frightened, holding out a box of chocolates. "Do you know me?" she asked. My sister's blurred gaze focused for a moment, her voice came clear, with a feeling that would have blighted buds. "How should I not know *you*?" After that, there was nothing to say.

When Mother died, a few years later, the nursing home said nothing to my sister. "What for?" an attendant asked. "She's out of it." I took Celia for a walk, holding her hand as if she were a child and speaking to her as if we were both children. "Celia, Mama died. She's dead. We'll never see her again." At first she kept her eyes fixed, as usual, on some invisible mote in the middle distance. Then tears squeezed out from under flaked dry lids. She turned to me and wailed, a child's cry with sixty-odd years of pain behind it. "Why did Mama hate me?"

This, then, is how I came to be so loved. I have heard of cultures in which mothers fashion a doll, a mock baby, to draw off evil spirits and protect the newborn. I think in our family Celia served that function. The accumulated poisons were drained off to her, making possible my mother's pure and total passion for her youngest child. If mine was the kingdom, the power and the glory, it was achieved at the cost of my sister's disinheritance.

Two Daughters

Rona

You always loved to act. Perhaps most children do — but
yours was a special passion, a strain and fervour and desperate-
ness that withered my green heart like an autumn leaf because
I knew it for no ordinary make-believe. Most of the time you
were a quiet child, and tractable. You did as you were told.
"How do you keep the baby from moving off the blanket?"
friends asked when, at nine months or so, you sat for hours
outside on a blue woollen square. I had no answer. You just
never moved, watching with cloudy brown eyes the stream of
life.

Then you discovered books, and a world you could be part
of. You became a princess, trailing about my kitchen in shabby
curtains with gold-paper crown and cardboard sceptre, star-
tipped, waiting for magic. You looked impatiently for friends to

join you in the castle, but nursery school was jungle gym and playing house. You never cared for domestic dramas ("I'll be the mother and you be the baby") and so, when I watched anxiously through the one-way glass, it was the others I saw busy with brooms and saucepans. You sat in Lion Cubby, a tiny stall where the stencilled lion marked Rona's coat and boots, and you were queen there, all alone. On the playground, four-year-olds whooshed down the slides or joined hands in singing circles. You raced back and forth with tense and fevered anima-tion, playing some kind of solitaire whose meaning I never could divine. I knew, by your excitement, the flapping at your skirts, that you were not running on a tarred playground. But where? What were the voices you heard, so insistent that when the bell rang you never responded, and the teacher had to lead you gently in for juice time? I had read about imaginary play-mates, but this was different. Even in fancy you had no friend. I imported little girls to play, driving them back and forth, but my urging was no catalyst. I always ended up baking cookies with Cindy and Kate while you drifted quietly back to your tower, raising the drawbridge and locking the heavy gates.

At four, you chose your first great role, Joan of Arc. An unlikely choice, on the face of it: was ever child less militant than you? Perhaps in a glossy modern book you never would have recognized your heroine. But someone gave us a beautiful tattered French edition — *Jeanne d'Arc* par M. Boutet de Monvel — and you passed through its green and gold-leafed cover as to a world remembered. Old favourites were abandoned; every lap time was Joan. I used to read aloud from a too difficult text, translating awkwardly as I went — "Everything was lacking: men, strength, the will even to resist..." — but words made little difference. It was the pictures that enchanted. Will I ever forget them, those drawings of a girl beleaguered, supported, inspired, driven, destroyed? On the first page, Joan stands straight as a stalk of young corn, her face composed under a smooth cap of hair, one hand on her heart and the other on a sword uplifted. In herself she looks defenceless. A delicate creature with fine small hands, how can she hold such a sword, let alone use it? But she is not alone. Behind and above, an angel stands, one hand on Joan's elbow, the other on her sword. Joan is in grey peasant wool, austerely cut; the angel flames in intricately draped orange and pink, her thick hair loose, her purple wings spread before a rising sun. The angel's face — did you sense it then? — is Joan's, only the angel's brows are drawn, the mouth set. On succeeding pages, Joan tramples a lion; she kneels, astonished, as the archangel Michael illumines the whole grove with blazing armour; she sits among toy sheep listening to heavenly voices; she moves serene among courtiers and kings, leads her army to victory and defeat, sinks disconsolate into the mauve and olive shadows of an English prison. Angel forms reappear — St Margaret and St Catherine now — but they float pale in a ring of flowers and Joan, chained to her bed, cannot touch them. The last page is all furious faces and the pikes of the crowd except where, in a quiet corner, Joan burns. I thought it an unhealthy ending for a child's book and improvised my own. "Then the angels came and carried her safely away, and punished all the bad people, and Joan lived happily ever after." You shook your head. "No, she didn't." And then, turning back to the first page, "Read it again."

All that year you were Joan. You wouldn't even answer to Rona. Other mothers, happy in children less astonishing, said, "What a wonderful imagination your little girl has!" It wasn't exactly imagination — at least, not in their sense. I knew you moved through a storybook landscape with the sense of *déjà-vu*. The voices announcing "You have been chosen" were familiar as the posts of your bed, and so too was the knowledge that victory trumpets led to the stake, that — as on the flyleaf of your book — the laurel wreath and the crown of thorns were one.

Had I read too many books, or too few? I worried that you might become transfixed in the martyr's role, pass through the looking glass. One day I said, "You can't be Joan. You're Rona. If people use other people's names, the police come and take them away." There was only a flicker of panic before you readjusted the mask. Within a week, exiled from France, you set sail for Russia. You were Anna now, and endlessly, on the living-room rug, you danced the dying swan.

Pavlova brought music into your life, as Joan had brought colour and line. You began with books — we left no biography unturned — but the black-and-white photographs were insufficient. Some even repelled. You turned away from pictures of Pavlova in recognizable real-world settings, passed over the fruity creature who danced a sensual Bacchanale, hair ribboned and ringleted, grapes held to parted lips. Your Pavlova was the nymph of *Dragonfly, Snowflakes, Papillon* and — epitome of all fragile, doomed beauty — *The Dying Swan*. Dreaming over a book of ballet stories, you became as familiar with Giselle and Esmeralda as your schoolmates were with the Bobbsey Twins.

That winter we drove hundreds of miles to see a performance of *Swan Lake*. Your ecstasy was frightening. Especially you were fascinated by the lead ballerina's dual role. "How can you tell the good queen?" you asked. A lifetime is too short to answer such questions, but I tried. "Watch how she moves," I said. "Odette and Odile have the same face, but Odette is gentle, soft. Odile is proud, and when she dances on point her feet are like sharp knives." We bought a recording of Tchaikovsky's score, and the role crystallized. Your home now was that mysterious lake created by a mother's tears; prisoner of a cruel sorcerer, able to touch but never hold a human love, you became the swan queen. No, it was more complicated than that. You played Pavlova playing Odile playing Odette — even that not the final reality, since beneath the swan maiden's feathers trembled the enchanted girl. In this game of infinite recession, you pirouetted down a hall of mirrors.

Unexpectedly, from the world of children, a friend appeared. She seemed an unlikely ally — assertive where you were shy, bold and confident and a little fierce. There was something Brobdignagian about her physical size and ruddy complexion; she seemed to scoop you up. And you, having waited so long for a knock at the door, were frightened when it came. For a long time you held back, while Christina clattered about examining your toys. "What's this dopey thing? Hey, you've got a talking doll! Come on, Rona, let's *play!*" But her persistence, and your need, triumphed. You introduced her to ballet, Christina a heavy-footed Siegfried to your Odette, and she taught you two extraordinary games. One was French Revolution; the other was Anne Frank. Listening to the enactments of torture and violent death, I tried not to worry. (A healthy release of tensions, perhaps? Children don't know the meaning of these things.... Anyway, Rona has a friend.) Then a new family moved in across the street with three lively children and a swing set. I heard Christina screaming joyfully in their yard and thought, "Maybe it will happen gradually so no one will be hurt". But Christina, a tidy child, hated loose ends. The day she told you she was going sailing with the Ryans and you said, "But you promised to play *Swan Lake!*" she cut free. "I hate you and I hate your stupid games! No wonder everybody laughs at you!" In a way, it was brilliantly done, so decisive, like the series of hard little whipping turns with which Odile spins away from Siegfried after she has betrayed him. You walked her to the door as you always had, and then, just as you had been taught to do, repeated the ritual goodbye. "Thank you for coming. I had a lovely time." Much later, I heard the Tchaikovsky playing, very softly.

After the Swan Queen died, you turned your back on heroic drama. You became a Good Girl in a performance so flawless that perhaps only I saw the strain of the role. "Rona is industrious, obedient, careful, responsible, co-operative…." Teachers sang your praises. I observed that your nails were bitten to the quick, your strange vague smile pulled tight at the corners — and that you always walked home from school alone. Was I wrong to push you towards the crowd? I made you march in the Memorial Day parade. "All your little friends will be there," I said, brushing the straggly curls back from the pale, solemn face. (Years later you told me, "I was afraid. They fired big guns, and there was a carload of nurses in Red Cross uniforms, ready. The Brownies were right in front.") I drove you to Scouts and Brownies for good fellowship, refusing to see that you came home beaten. When it was your turn to take cookies, I sent a platter of delicacies that returned untouched. "Jennifer's mother bought fig squares," you whispered. "Everybody liked them best." "All the better for us," I said, false-hearty. But I didn't insist any more on Tuesday Scouts. You begged me not to give birthday parties; I understood. As years passed, I listened to the happy complaints of other mothers — "Kit spends all her time on the phone!" "I've had to limit Wendy's dates to weekends, her grades are slipping so." "I don't like to see them going steady, but what can you do?" We had no such problems. Behind the closed door of your room, you read, listened to music, drew.

In high school, you tried out for your first play. I was delighted, because a play meant rehearsals, gaiety, people, life, and you had always loved to act. You didn't get the part you wanted — "There's this girl, a real ugly duckling, who gets made over on a trip to New York" — but a character role was better than nothing. I noticed that you took your books to rehearsals. ("I might as well get some homework done while I wait.") The play was a great success. Everyone admired your acting. I wasn't surprised — a girl with your experience. No-one seemed to notice how strangely you played the role of the mother. The voice carried beautifully, yes; the manner was confident, even authoritative — but it was a solo performance. When you spoke, you addressed the audience, eyes fixed on some distant point.

After that, you were in all the plays and usually, it seemed, playing mothers. Certain kinds of mother-things you did painfully well: the stance of nagging, intolerance, stubbornness, authority. But still the role lacked conviction. I could believe that the untidy youngsters who fumbled their lines were members of the stage family. Not you. Whatever the part, Mrs Gibb in *Our Town*, Eliza Gant in *Look Homeward, Angel*, you were Rona performing. Remember the time you played in *A Happy Journey*? Watching you, I was puzzled. Thornton Wilder *couldn't* be satirizing motherhood. Yet what a strange mother! Visiting a daughter who has just lost her firstborn (and barely survived herself), this woman behaved like a social worker inspecting a troublesome case. There was a moment, just at the end, when Beulah put her head on Ma Kirby's shoulder and wept. "It was awful, Mama. She didn't even live a few minutes." You pulled away and your voice, when it came, was edgy with distaste: "What time did you put the chicken in the oven?" The audience thought this must be comedy and laughed obligingly.

So when you were chosen, in the last year of high school, to play Helen Keller in *The Miracle Worker*, I was frightened for you. A part involving all that passion and speechless violence? A part without lines, when clear articulation was your strong point? Rehearsals began. You joked, "At least I know my lines.

I've got just one word — in the last act," but your anxiety was visible as smoke. You came home bruised from the practice battles with Annie Sullivan. When you got a cut over the eye, I asked, "Couldn't the girl playing Annie let up a little? You're taking a frightful beating." "It's not her fault," you said. "I can't seem to hit back. Maybe I'm not right for this part. At the big moment, where Annie finally gets through to Helen and Helen speaks, I have to say 'Wah-wah.' I just can't *do* it. People will laugh." I stopped asking, "How did things go today?"

Then, one afternoon during a snowstorm, you phoned from school. "Can I bring somebody home for dinner and overnight? It's a new girl, and she's stranded." My excitement was preposterous, I suppose, but in sixteen years you had never, unprompted, invited a friend. I got out the good china and made a quick trip for candles, speculating all the while. This girl would have to be sensitive and intelligent. Probably good-looking, since hair and clothes had always mattered to you. I pictured a slender, elegant creature with a vaguely poetic melancholy and a cosmopolitan background. Artichokes…Rilke …incense…velvet…Scarlatti…. The picture formed in my mind. So it was a shock when I saw Randy, a short lumpy girl, alley cat to your Siamese. Everything about her — bad teeth, greasy hair, laddered stocking — spoke neglect. The manner, though, was jaunty, and there was an extravagance of speech, gesture, laughter even, that dazzled. After dinner, she bounded first up the stairs: "Let's see what you've got in records!" The phonograph, which had always played softly behind closed doors, blared and shrieked. The ceiling trembled. I thought, "My God, they're *dancing!*"

It was probably only a month that Randy lasted at the high school before she broke one rule too many, was suspended, and vanished. But it seems longer in my memory. You went skating on the mill pond together, hitchhiked to a basketball game, wore togas to Latin class, explored local coffee houses, organized a talent show — all the wild, improbable things. When Randy wasn't at our house, you were on the phone, talking for hours about nothing in particular. Two days before *The Miracle Worker* opened, you announced flatly, "The principal found out who stretched plastic over the toilet in the teachers' john. He put Randy on probation — and she's left." "What do you mean, *left*?" I asked. "Gone," you said. "She didn't get along with her stepmother anyway, and she's taken off. Maybe New York, maybe San Francisco." "But you'll keep in touch with her?" You were halfway up the stairs, but you turned with an inscrutable smile. "You don't keep in touch with people like Randy."

We went to your play's opening on a damp April night. One does not expect great experiences from high-school plays. If they move, they do so incidentally — because a spirit trembles beneath even the most inept *Hamlet*, or because the matter of the play touches close to home. *The Miracle Worker*, on the face of it, threatened no violence to the emotions. Nothing in the situation of its heroine suggested yours. Still, my detachment wavered when I watched you, as Helen, with your sighted comrades. The other children played and chattered over the paper dolls; you reached from one to the other, tracing lip movements, and finally, in baffled rage, lunging with the scissors. I shrugged away unease. Did I, perhaps, recognize the mother who met a child's terrible gropings with yet another peppermint drop? But we are all of us like that. Most certainly I did not know the furious little animal who scratched, kicked, bit, wrestled her way through all those scenes where crockery smashed about the two principals. I only wondered that you could act so well. Because I *was* convinced, no question. The child who reeled about the stage was deaf and blind and mute, and the words Annie Sullivan spelled into her hand were raindrops on a tin roof. All the voices around her — gentle, exasperated, cajoling, desperate — died on the wind. Until that one moment. There was Helen, defiant, ringed by her protective family; and there was Annie Sullivan, herself afflicted, stubbornly, indignantly refusing to play the easy game. "I treat her like a seeing child because I *ask* her to see, I *expect* her to see!" I watched Annie drag Helen to the pump, forcing the child to work the handle up and down, up and down. The water gushed. The teacher's fingers, spelling, pressed into Helen's hand, *your* hand. "Water. W-A-T-E-R. Water. It has a *name*." And then the miracle happened. The child speechless from infancy articulated with enormous difficulty two syllables: "*Wah wah.*" It seemed to me a sound like the cracking of ice-bound rivers in a spring thaw, as sharp and tearing as that. In the applause that followed the final curtain, I could not clap. How many years had I been at the play?

Joyce

I dream of you often. In my dreams, you are always doing something breathtaking — and dangerous. You are walking along dark Manhattan streets, barefoot, wearing that long black chesterfield coat you bought years ago, and I can tell that underneath you are naked. At midnight, in New York. You are driving our old grey Buick down an icy road, much too fast. You are diving at Mendem's Pond, reckless and laughing; only I know about the jagged rocks. You are hitchhiking, hopping up into the cab of a trailer truck, eyes widening as your realize this is definitely not the road home. You are eleven years old, in Mexico; you have set off for the market yourself, just to buy a string of beads, and you've been gone much too long. Now I am running through the streets of Oaxaca, bumping into tortilla makers and chiclet sellers, calling out in my pidgin Spanish, "*A visto una nīna en minifalda?*" Have you seen a little girl in a short short skirt?

Daring, danger, rescue: the theme of our life together. Only in these last years have I begun to understand how I trained you to need me, because I needed you. Second child, second daughter, you were born when I had no more hopes for my marriage; you would be the last baby. So I went on breast-feeding even after you had clearly signalled your preference for bottles. When you cried at night, I rushed to pick you up and took you to the kitchen, where the carriage awaited. I pushed you back and forth, talking and singing, until you dozed off. To other young mothers I complained about this child who would not sleep through the night, but the truth is, I often lay awake waiting for your call. Very early, you learned to call.

That I chose you, rather than your sister, as the one I would rescue, might at first glance seem strange. It was Rona, born four years earlier, who appeared timid and fearful, needing support. But Rona from birth would not be possessed. When I tried holding her close, she arched her back. Her first words, at ten months, were a declaration of independence. "Hot face!" she protested, pulling free, when I placed her cheek against mine. You, on the other hand, were from the first a cuddler, fitting your body to the holding parent, clinging and patting. Long before the invention of infant carriers, and long past infancy, I carried you everywhere. "Sense of security" was a fashionable concept in the 1950s, and I adopted it gratefully to explain my hovering protectiveness. If I were only going to hang out the wash, I took you along, lest you note my brief absense and feel *insecure*. You were a bold toddler, an enterprising three-, four-, five-year-old. Torn between admiration of your spirit and fears for your safety, I sent in a hundred little ways a most complicated message. *I love you unreservedly. I will support anything you choose to do. And if you get into trouble, I will save you.* To your sister, meanwhile, I said in the secret language of mothers, *I love you, but you must be responsible or suffer the consequences.* I think now that I was a strange mother to both my children, but Rona was the more fortunate.

You were much loved, the family darling. Even before you were born, Rona, a shy loner, chattered happily about how, when her baby sister came, you two would go down the street together "and the baby will hold my hand." A fantasy that came true. As soon as you could walk — an easy, outgoing, affectionate little girl — Rona took you along when she went out to play, as her offering to rowdier companions. "Here's Joycie." Your father adored you from the beginning — because you were Joyce, named for his beloved dead sister, and because you responded so tenderly to the family embrace. (By his first daughter, early and late, he felt judged.) I loved you with a passion I did not then see as dangerous. You were the child who would redeem a disastrous marriage, gratify my parents, enrich and justify my life. Each of us, in our way, offered you to the hostile world. Dance, sing, talk, laugh, clown, delight. *Here's Joyce.*

Like most second children, you admired and imitated the first — with a notable difference. You pushed harder, farther. When Rona drew or painted, her pictures went up on the refrigerator. When you made pictures of your cat, your best friend, yourself with bangs and wide smile, you gave them price tags — 1¢, 3¢ — and trotted briskly down the street with your clutch of papers, selling. Myself the cautious child of a cautious mother, I was dazzled by your boldness and set no limits, even when I knew your reach exceeded your grasp. At eight you went into business, putting up a sign in front of our house: TOMATOES, $2 a bushel. The tomatoes grew in your father's garden plot, several miles away; you were almost always at school when customers appeared. But I would drop everything and race off in the car to pick. At eleven, you established your own baby-sitting agency, with placards advertising a variety of services. *Reliable child care. Stories, crafts, games, excursions.* You returned from your first job badly shaken: a whole day in charge of five children, the youngest an infant and the oldest a year older than you. I said, "What was that mother thinking off?"

I chose you to be happy for us all. Do you remember the story of Baldur, the Norse god so handsome and good that he was called Baldur the Beautiful? His mother travelled all through the world, extracting from every person she met, every stick and stone, a promise never to harm her son. She overlooked — it's the way of the world — a sprig of mistletoe. There came a time, at a feast of the gods, when the sport was to hurl missiles at Baldur the invulnerable. Knives glanced off his delicate flesh, thunderbolts exploded harmlessly at his feet. Then demon Loki aimed a sprig of mistletoe, and the young god fell dead.

I was like Baldur's mother. When you came home from kindergarten in tears — Sammy had snatched your new hat and thrown it in the mud — I ran myself to the school, found Sammy on the playground and tossed *his* hat. It did not occur to me that you would be ashamed rather than gratified.

I was as vulnerable to your gallantry as to your tears. There was the time the first grade's social star — Sherry? Cindy? Linda? — circulated daily bulletins about her upcoming birthday party. "She's inviting me," you said. Time passed; two days before the party, and still no invitation. On the last day, home for lunch, without appetite, you picked up a reversible metal button designed to be used with a subscription offer for *Newsweek*. One side said ACCEPTED, the other REJECTED. You slipped the button in your pocket. "Maybe she forgot to invite me," you said. "I'll ask her at recess." In mid-afternoon, you came down the front walk, affecting jauntiness, with *Newsweek's* button pinned to your coat. REJECTED. You didn't want a chocolate-chip cookie. When you went to your room and shut the door, I phoned Sherry-Cindy-Linda's mother.

You were only days old when I wrote in my journal lines for the newborn that ended with a touch of the infant cheek:

> *I cannot bear*
> *That any tear*
> *As yet, should wet it.*
> *Ask me, my dear*
> *For the bright moon*
> *And I*
> *Should try*
> *To get it.*

With your sister I was demanding and strict. "Christina doesn't want to come over? I told you, Rona, you have to share toys, you have to take turns choosing or kids won't play." Life lessons. You I protected from all such lessons. If I couldn't deflect the arrows, I shifted blame. "Mary and Margie won't play with you?" I had seen how you ordered them around. What I said was, "Never mind. They're mean. Would you like to bake with me?" I set myself up as personal guarantor of your happiness. Is it any wonder that for so long you believed in mother-magic? When your parakeet keeled over on his perch, I drove from one pet shop to another to find a convincing replacement before you got home from school. When you wrote unhappy letters from camp — other children's poetry and dancing were praised, nobody paid attention to you — I said, "I'll come and get you."

In small and large ways, I made myself indispensable. Food was the most obvious of these, a small matter that became large, bondage for us both. You didn't eat what other people ate: that started early. So I cooked specially for you the one or two foods you would tolerate. Acceptable foods varied over time; there was a long period when you lived on fried chicken wings and fritos, another when the daily fare was pork chops. Occasionally, out of concern for good nutrition or from simple exasperation, I would rebel against the tyranny of your diet, announcing, "You'll eat what we eat or go hungry!" You went hungry — a large-eyed delicate-featured skinny little girl sitting melancholy at our table — and always I relented. When I took you and your sister to Mexico, friends said, "Now Joyce will have to eat what's offered." Not true. In every town, we located restaurants serving *pollo frito*. When, in San Cristobal, we stayed at a fixed-menu pension, you sipped water while others ate. After you fainted in the street, I initiated a new routine, walking several miles with you in siesta hour, the heat of the day, to a hotel where a friendly cook prepared chicken wings. Looking back now at my lunatic excess, I am struck by the vision of myself as still, through the years, a nursing mother. I made myself your lifeline, a posture appropriate for the mother of an infant, but scary for us both as time passed without separation. Still I did not for years understand your unhappiness, the new sharpness and withdrawal. "How can she be unhappy," I would say to your father, "when I do everything, everything to please her?"

I felt your pain as mine. When you got too few valentines, I felt rejected. When you were passed over at school for honours or special privileges, I cried. You walked alone to high school dances and came home alone and I experienced an adolescent grief and rage. I thought my involvement natural, a mother's natural response. I did not see how I was repeating my own mother's pattern with a daughter — you are my life, live for me. Supporting you, I acquired an illusion of control when so much else in my life remained catastrophically out of control.

So you see, I could not let you fail. I encouraged grandiose schemes, let you undertake too much — and then, when I saw it was too much, moved in with lifeboat or tugs. Remember the muscular dystrophy fair? I was proud when you came to me, a fifth grader, to say that you had written to radio's Uncle Bob for a carnival kit to help you raise money for sick children. My daughter the humanitarian. You raced daily to meet the postman, then, deflated, showed me Uncle Bob's suggestions. A lemonade stand. Cookies. A raffle. "It's old stuff," you said. "I thought there'd be something really interesting." I listened with half an ear as you made plans. Could you use our back yard for the carnival? Of course. Would Daddy and Rona and I help? Of course. Not that you'd need much help. You'd be enlisting school friends, the members of the Unitarian Fellowship....

Weeks passed. I heard murmurs of plans and prospects, but didn't really pay attention until a friend told me there were notices *all over town*, everyone invited. No longer a back yard affair, the carnival was to be held on church grounds. Local merchants had donated goods for an auction. There would be bingo, a Gypsy fortune-teller, games of skill and chance, a food sale — all of this co-ordinated by Joyce Maynard, aged ten. The day of the carnival, I looked at you and saw panic. Promised help had not materialized. The phone rang constantly. People were coming, from all over. Who was to make the brownies, the punch? Who would tell fortunes? Who would act as auctioneer? "Don't worry," I said. "We'll manage." Your father, an unlikely recruit, made gallons of punch and donned a top hat for his vendor role. Rona baked. I shuttled between the bingo game and the fortune-telling booth, my head bound in a silk bandana. You auctioned off the donated merchandise. By day's end, the take stood at several hundred dollars for muscular dystrophy.

So I shouldn't have been surprised that the next year you advertised a spaghetti supper to raise money for welfare mothers, everyone invited. The actual supper has mercifully faded from my memory, a blur of faces and plates. But I recall a brief exchange that afternoon, as you were arranging forsythia for the tables and planning to make aprons — *make aprons* — for the waitresses.

"Joyce," I said, "Have you any idea how many people are coming?"

"How would I know?" you said.

"Do you know how to make spaghetti?"

"Boil it?" you said. "And put sauce on it? I think Leslie's coming. She knows."

Every near-brush with disaster, every miraculous escape, fired more ambitious plans and confirmed your sense of invulnerability. I don't know when unease about my own role surfaced; I suppose it had been gathering gradually, a subterranean counter-rhythm to triumphs. Certainly the Mexican summer contributed something. At the San Cristobal pension where you wouldn't eat, a psychiatrist sitting at our table expressed concern. "Does your daughter eat normally at home?" "I cook for her," I said. "Special things." "And here?" he persisted. "Here I *find* special things." There was a long silence. "You feel that's your responsibility as a mother?" I chose to receive that as statement, not question, and we said no more about the problem, yours or mine.

Then there was the matter of purchases. I had announced at the beginning of our trip that we would carry one suitcase each, and acquire no more than one suitcase would hold. Your acquisitions didn't lend themselves to suitcasing: an enormous *papier-mâché* doll, a Chamula Indian harp and then, in Mexico City, a fantastic birdcage, a bamboo palace. "Oh, Mummy!" You knelt on the sidewalk, examining the turrets, the perches, the tiny swinging doors. "I could have little birds to sing to me in my room." "Joyce, don't be ridiculous," I said. "There is no way we could carry that cage. You already have a harp and a doll." "I could strap the harp to my back —" you began. Your cousin Gail moaned, picturing the scene; Rona said, "Mother, you aren't going to let her!" But in the end, I couldn't bear to say no. My heart's heart, my darling, little birds to sing in her room. ...

The morning of our departure from Mexico, you approached the plane with the Chamula harp on your back, the doll emerging from your suitcase, a helium balloon tied to your wrist — and a bamboo birdcage in your arms. Three flight attendants barred your way. "No, no, *señorita*, impossible!" A steward took hold of the birdcage. You called out, "Mummy! my cage!" "I'll take it to the baggage compartment," I said. "Impossible," the steward said. "This minute we are leaving." I snatched the cage and ran with it, under the plane's nose towards the just-closing baggage compartment door. I heard the whir of propellers and the screams of "*Señora! Cuidado!*" But we got the cage home.

The dynamics of a mother-daughter scenario like the one I created are very complex. In theory, there's a rescuer who dashes eagerly forward at critical moments, and a grateful rescuee. What in fact happens, over time, is that the rescuer tires of running with rope ladder or net — and the rescuee becomes resentful, fixed in the role of one who can't quite manage on her own. You would send up distress signals, then be angry when I appeared. Or, having allowed me to help, you turned melancholy.

Ultimately, you obliged me to see. The decisive moment came in your seventeenth year. You had at last realized an old dream, leaving the public high school where you felt labelled and left out, and going to Phillips Exeter, one of the country's best preparatory schools. Here at last you would come into your own. Friends, recognition, opportunities in music, drama, dance...*Here's Joyce.*

Perhaps the dream was doomed by the intensity of your wanting. Just before term started, you walked into a patch of poison ivy. That first warm day of classes, you set off for Exeter wearing sweater and tights to conceal the blisters on your legs and arms. It seemed an omen. Soon I was hearing the horrors of the dining hall: other kids laughing and talking together, everyone else had friends.... You plunged into school activities with a passion that seemed more desperation than pleasure. You joined the newspaper staff, sang in the chorus, entered the oratory competition, performed with the drama club. You left early in the mornings, always in a flurry of costume changes, and returned late. You ate standing up at the kitchen counter, spoonfuls of peanut butter from the jar.

On the morning I remember, you seemed more than usually keyed up. You wailed that your hair was greasy, and there was no time for a shampoo. You tried and discarded the leather miniskirt, the crocheted dress, the velour pantsuit. "Joyce," I said, "it's late," and then, as you dashed out the door: "Drive carefully." Half an hour later, the phone rang. I was not really surprised, only terrified, when your voice came thin and strained. "I've had an accident." What happened was a near miss. Speeding along treacherous winter roads, you came up behind a school bus, stopped, with its door open. You moved to pass — unthinkable, but you were not thinking — and a child darted out from a roadside house, heading for the bus. You swerved just in time, took the car into a ditch. You didn't need the bus driver's tirade to tell you what might have happened. After you hung up, I was as shaken as if I had myself been at the wheel of the car. I thought about that child, that child's mother, all the what ifs. And then, thinking how frightened you must have been, contemplating the likely possibility that you might lose your licence, I went out — and bought you a present. That night, when you unwrapped the little box and saw the silver starfish brooch, you said, puzzled, troubled: "Mummy, you are rewarding me for being bad."

Passions
Spin the Plot

---◇─◇─◇---

I remained in my marriage for a quarter of a century, until 1973. By then, Rona was married, with a child; Joyce, after a year at Yale, settled in a New Hampshire country house bought with the proceeds of a precocious writing success. I had an established career as educational consultant and writer. The course of Max's life — emotionally, physically, professionally — was down. Depressed and desperate, he was drowning in drink; I assumed, as I had for years, the martyr stance, a woman valiantly struggling to keep a self-destructive man from total ruin.

The first challenge to this flattering view of my own role came when, after my marriage ended, I consulted a therapist. I knew I needed help in dealing with my bitterness and rage, after all those civilized years an avalanche of fury. I hoped for a deeper understanding of what had gone wrong. Certainly I expected sympathy. The therapist listened, inscrutable, to my indictment of Max: his drunkenness, his irresponsibility, his grandiose pretensions, his childlike egocentricity. "You stayed twenty-five years?" he said at last. "Well. You must have been getting something out of it."

Of course the therapist was right. No woman puts up with such treatment unless, beneath the obvious cost, there's a payoff. I used to tell myself that I stayed because I loved Max and he was, so much of the time, a charming companion. Because I wanted the children to have two parents. Because I hadn't the money to pick up and go. Because I couldn't bear to tell my parents the marriage was a disaster. Beneath all such real considerations, the profounder reality, the ultimate payoff, was power. I controlled the money. The children were mine. I chose the house and everything in it. I planned the parties, chose the guests. Always I enjoyed the position of moral superiority that comes from living with an alcoholic. Max drank, ignored obligations, alienated friends, wasted our small substance. Frugal, temperate, conscientious and cautious, I was — it became a family joke — *always right*.

Of course this sort of power is illusory. Weakness can be a most effective strategy. The individual who declines the struggle for conventional goals — money, prestige, security — is free to chase butterflies, confident, often, that someone else will put bread on the table, keep the house in order. Though I may have imagined myself in charge, Max effectively controlled me by his dependence. While he performed on the high wire, I acted as safety net. I excused or covered up his delinquencies, catered to his moods, accepted restrictions on my own life so that I might be available for his. For twenty-five years, I stopped whatever I was doing in mid-afternoon to make sure that Max would have dinner before he had time to get drunk. When, in the later years, I was obliged to go out of town, it wasn't really the children I worried about and rushed home to rescue; it was the children's father. Power? I carried a big stick and danced to his tune.

Once I had admired Max as the most singular of men; now I saw him as absurd. The visionary in his singing robes had become Gimpel the Fool, or the simpleton in *The Vicar of Wakefield*, who trades the family's entire substance for a gross of green spectacles. The tender protégée, once so grateful for protection and inspiration, emerged as Taskmistress.

This transformation, which occurred early in our marriage, was not black magic but a reversion to deeper reality. Those other selves were present all along, waiting in the wings for their cue. A dispassionate reader of our correspondence could hardly miss his wavering and unease, her firmness. Max had always been looked after, managed, by women. So it is perhaps not surprising that when the race was over and the prize won he collapsed, reverting to a helplessness learned long before. No doubt I crystallized the role for him. Life is a comedy to those who think and a tragedy to those who feel. I had either to accept a vision of my marriage, my life, as tragic − or, unconsciously self-protective, to make it a comedy with Max as its bumbling star. I had my own models here: powerful mother, lovable-impractical father. Max accepted, may on some level have welcomed, this stroke of casting genius: it let him off the hook. Incompetent, irresponsible, ridiculous dreamer, how could he be expected to toe the line or, in crass terms, to *produce*? The role offered opportunities for a kind of nobility; a man who cannot cope with practical matters has, by implication, set his mind on higher things. We made fun of Max. Rona and Joyce, growing up, called him Mr Magoo after the endearing near-sighted cartoon character who mistakes streetlamps for policemen and strolls jauntily over the edges of precipices. But we also deferred to him as the expert on truth and beauty and goodness. The fact that he could not balance a chequebook somehow attested to his spiritual credentials.

Even before we married, Max displayed occasionally a startling, dead-serious absurdity. He proposed getting me pregnant as a way of overcoming my parents' opposition to our marriage. (*My parents* — with their feelings about their precious virginal daughter, their sense of family honour.) In the kitchen of the house where he lived during his bachelor days, I saw ants swarming about an uncovered jam jar; when I moved to cover the jar, he said, "No, no. I leave it open on purpose. That way the ants concentrate on the jam instead of getting into all the other stuff."

It was after we married, though, that ineptness, lovable or outrageous, became a way of life for him. There was the Maynard bus to Boston. As deviser of a humanities course, Max set out to acquaint small-town New Hampshire students with their cultural heritage. When he found that many had never travelled to a city larger than Manchester, never been inside an art gallery, he arranged for a day's outing. He would take these innocents to Boston, show them Faneuil Hall, the Museum of Fine Arts, the Gardiner Museum. One day he rushed in with, "My dear, where's the chequebook? I have to pay for the bus, $150." One hundred and fifty dollars being the equivalent of three months' rent, I protested. Surely the university, which provided buses, would give credit? Why not collect from the class first, and then pay? Max was impatient with my "pernicketiness." "My dear, that has no style at all. I'll write the cheque, and students will pay as they get on the bus." The day of the outing, Max (at the bus door) was practically knocked down in the stampede for seats. Word had spread to other classes: a free bus to Boston. Home from a wild ride with happy revellers, Max was shaken but reassuring: "I'll collect from the class next week."

Next week, and the next, passed. Students hadn't the right change, they denied having been passengers. When we closed the books on the culture expedition, Max had collected $14.25.

Over the thirty years of our closeness, Max accumulated losses and I accumulated resentments. He lost money. (Once, when he claimed he didn't know how to cash a cheque, I demonstrated and sent him to the bank. He returned triumphant. "Nothing to it." "Where's the money?" I asked. He clapped his forehead. "My God! I left it on the counter." He left trousers in hotel rooms and raincoats in the park. Once he came home from a concert in a state of high excitement. "The Bach was superb! But Rubinstein simply doesn't understand Chopin — all the delicate living little flowers turned into solid brass." "Max," I said (another flower-crusher), *what on earth are you wearing?*" He looked down. A long, shabby, totally unfamiliar raincoat flapped about his ankles. "My God! I didn't notice. It was the last coat on the rack." Visiting a friend in New York, he called me from a pay phone: "What's Dave's address? I've been out for a stroll, and I've forgotten where he lives." He went to England, cabled "SEND MONEY AT ONCE." I dispatched a money order to the address given. After two more cables and a transatlantic phone call, we discovered that he had given me the address of Harrod's department store.

Max and I maintained, on the surface, a civilized cool. There were no raised voices in our house, no slammed doors. We exchanged, indeed, ritual assurances of regard. Max said regularly, "You are the most wonderful woman in the world" — to which I regularly replied, "I love you." Neither said what the other wanted to hear. Out of this mutual frustration arose all kinds of subterranean struggles, like the one over keeping up appearances. He thought me delinquent in this area; I thought him meanly preoccupied with trivia. Here was a man who worshipped Beauty and Truth, obsessed with keeping up with

— well, not the Joneses, to be sure, but with Important People. Did the Howlett children take French lessons? Well, then, our children must too. The Heyworths had living-room furniture that *matched*. They had a *colour scheme*. We must get rid of our cheerfully eclectic belongings (this in the days when we could barely pay the grocery bill) and acquire a proper living room. "We owe it to our friends": Max could deliver that line without a trace of self-consciousness or self-questioning. Other things we owed to our friends were the most expensive French wines, as opposed to our usual California potations, and lights on the front-yard trees at Christmas. One of our few open battles occurred on this point. I maintained that, as a Jew, I did not celebrate Christmas and could not countenance outdoor decorations — also that we couldn't afford them. Mention of *affording* was a mistake, reducing my argument from principle to vulgar expediency. Max got in the car, drove furiously down an icy road — and demolished the Buick's front end. But we had lights on the trees when the Dean of Liberal Arts arrived.

Before a party, Max was always in a state of nervous agitation. Was I serving real meat, not a "concoction"? Would there be enough food? What did I plan to wear? Surely not *that*. While I cooked and cleaned, he would be rearranging the paintings for best effect. On more than one occasion, he climbed a ladder to a second-floor window to remove an offending cobweb. He objected regularly to the books in the downstairs bookcase; they were paperbacks, mostly psychology and sociology. "What will people think?" I insisted that this was my working library, located for easy access. "My dear," he announced, as gravely as if he had just discovered the Pythagorean Theorem or the Law of Conservation of Mass, "People judge you by your books. We should be building a distinctive collection — modern American novels, perhaps." (I had never known Max to read a modern American novel. I read little fiction.) He bought a sun lamp because he was convinced that details like a winter tan affected his chances of promotion, but he never used it. Twenty-five years later, when he left, the lamp was still in its carton. A man whose intellect and gifts qualified him for attention in any company flaunted pseudo-qualifications: he was descended from the noble Shrewsburys, he had once shared a train seat with the university president (a complete duffer), he had a friend whose government sent him annually to Paris to inspect a gold brick for the Department of Weights and Measures. He knew gold and deferred to dross. Admiring the heroic gesture – Sydney Carton on the scaffold, Oates striking out into the Arctic night so as to leave provisions for starving comrades – he struck poses comically inappropriate to the occasion. I remember a typical incident at the time of our first move, from a small apartment to a modest house. Though we owned almost no furniture – a table, a bed, a few chairs, some lamps – Max had engaged the services of the town's professional mover, Forrest Smart. Then a friend offered the use of his truck. "We can cancel Mr Smart," I said happily. Max confronted me, arms folded, feet slightly apart, with an expression of proud resolve – Churchill in the Battle of Britain, Nelson at Trafalgar. "*Never*," he said. "I will not turn my back upon Forrest Smart."

Meantime, an appearance that matters in any marriage – the appearance of relative husband-wife success – had drastically altered. Max had come to the University of New Hampshire in 1947 as a phoenix, a rare talent respected and admired by more prosaic colleagues. Respect endured; he remained formidable as a force in department policy and as a teacher. As years passed, however, and his alcoholism became widely known, the admiration of colleagues changed to apprehension and, in many cases, distaste. He was given tenure, but kept for humiliating decades at the rank of assistant professor and then associate. Still a charming social presence when he chose, Max became increasingly short-tempered, fierce, intolerant, irrational, extreme. He saw new Ph.D.s, men he regarded as less able, promoted to higher rank and much higher salaries. Even his wife, his protégée, earned more than he and was acquiring a reputation as a writer. Maynard the writer had not, after all, published novels or critical studies. As for Maynard the painter — who cared? "So you paint, Mr Maynard," faculty wives murmured. "That must be such a fascinating hobby." When he asked the university art gallery to arrange a show of his paintings, he was told, "We don't show amateur work."

In this climate of failed expectations, a shrinking world, Max's lifelong hypochondria intensified. Small ailments were magnified and dramatized. If his head ached, he flung himself on the couch. ("Oh God, I would welcome a nice clean decapitation.") He experienced panic attacks during which he shouted for me to call an ambulance, he couldn't breathe. On one such occasion, after I'd called the ambulance, I rushed to Max's room and found him choosing a tie for the journey. To the best of my knowledge, he suffered in his lifetime only two chronic afflictions, both classic responses to stress. As a young man, he was subject to blinding migraine. I remember him writhing on the floor, begging me to call the doctor for a shot of ergotamine. (The doctor, when he came, said, "Strong as a horse. He'll outlive us.") In later years, as arthritis gradually froze his hands and feet, he became obsessed with socks and shoes — the softest cashmere, the most flexible leather, accumulating a vast collection of footgear strewn about his study in readiness for therapeutic substitutions. The study became a kind of personal pharmacy which filled the drawers of a big oak desk. He bought (but seldom took) any patent medicine advertised for chilblains, headache, neuralgia, heartburn, stomach upset. When the theme was feet, he would acquire every article produced by the Johnson company — not only the corn pads and bunion

removers, but arch and metatarsal supports, powders, oint-
ments, elastic bandages. When the theme was staving off decrepi-
tude, he bought Geritol and every vitamin in every conceivable
strength.

Most people dread institutions and would go to considerable
lengths to escape a hospital bed. Not Max. A cough, a sniffle, a
stomach upset or a persistent headache was likely to provoke
the announcement, "My dear, I must go into hospital." One
year he decided nothing less than a prolonged stay, with multi-
ple tests, would solve the problem of his delicate digestion. He
checked into New England Deaconess, in Boston (a safe distance from harassment). When a week had passed without
word I telephoned, alarmed. Had the doctors found serious
trouble? Heavens, no. "They say I'm in superb condition," he
announced from his private room. "But you know, it's awfully
pleasant here. The nurses are charming, so attentive. I've decided
to stay on a bit, just to rest." At the end of ten days, he was
wheeled out the front door, where we waited, by one of the
attentive nurses. Then, like the wolf in Red Riding Hood casting aside grandmother's bedclothes, he bounded out of the
wheelchair, heading for the car and home.

By the last year of our marriage Max, semi-retired, in deep
depression, had all but taken leave of reality, the demon lover
become a Yeatsian old man, Timon or Lear who beat his head
upon a wall till truth obeyed his call. He flew to England to
consult a famous homeopath without the elementary precau-
tion of an appointment; in London, he found the homeopath
had just left for a month's vacation. Convinced that he had
cancer, he worried briefly about hospital costs and then came
up with an inspired solution. "I will insure myself heavily, find
out which are the most dangerous air routes, and keep flying
till I crash." Once I had argued with him, pleading for common
sense. At the end I scarcely looked up from shelling peas when

he stood over me in the kitchen, a frail figure but striking a
Byronic pose, to announce: "I am going to Antarctica. It will
be difficult and dangerous, but I must go." He drank openly
now, for the first time in my experience, and when I said, "Max,
you're not even *trying*," he said, "You're right. I'm not." My most
chilling memory of that last winter is shovelling through a
storm. While sensible citizens sat by the fire, Max and I plunged
through drifts with shovels as the snow fell around us, I
protesting and reluctant, he frantic. A firefighter or a physician
could not have been more passionate about keeping the driveway open. This need came from a generalized fear of confine-
ment, no doubt, but also quite specifically from that map in his
mind, the elementary geography connecting home with the
liquor store five miles away.

When I think, now, of my twenty-five-year marriage, I am
surprised to realize how small a part Max plays in my memories of good times. My image is of dashing off with the girls — to
a ballet, a shopping mall, a movie, and — one whole summer —
to Mexico, waving to Max as he set up his paints. Privately, we
felt that Daddy was not much fun. He wouldn't drive the car on
holidays (too risky) and preferred not to drive on weekends
(heavy traffic, also dangerous). He was always expecting rain.
He never played active games with his children — neither
peek-a-boo nor, later, baseball. Both girls, I think, secretly
longed for a Norman Rockwell father, an all-American regular
guy. They were mortified by Max's walking stick and his bathing cap, always the only one in the swimming pool. What I
remember affectionately is his tenderness with the children,
the way he taught them to look and really see. A walk with Max
was an experience in light and shade, bird calls, felt sky, the
tracks of rabbit or raccoon. Poetry came as naturally to him as
speech: he linked it with the natural world ("A rainbow and a
cuckoo — Lord, how rich and great the times are now!") and

with small daily rituals — Herrick's prayer at suppertime ("Here a little child I stand. Heaving up my either hand...") and Blake's Little Lamb at night.

And this is odd, odd....Though I have never had much empathy with dogs and cats (would not, on my own, choose to have pets), some of my most cherished memories of Max involve his feeling for animals. He would climb an awesomely tall tree to rescue a kitten which clung to a top branch, mewing frantically. When Joyce's parakeets escaped their cage and flew about the rooms, he could whistle them back to their perch. He treated our scruffy black poodle with affectionate dignity, as an old and valued friend. Often savage with humans, he could not bear to see other living things in pain, hated Mexico for its cockfights and, in the market, the dreadful spectacle of turkeys with legs tied together, panting in the midday sun. One evening, as we sat, all of us, reading in the living room, something small and grey flashed past. "A mouse!" Rona shrieked. Max looked with interest. "Good heavens — *a shrew*. I wonder what brought it indoors." By now both girls, in no mood for speculation on the habits of shrews, were up on the couch, screaming. "Don't be silly," Max said. "The poor little thing is terrified. It won't hurt you." More shrieks. "Get it out, get it out!" Reluctantly, Max went for his walking stick. "All right, I'll try to urge it along." He made a few passes with the stick, to move the shrew doorwards. In a frenzy, it darted along the floorboards. As the girls' voices rose in a crescendo of alarm, Max moved the stick sharply. The shrew spun in the air, then lay still. He was appalled. "Dear God, I've killed it." He picked the creature up and carried it outdoors. When he returned, he didn't look at any of us.

And then there were the starlings. Knowing nothing of birds, but liking the idea of a nesting robin, say, within view, I announced one spring day, "There's a sweet little bird building a nest right under the porch eaves. Look — here she comes with a bit of straw." Max groaned. "My dear, that is not a sweet little bird. That is a starling. Starlings drive away the robins, and they're a dirty lot. A nest under the eaves will cover the porch steps with bird droppings. They'll be back next year too."

He was right. The baby birds squawked loudly and befouled the steps. Pale blue eggshells appeared on the grass: farewell to the robins. And the following year, the starlings returned, with friends. The third year, I said, "You've got to do something." Max got up on a rickety ladder, poked around and said, "There's already a new nest here." "Throw it out," I called. He hesitated. "I think, if I just block the entrance, they'll go elsewhere to build." He blocked the aperture with crushed paper — a whole weekend's worth of *The New York Times*, carefully balled. Next day we watched as the mother bird tried to reach her nest, swooping and pecking, then circling back for another attempt. "An optimist," I said. "She's got a twig in her mouth." "I wish you were right," Max said. "I'm afraid it's a worm." We were silent a moment. "Well," I said, "the eggs can't hatch if she's not sitting on the nest."

Next morning, just past daybreak, I heard Max going down-stairs. I found him on the porch, barefoot and pyjama'd, transfixed. "What's the matter?" I said. "Sssh," he said. "Listen." Sure enough. From the blocked nest, through the Book Review section and the News of the Week and the Classifieds, we heard a tiny, persistent cheeping. And here came the mother bird again, worm in beak. Max headed for the garage. "Where are you going?" I said, but I knew. He came back with the ladder. "I'll clean the steps this year," he said.

"I had no idea he was a depressive," I told my therapist after the marriage ended. "I didn't know how much he drank." He sighed. Therapists must hear that sort of thing a lot. "You knew," he said.

Reflecting now on our long courtship, I see that he was right. Whisky is a constant minor theme of the letters. Despair hovers. "The spectacle of anyone going down the drain touches me too near," he wrote once. "I love you, darling, but I begin to wonder whether I don't carry a load with me that you ought to have nothing to do with." On some profound level Max and I both knew — and wanted — just what we were getting.

A neurotic collusion, I once read, occurs when the rocks in his head fit the holes in hers. That pretty well describes our marriage. Some people (my parents, for instance) saw us as a total mismatch, but in fact we fitted well: practical spirit and dreamer, managing woman with childlike man. This arrangement might conceivably have gone on until death, had we both remained as we were. I think Max didn't really change; he just got older. But I was forced, by the conditions of the marriage, to grow up. In very important ways, I got more out of it than he ever did.

As it had begun, my marriage ended with a letter.

The first letter ("Here I am, with this clever little Jewish girl") appeared without precedent and almost without warning. The final one, last in a long series of late-night missives, came as a shock but not wholly a surprise. Like a single crystal added to a supersaturated solution, it revealed — and ended — overload. Elements previously held in perilous suspension, released, appeared as issues that had at last to be faced.

For months before our marriage blew up, Max had been in a state of unrelieved black depression. About to retire from teaching, he faced the loss of his student audience — and the challenge of beginning, so late, life as a painter. His daughters had moved off into lives apparently complete without him: Rona had her new baby, Joyce a new love. I had published a book, claiming territory once regarded as his. Arthritis, doubtless aggravated by anxiety, flared up ominously; some days he could not hold a pencil. He drank as never before — not just in cycles now, but constant, night-after-night blackouts. I tried humour — "At this rate, your blood must be 96 proof. I could flame a pudding with it." I tried pleading — "You are destroying yourself" — and he shrugged, "The girls don't need me. You don't. Nobody needs me." When I threatened to leave, he said, "I honestly don't care. I don't feel anything any more."

Our social life had effectively ended. Most people were unwilling to risk the potential embarrassment of Max Maynard at a cocktail party. Even intimate dinners posed a danger. Weeks before the end, we spent a rare evening out with David and Ilona, close friends. Over the wine, Max embarked on a long, sentimental reminiscence of his first marriage — what a delightful person Evelyn was, how happy they might have been. As our hosts stared into their soup, I found myself becoming dizzy, then faint; I spent the rest of the evening, half conscious, on a couch. When I came to, Max was standing over me. "Look here," he said, "are you well enough to drive me home?" His one comment on that strange evening was an elegiac reflection over breakfast next day: "Ilona and David will remember us as people they knew long, long ago."

Max's persistent hypochondria now acquired a new, sharper focus. A small sore on his forehead, slow to heal, must be malignant. He brooded endlessly on his imminent demise. I persuaded him to see a doctor. He drove off like a condemned man, returned in a rare state of euphoria — "It seems we Nords have sensitive skins, nothing to worry about" — and celebrated his deliverance in what had become his chief, his only mode of celebration. All night I heard him banging about the study, weaving down the hall to the bathroom, falling on the stairs. Next morning, a new midnight letter lay on the dining-room table. "My own darling," it began. So many phrases were familiar — "With you beside me I can do anything, without you I am nothing" — that for a moment I thought the letter a hallucinatory remembrance of things past. Then I saw references to passion on the shores of Great Bay, a glorious meeting in New York — and a name. "Sarah, Sarah, I love you, I cannot live without you." I knew then that Max had introduced into our lives an element that could not be dealt with tidily. I knew Sarah.

Max had first spoken of her about a year earlier as a new admirer, an intense young woman who followed him about the campus, invented pretexts for conferences, brought him small awkward touching gifts — a dozen wild strawberries on a nasturtium leaf, a card decorated with cutout heads from Renoir reproductions, a beeswax candle moulded in a jelly glass. Once he pointed her out to me on campus — a curious anachronistic figure, style *circa* 1960, in high laced boots with trailing skirts and trailing hair and a rangy dog whose name, I learned, was Dog. "She looks a bit — off-centre," I said. Ah, Max said, she had a sad history: alcoholic father, lesbian mother, an early marriage to a manic depressive who tried to kill her, a nervous breakdown, time spent in mental institutions. "If I were you, I'd be careful," I said. "My dear," he said, "this is a very unusual young woman. Pathetic, but genuinely spiritual. Of course I don't encourage her, but she is *devoted* to me." From time to time I heard more about Sarah. She was an anthroposophist, a follower of Rudolf Steiner. She believed in spirit visitations and transmigration of souls; she conducted mystic rituals by moonlight, believed in the literal existence of the Holy Grail. She heard and followed angelic voices. Max reported these notions with a combination of amusement and affectionate indulgence. "She's completely naïve, you understand. She does nothing well — she has no *gift* — so it would be easy to underrate her.

But she's really…*sweet.*" That these qualities would have led a 70-year old man to reckless passion and promises I never imagined.

Yet that is what had happened. When I confronted Max with his fatal letter, he at first said, "A fantasy," then admitted the fantasy's real-life basis. This was no forced confession. He badly needed to let me know that, whatever I thought, he was seen as an object of desire by a woman half my age. Yes, he was having a love affair, with secret meetings and a plan for a spring rendezvous in England, where Sarah had gone to pursue her anthroposophical studies. Yes, he loved the girl. Stunned, but experiencing a kind of eerie clarity, I said, "Then you must go to her." He protested. Good heavens, he had no intention of leaving his marriage. ("I have always loved you above all.") On the other hand, he could hardly abandon this young acolyte. He would go to her in the spring, spend a few months ("until the fever dies down"), then return to Durham. From time to time he would see Sarah — she was his responsibility now — but our life together would continue essentially as before.

When I told him that our life together was over, the triumphant lover was transformed into a terrified child. "You don't mean it," he said. "I want you to go and never come back," I said. When he saw that I was adamant, he wept. "Please don't send me away. I'm old and tired." Because I could not bear his grief, could not trust my own resolve, I ran into the bedroom, leaning against the door to prevent his coming in. He knocked timidly. I opened the door and he said, "Only take me back and I will be *so* good," and I shut the door and that was the end. The only thing he took with him from the house was a grotesque green and red wooden animal sculpture he had bought in Mexico — over my objections.

Max spent the next five years wandering, like Cain in Hugo's "*Conscience*," fleeing the eternal Eye, *Muet et pâle et frémissant aux bruits*, looking for solace. *Laissez moi m'endormir le sommeil de la terre!* He flew to England, lived briefly and disastrously with Sarah in a Sussex farmhouse and returned with tales of abuse. Sarah beat him with his own walking stick, he said. She flung her heavy boots at his head, attempted to kill him by driving the car into a tree.

He tried living in a Durham guesthouse — humiliating for a man who had once been lord of his own manor. He moved to Wilton, New Hampshire, where Sarah now had a teaching job. More trouble. He moved to Peterborough. He moved to British Columbia, decided after a short stay that Victoria was sadly changed, stagnant, impossible. In New Hampshire again, rootless and wretched, he reconsidered his options, headed back to Victoria.

And here, second time round, a great thing happened. Max's grandnephew, a young man with a cultivated interest in painting, saw for the first time the pictures Max had brought with him to British Columbia. He arranged a small show in his own house. People came, admired, bought, and the word spread: Max Maynard, friend of Jack Shadbolt and Emily Carr, was painting again. Within a year, galleries were begging for his work. The government of British Columbia bought paintings for its offices in Canada and abroad; the government archives established a Maynard collection (where, not long ago, I had to don white gloves in order to handle the notebooks I used to toss about in Max's studio).

Max's personal life, meanwhile, appeared on the surface at least less tumultuous. Sarah had left him for another elderly sage. He had, however, found a new circle of female admirers and a new audience, the members of Alcoholics Anonymous (joined, it appears, at Sarah's insistence). The evidence suggests that Max never entirely gave up drink, and certainly his AA testimonials smacked more of theatre than true confession. But he attended meetings faithfully; in general, he stayed on track. Those of us who had believed Max Maynard could never manage on his own were humbled by the sight of a man painting steadily, using a palette knife when he could no longer hold a brush, taking an Arctic cruise so that he might sketch, on deck, the landscape he loved, making money and looking after his own financial affairs.

In the first years after our separation Max wrote me often, with the old warmth and charm but with distance carefully controlled. ("The fact is, I am afraid to let myself go.") The tone now was not passionate suitor but penitent eager to prove his worth and devotion. I wrote of my feelings; he responded with logic and elegant argument. Sex? "When people are honest with themselves," he wrote, "they see clearly that sexual joy is a fugitive thing, a concomitant of beauty and youth – largely an aesthetic experience." Betrayal? (When I had spoken of myself as "most intimately betrayed.") "Betrayal of one sort or another is terribly, terribly common – almost, it seems to me, inevitable. That is why compassion and esteem and patience and a kind of basic loyalty are so important." As for the "sad and terrible knowledges" which I felt had been forced upon me: "Are they really so much worse than all the other terrible knowledges that are forced upon us as the substance out of which we must construct our meanings and forms? And anyway, aren't they really knowledges of particles rather than wholes?"

This sort of talk, which had once enchanted me, I now found curiously irrelevant. I was tired of meanings and forms and aesthetic experiences. So our correspondence, like our occasional meetings, followed a pattern common to couples with a long history of pain: attempted rapprochement, affection, tension, misunderstanding and finally a blaze of anger. After each spat, I vowed, *Never again*. I won't write, I won't answer his calls. And time would pass, and he would send me a pot of white cyclamen, or a drawing, or a letter that smote me with its sweetness and sorrow. "You will always remain the most important person in my life, the most dearly beloved. I face this new life with sinking heart." A grateful acknowledgment from me would be misinterpreted: we must meet. I would decline, he would feel rejected, and hostile silence descended once again.

I had hoped, after the post-divorce ups and downs, that Max and I might find our way to some plateau of ease and friendship. That never happened. Our last encounter occurred in 1982, a year before he died. I was living in Toronto. He had flown from Victoria to see me; I realized, from letters and phone calls, that he Had Hopes. (Was he not now a well-known and successful painter? And surely, after ten years, I would have come to my senses.) We had not met since Joyce's wedding, four years earlier. He appeared at my door a small, frail figure, very like the photos of Thomas Henry Maynard in old age, leaning on his stick. He did not see me at all. He walked past me to a wall hung with his early watercolours. "My God!" he said. "I had forgotten how fine they are!" It was only after long contemplation of his work that he looked around at the house. I sensed his reluctant admiration — and disappointment. Things were too good with me. Seated in the living room ("Very nice, very like you, my dear"), he began to tell me of his latest book project. Perhaps he felt my disbelief. Or perhaps he remembered his object in coming. He broke off and, almost looking at me, said, "I know, my dear, I was a very poor husband. Self-centred, irresponsible. But if I were given another chance, I should do very much better."

"Max," I said, as gently as possible, "I hope you will never again be anyone's husband. The role doesn't suit you." After that, there was nothing to say. I served dinner, his favourite foods, and he said, "I have no appetite. I'm afraid I must go and lie down." We drove to his hotel in silence. When I parked the car, he did not at once move to open the door. "I am not in love with you any more," he said finally. "But I still love you." I could not speak the words he wanted to hear. "Max, I have never regretted marrying you," I said. "And I don't regret leaving the marriage." I wish now I had remembered his own precept — *The truth is for those who deserve it.* He pushed out of the car, shaking off my arm. He looked old and sick and angry. Next day, lunching with Rona, he said, curtly, "Your mother is depraved."

Max never wrote or telephoned again. When he died, I mourned the young lover and the sad old man, and the waste in our years together. But looking now at his paintings — the early lyrical watercolours and the late rich, dark, passionate oils — what strikes me is how much he salvaged, what rare fragments he shored against his ruins.

As for me — well, the young woman who loved Max Maynard is dead. I have often said this is the best time of my life, and by most accepted measures, that's true. I have health, love, security, good friends, a dear family, deeply absorbing work. My pleasure in the light sweet fragrance of a peony, the feel of sun on my face, the opening flare of a Mozart concerto, is rich and sustaining as ever. Still I know some profound joys are gone from my life forever. Some fire is extinguished. I remember I once thought the world well lost for love, but can't recapture that feeling. I know there was a time I walked the streets and thought surely anyone who passed would see I was on fire, burning with delight. "My heart is like a singing bird Whose nest is in a watered shoot; My heart is like an apple-tree Whose boughs are bent with thick-set fruit…"; I read those lines and wept for my own luck, my amazing unlooked-for happiness.

Before we married, I ran daily to meet the postman for fresh assurances that I was wildly, rapturously loved. What I lost, in the first days and months of my marriage, was not just love; it was also the beloved. In a melancholy inversion of those fairy tales that nourished my romantic dreams, I married the prince and found in my bed — not the Beast or the frog, to be sure, but a raging, bitter spirit who identified me as one source of his pain.

So I sealed off the most intensely alive part of myself, buried it in an unmarked grave. I have learned, over the years, never to go near that plot where no grass grows. Sometimes, though, I am caught unawares, like the time I flew to the West Coast for the first retrospective show of Max Maynard's painting. When Max died, months before the show, it seemed to me I felt little. I did not attend his funeral. Then I walked into the art gallery in Vancouver, and the first thing I saw was a billboard-size photograph of Max as a young man, intense and inscrutable, the very picture I had kept on my desk for years. I tried, in the opening ceremonies, to deliver my carefully prepared speech — Mrs Max Maynard reviewing her late husband's career — and then Fredelle Bruser suddenly came out and cried for Max.

Long after I had left Max Maynard, after he was dead, his friend, the painter Jack Shadbolt, said, "Poor Max. He always gave more than he got." "Not to me he didn't," I said. "Oh, I didn't mean in any practical sense," Jack said. "Of course he was ruthlessly self-obsessed. He disrupted the lives of every-one he met — but he also touched those lives with genuine creative passion. That's a great gift." I know this to be true. I see the trees and the sky differently because I knew Max Maynard. He deepened my response to painting and music, he affected even the rhythms of my speech. Though the cost was high, I no longer try to assess losses and gains. Long past the orgies of blame and self-blame that accompanied the collapse of our marriage, I think now that what happened was no-one's fault.

> *In tragic life, God wot,*
> *No villain need be! Passions spin the plot.*
> *We are betrayed by what is false within.*

Kaddish
for My Mother

Somehow, the time was never right. The weather was too hot or too cold. I was working on an article or planning a trip. Lots of dinner parties coming up, what would I do with Mother? On weekly phone calls I would wave the possibility, a small flag of hope. She played the game with me. "I want you to come very soon," I'd say. No date mentioned. "Well, you know, dear, I haven't been feeling too well. When I'm stronger...." If I said, "I'd love to see you, but I'm deluged with work," she would say, "I understand."

Just when my mother's love and pride became for me more burden than gratification is hard to say. I remember being frightened rather than pleased when she said once, "I wouldn't die for Papa, but I would die for you." I remember stirrings of unease in late adolescence — when, for instance, I sensed Mother's jealousy of my friendships. "That girl you can't trust," she would say when I'd spent an afternoon happily exchanging confidences with a schoolmate. "I can tell how she begrudges." During my twenties, a friend who visited Winnipeg met my mother and responded in unsettling fashion. "Your mother is wonderful and charming, etc., etc.," she wrote. "The kind of person you get entangled in. I see you as enmeshed in a net of surprising softness and fineness, of bewildering softness and strength." Around the same time, my father gently reproved me for not writing home more than once a week. "There is no better tonic to strengthen Mother's nerves and uplift her spirits. I often think she just lives for you and with you; no greater love and self-denial ever existed."

Rebelling against love and self-denial is singularly difficult. I came to envy daughters less loved than I, less sacrificed for. When, over the years, I went home for summer visits, Mother required my total attention – and my children's. The year they brought French books to help pass the time in a small city apartment, she said, "Do you come to visit your grandmother or to study French?" If I took an occasional hour off to see friends, I would return to hostile silence, my mother scrubbing a floor that didn't need scrubbing in mute accusation. The reverse situation – Mother visiting us – was no easier. Never, during the years when I was housebound with young children, did she offer to take over while I went on vacation. If she came, she came to see *me*. She would follow me through the house, talking, talking – often while two little girls waited hopefully, trying to get a word in. If they presumed to break in on a monologue about uncles and cousins unknown to them, my mother would say, "Your mama never interrupted when she was your age."

So I came to dread her visits. Critical observations accumulated during a lifetime and swiftly buried began to surface, form patterns. Now I saw my mother's apparent self-denial as narcissistic self-serving; refusing to accept my separateness, she had dedicated herself to *our* triumph. My push for autonomy, appearing as it did so late, came accompanied by disproportionate rage. At fifteen or sixteen, I might have said, passionately but without rancour, "Let me go!" Delayed until I was past thirty, my rebellion was blind as my devotion had been. Though I never wholly abandoned the good-daughter pose, I could hardly see, now, the good mother of my childhood. So I cut my mother in small mean ways — which she pretended not to notice. "Fredelle tells me everything," she would tell friends. "I see all her writing before it's published." And I would say coldly, "That's not true." She would embark on an anecdote — I used to love her stories — and I would cut her off with, "Mother, you *told* me that." One day, in her seventies, visiting Durham, she became frantic because I'd been gone in the car for perhaps two hours, shopping. As I entered, she burst into tears. "Where were you? I thought maybe an accident. I was just going to phone the police." I didn't give her a hug or comfort her, as I would once have done. I said, "For heaven's sake, Mother, don't be ridiculous!" and walked right past her, a flagrantly independent spirit going about her own business. Where once I sang my mother's praises, now I complained — to my children, my husband, my friends and her friends. "Mother is *impossible!*"

And then her health began to fail. This should have been no surprise: she was over eighty. But I had grown up with the legend, and the evidence, of her strength. My mother could crack brazil nuts with her teeth. Once, when a friend's car got stuck in spring mud, she lifted the whole rear end of the vehicle and pushed it to dry ground. I had seen her face down every kind of difficulty; she had nursed friends and family members through illnesses, preserving always her good spirits and good health. So I was not prepared for the new hesitancy in her voice and manner, the quietness. She no longer tried to hold me on the phone when I called. Where once she talked on and on, preventing my "*goodbye*," now she cut short conversation after the first moments with, "Well, dear, thank you for phoning."

It was then, nearing the end of her life, that my mother gave me what I needed to love her again. She began to let me go, for the first time in our shared experience gently but firmly disengaging. Mortally ill, she urged me not to linger by her bedside. And then she summoned all her forces — instinctively or consciously, who knows? — to die well. In place of the tedious old woman who had alternately bored and enraged me, I found once again my mother, my extraordinary mother.

By the time my parents sold their Grandview store and retired, my mother was sixty-one, my father an ailing sixty-eight. Settling in Winnipeg, for good (we had lived there only briefly, during the thirties), was an old dream, the last of the dreams that had carried my mother through a lifetime of adversity. Quick, clever and gifted, with a head for organization and, as my father used to say, "golden hands," she had grown up in a world where marriage must have seemed the only possible fulfilment for a woman, however strong and ambitious. Essentially uneducated (she was allowed to attend school for just six years, walking five miles each way), she somehow kept her curiosity and spirit alive in a household whose only concern was *parnosseh*, earning the daily bread. When the family moved from a Manitoba farm to Winnipeg, where my grandfather developed a wholesale tobacco business, she did what she could to improve herself. She went regularly to the opera (though as far as I know, she had no ear for music). She attended educational lectures at the Walker theatre. Meanwhile she had become, in the city's close-knit Jewish community, a famous beauty, a *catch*. From a field of promising suitors — business-men, scholars, a rabbi even — she chose a penniless Russian painter. What drew her to my father? Certainly she valued his gifts of intelligence and feeling (not to mention his dashing good looks). Also, I think she must have been stirred, this girl who stood at the back of the concert hall to hear *Tosca*, by the thought of an artist husband. Innocent as she was of the arts, she may have imagined wealth and vicarious fame.

Instead, she found herself transported to a series of remote Saskatchewan villages, living in primitive conditions and working in my father's general store. In the beginning, she saw her exile as temporary — just a few years, until Boris established himself. As the years passed, with business failures and moves only to other, even poorer prairie towns, the dream of life in Winnipeg with her family faded and changed. They would retire to Winnipeg. When, however, they moved to Winnipeg in 1953, it was not to a dream home.

Their apartment — three rooms in cheaply constructed postwar housing — overlooked an alley, a parking lot and a tumble of garbage cans. No lawn, no garden, Still my mother rejoiced in the prospect of a new life. Back in Jewish Winnipeg, she would be near her sister and her girlhood friends; my father could join a *shul*, return to his Talmudic studies. Or perhaps he would take a part-time job in a North End department store, "bring in a little extra." She would entertain. She bought furniture, two matched suites — pale oak for the dining area and a voguish greeney-white for the bedroom. She bought new dishes, a set of community plate, passing on to me her beautiful wedding china and silver, which she now saw as not modern enough. She installed wall-to-wall carpeting, evidence of improved station. She started a whole new collection of plants — cuttings of begonias, philodendron and dieffenbachia that proliferated with accommodating speed — and began to consider the possibility of a small flower garden outside her window.

Then came the accident. On a celebratory visit to Florida — my parents' first trip together, ever, since their wedding thirty-seven years before — my father was struck down by a drunkenly speeding driver. He spent six months in a Miami hospital, with a compound skull fracture and two broken legs. Doctors my mother had never seen, never heard of, sent bills, claiming they had assisted at the scene of the accident or been called in consultation. Money saved from years of work and scrimping melted away. My father came home on crutches and settled into an armchair, where he dozed a great deal. There was no more talk of part-time jobs. Mother made plans for "when Daddy is better," but gradually it became evident that he would never be better, the trouble went deeper than broken bones. Tests confirmed what we had begun to suspect from his strange stillness, his forgetfulness and disorientation: senile arterio-sclerosis, progressive.

So there were no dinner parties or bridge games. "If people didn't know Boris before, when he was well," Mother said, "I don't want them to see him now." My father spent ten years in his armchair, in the city apartment where my mother had planned the new life. When, incontinent and unsteady on his legs, too heavy for Mother to lift when he fell, he was moved to a nursing home. My mother's beloved younger sister Lucy was found that winter to have stomach cancer; she died before the snow melted. My mother's life shrank to a daily ritual of trips to the nursing home with a bag of treats. Though these visits depressed her — husband and lover become a child again — they gave pattern and meaning to her life. When my father died, she was desolate. She carried the new dishes and silver to her basement locker for safekeeping. She laid out old photographs on the dining-room table (never used, the extension leaves still in their box) and put a sheet of glass over them. She ate in the kitchen, a single place-setting on a plastic mat. Above the table hung a piece of needlework executed in more hopeful days — a cornucopia of appliquéd fruits and vegetables with the legend WE MUST EAT TO LIVE, NOT LIVE TO EAT. Except when she was invited to weddings or bar mitzvahs, she no longer cooked — and what was there to shop for? She cleaned, read old letters, watched TV.

My father's death left my mother lonely, querulous and melancholy. Her relationship with my sister became more contentious. I, meanwhile, had distanced myself, writing less frequently and "forgetting" Mother's Day. I went on trips, out of touch for weeks.

Occasionally — this as close as she ever came to criticism — Mother would report queries real or invented. "My friends want to know, how come your daughter has time for Mexico but not Winnipeg?" Immediately, though, she'd throw planks across the open pit. "I tell them, Fredelle has assignments." *Assignments* was a proud word for her; it meant money, public performance, success. On some profoundly subterranean level, she experienced my busyness as battle for her sake. Like reciting, like coming first in class; my triumphs were hers.

Finally, of course, she had to visit. I'd clear a space, anticipating frailty, my unease fuelled by the time it took, now, for her to answer the phone, and her tremulous voice. I'd arrange for a wheelchair at the airport, brace myself for the sight of a mother tottering and vague. And then she'd walk off the plane like a queen, a small woman but compact, commanding, assured. In summer, she wore her turquoise silk with matching coat and tam, in winter her mink. Dress oxfords, for arrival. (She would change, as soon as we got to my house, into the *chubatoras*, heavy laced shoes with elaborate architecture of metatarsal lifts.) In her eighties she remained so fresh, so perfectly groomed, that instinctively I'd adjust my scarf. Her look when she saw me was radiant. I could hardly bear it: tenderness, pride, eagerness, joy, *love*, just what it had always been. There was one notable change. Where she used to announce, at a visit's beginning, the date of her return ("I have to be back for Ernie's bar mitzvah"), now she'd ask, as soon as she had unpacked: "When do I have to go?"

Fearful of overstaying her welcome, she was from the first day getting ready to leave. No longer able to help around the house, she made the only contribution possible: she stayed in bed mornings, so I could get my work done. When I brought her coffee, she'd ask, the verb having no object: "Well, have you *achieved*?" We talked about safe subjects. Conscious of failing memory and small confusions, she was nervous about her departure date. "Is it tomorrow I go?"

From her last visit — we didn't know it would be the last — two moments stand out. One was the night I wakened to find all the lights on. I found my mother sitting on the sofa, looking around, taking it all in — the white Haitian cotton upholstery, tropical plants, Mexican pottery and Polish wall hangings. She reached out to touch a painted Kashmiri box that stood on the glass table. "Is this the upstairs living room or the downstairs one?" she asked. And then, half aloud, to herself: "Friedele has *two* living rooms. If only Boris had lived to see it."

The other moment occurred when I embarked on a plan to rouse her from a new, ominous lethargy. On this trip, she made none of her usual phone calls. She slept a lot. She had no shopping commissions, no gifts to buy, and when I proposed expeditions she begged off. "Maybe tomorrow I'll feel up to it." Just before she was to leave, I asked if she would bake. Could she show me how to make *sucherlach*, her special cinnamon rusks? She looked defeated and sad. "I've forgotten the recipe." I told her I knew how to prepare the dough; it was shaping and handling I wanted to learn. No use. She couldn't. One morning I took out the flour, sugar and eggs. By the time Mother appeared,

the kitchen was sweet with the live smell of yeast. She walked
slowly over to the brown earthenware bowl and lifted the linen
towel, already quivering slightly with the rising dough. She
bent over it and breathed deeply. Then, as if in a trance, she held
out her hands. "I need melted butter. You have loaf pans? Now
the cinnamon and sugar. No, No. *Fine* sugar." She rolled, cut,
dipped, sprinkled, lined up buns in pans. Through two risings,
baking and then drying the rusks, she busied herself in the
kitchen, cleaning up as she worked and polishing the stove's
chrome trim. "Tomorrow, if you like, I'll make another batch."
Next day she never left her bed.

She returned to her apartment, but the signs of trouble now
were unmistakable. She would phone three or four times with
the same question (and the same urgency). Winnipeg friends
expressed concern. "Your mother gets dizzy spells." Once a
neighbour found her lying on the bathroom floor; several times
she called an ambulance herself. She forgot to pay bills and the
telephone was cut off; social-security cheques were mislaid. A
cousin who stopped by during a freezing cold spell reported
that she found Mother with no food in the apartment. Afraid to
risk the icy streets, she was living on dry cornflakes. Her doctor,
after a routine check-up, called me to say that her blood pressure was dangerously high. "She forgets to take her pills," he
said. "Your mother absolutely cannot go on living alone."

I flew to Winnipeg. The doctor, the friends, were right. The
apartment's condition might have satisfied my own casual
standards of housekeeping, but not my mother's in the old
days. Objects had been dusted around, a glass from the cup-
board felt sticky, the oatmeal was infested with weevils. A pot
lid from the prized Wearever aluminum set had a jagged hole
in the metal. What happened? "I left it sitting on an electric
burner and forgot to turn off the stove." Obliged at last to look,
really look, I saw that I had neglected her. Her shoelaces had

been broken and reknotted so often they no longer passed through the eyelets. Her oxfords were scuffed, the heels worn down. She had used up all her lipsticks, reaching down into the empty tubes for what dabs of colour she could salvage. Her purse wouldn't snap shut; she held the clasp with an elastic band. "I'd like to get another purse like this," she said, "but it's hard to go downtown." "For goodness' sake, Mum, you can't replace a fifteen-year old style," I said. She took the implied reproof in silence. Her figure bulged in strange places. When she undressed, I saw that her ancient corset had stretched beyond all usefulness; the elastic sagged like cheesecloth. Her bloomers were mended with large coarse stitches. I remembered how, years ago, she embroidered even the edges of my petticoats with flowers and hand faggoting.

As gently as possible, I raised the possibility of moving to a senior citizen's home where all her needs would be taken care of. "You mean the old folks' home," she said, scornful of euphemism. "I'm not ready yet." "These places won't take you the minute you decide you're ready," I said; she had already shut off the discussion. So I quietly initiated procedures — a smooth official phrase for filling out the forms, making the telephone calls that would put Mother's name on a waiting list. A social worker called to evaluate the case. Sensing danger, my mother at first put on so good a show that I feared the investigator might underestimate the need. But as she stayed on, Mother became more anxious and began repeating herself, a needle stuck in a groove of bravado. "I like living here by myself. I have so many friends." She asked, "Do I look like somebody who has to be looked after?" and the social worker said, "We all enjoy being looked after at times."

On one point my mother was adamant. She would not enter a gentile home. "I have nothing against goyim," she would say. "I've spent my life with them. But when the time comes for me to push daisies, I don't want to see any crosses. I want to die with my own." A year passed before I received an urgent call from a Winnipeg cousin. "Your mother's been given an interview appointment at the Sharon Home. She's very upset. You'd better come." I found Mother tearful and refractory. "I don't have to go. It's ridiculous. Look how I keep this place." I described the pleasures of living in luxurious surroundings, Jewish friends all round. "Friends!" she snapped. "*Yachnas. Alte lieten.* Gossips. Old people. And Sundays, everybody else with the children coming, I'd have nobody." I pointed out the economy of the arrangement, food and medical care provided. She was not impressed. "I have money. I don't depend on anybody. I won't live to use up what I've got." Finally I said, "Mum, do it for me. Can you imagine how I worry, thousands of miles away, knowing you might take sick when you're all alone?" This argument, which I had not expected to carry weight, silenced her. She needed to believe my peace of mind depended on her welfare. "All right," she said, meek, like a good child. "I'll do it for you."

The morning of the appointment she lay trembling. "I can't get up," she said, barely audible. "We'll have to postpone. I'm not well." "There may not be another chance," I said. I lifted her to a sitting position, pulled on her corset over stiff legs, drew up the stockings and snapped the garters. When I knelt with her bloomers she said, "I'm not helpless yet." I watched her, tottering slightly and holding the bureau for support and thought *They'll never take her. The social worker says they want brisk decorative old people for the ground floor.* But when I announced, "Mum, it's time," she said, "I'd better wear my mink."

No-one watching my mother enter the Sharon Home that day would have guessed how she had wept in the cab, begging me to tell them she'd need time to adjust. She walked like the Queen Mother reviewing the troops. Throughout the interview she sat attentive and composed. I had a bad moment when the director's wife, with sudden intuition, said, "Mrs Bruser, I get the feeling you don't really want to live in our Home. And of course we have hundreds of people waiting who are eager to come." My mother scarcely hesitated. She turned to me, embracing me with her look. "My daughter thinks this is the best place for me," she said. "And I trust my daughter."

Of course they accepted her. A woman almost ninety who talked like that, walked smartly and was a well-groomed beauty besides. At one point Mother said, "I must have my privacy," and the director said, "We can't guarantee a private room." But his wife instantly reassured. "For Mrs Bruser we'll find a private room." After the interview the staff gathered round to meet Mother, admiring her as if she were a new item of furnishing — which in a sense she was. She would look good in the lounge. The director took us on a tour of the building. I asked to see the crafts room, saying my mother was wonderful with her hands, I hoped she'd go back to knitting and sewing. Walking past tables where old ladies worked at bean bags and pipe-cleaner dolls, Mother said nothing. I wondered what passed through her mind. The hand-painted pillows she used to make, water lilies with a shimmering butterfly poised on one silken petal? My baby dresses, white rosebuds satin-stitched on batiste, with hand crochet edging the tiny puffed sleeves?

We paused by a woman gluing lollipop sticks together to make a napkin holder. "Mrs Shimer!" I said. "Remember me? I went to school with your son Leo." She made a throttled angry noise. "Leo is in heaven," she said. I apologized, I didn't know. Perhaps he had left children? "A son a hooligan," she said. "A daughter who knows where? Me she never writes." Struggling for safer footing, I performed introductions. "My mother's coming to the Home soon." Mrs Shimer fixed her with a bitter eye. "Keep out as long as you can," she said. "This is *gehenna*, hell."

On the way home I said, "You're lucky. The Sharon Home is exceptional, the best place I've seen." "Beautiful," my mother said. "Like a hotel."

I had hoped for a period of weeks before the actual move – time for us both to get used to the idea. But the very next day Mrs Faintuch called. A room had just been…vacated. Come at once, or lose your turn. Mother panicked when I told her. "What will I do with my things? I've got a lease." When I assured her I'd attend to everything, she fell silent, watching as I packed. "I can take all my pictures?" It was not really a question. "My plants? My rocking chair?" Pictures and plants yes, I assured her. As for the rocker – Mrs Faintuch had said no furniture, the Home provided everything necessary. "Without my rocker I don't go," Mother said. "I sit there nights when I can't sleep." "We'll see," I said. "We'll discuss it." I had learned that ploy from her, and practised it on my children. Let the dust settle, people forget. One more river not crossed.

Two days after the interview and acceptance we sat waiting, my mother and I, for a cousin with a station wagon. The apartment felt unbearably hot. Mother had turned on a fan, and the schefflera shook in the breeze. She reached out and touched the top of a leaf. "Don't worry," she said – as one might speak to a child, to a small frightened animal. "You're coming with me." She reached into her purse for a handkerchief. "I'll tell them at the Home, I'm not crying because I don't like their place. I'm crying…." She shook her head hopelessly. "It's good, I'm lucky. Why am I crying?"

When I cleaned out my mother's last apartment, I found the familiar combination of order and fullness. The basement locker was packed with supplies, enough detergent and canned tomatoes for the entire building. Her drawers were impeccable, as they had always been: stockings rolled, gloves properly mated and layered in tissue. Fine white linen handkerchiefs (my mother the only person I knew who still used them). Pink bloomers in the style she preferred, with elastic at waist and knees, carefully mended because such garments were no longer made. A petticoat with lace trim, several sizes too small, kept no doubt because the lace was still good. Dozens of little chiffon scarves, every shade of lavender, blue, grey: one of her few indulgences. Four pairs of gold-rimmed eyeglasses. She had a theory that unless you claimed your old spectacles the optometrist might fob off on you your old lenses, recut to new frames. Pill boxes full of metal snap fasteners, pill boxes full of pills (R. Bruser, two at bedtime, 1956). Though she hadn't for years used hairnets or hair colouring, she had large supplies of both. Then the records: my father's love letters, folded in chocolate boxes and tied with taffeta ribbon; my first poems and stories; my school report cards; newspaper clippings of university awards; my letters home, three decades' worth; my published articles; old photographs — everything kept with the devotion of a fan and the care of an archivist. Dispatching these familiar treasures to my home address, I seemed to be packing up, putting away, my mother's real life. No longer the inspiration of child or lover, she had become an old woman in an old folks' home, waiting for death. I remembered how, sitting in my kitchen the year before, she watched me take out one of her Wearever pans. "It's kind of nice to see you use my things," she said. "But it's sad too."

Her room at the Home was as pleasant as such rooms can be. Sunny, with a broad windowsill for plants. A small refrigerator, a bed, a bureau, a night table, two chairs — all new-looking — and a private bathroom. "Where's my bathtub?" Mother asked. "Oh, Mrs Bruser, you won't be bathing yourself," the nurse said quickly. "You'll have a regular bath night. I'll come to get you." I didn't dare look at Mother's face. (Image of my mother in the tub on summer afternoons, luxuriantly soaking. She took a sensual pleasure in hot water and perfumed oils.) I broached the subject of the beloved rocker, pleading medical reasons. "Mother has a bad back. Her doctor prescribed this rocker." The nurse sighed. "Not a chance, I'm afraid. If everybody brought a rocker, can you imagine what the baseboards would look like?" Ever a pragmatist, my mother retreated. *No is no.* "But my daughter can stay with me a while?" Of course — at least until dinner. No visitors in the dining room. A handyman was summoned to put up my mother's pictures: her wedding photograph; my father's framed proposal-by-mail, a painting of his hand holding a gold ring; a large portrait of me as a young girl; paintings by my children and my sister's artist daughter. Mother laid out on the bedside table her copies of my books, wrapped in plastic. "People should see who I am." And then the housekeeper came, pushing a cart, to collect her clothes. "What is she doing?" Mother asked. (It was her habit, when alarmed, to speak through me, as though she required an interpreter.) The housekeeper explained. In this new world everything — every stocking, every handkerchief — must be labelled and stamped. *Rona Bruser, Room 204.*

Living in the Sharon Home, my mother became oddly quiet. Always active — a woman who had tirelessly cooked, cleaned, sewed, scrubbed, knitted, gardened, entertained, clerked in the store — she now sat all day, surrounded by photographs, my father's letters, my published work and my children's. She did not attempt to make friends, and discouraged friendly overtures from other residents. "It's all over now," she said one day. "I raised my children and then *plumfp*, I went down myself. It's just like a wheel turning."

The pattern of our relating, once so rich and complex, had simplified. I telephoned weekly. She did not tell me that her

days were empty, that she was unbearably lonely and afraid of
dying alone in the Sharon Home. ("Don't call it *the Home*,"
she'd say. "Just '128 Magnus.'") Instead, she told me how good
people were to her — evidence, this, of *her* goodness. How the
director's wife never failed to stop by on her rounds. ("The
other women, *yachnas*, gossips, are jealous because she favours
me.") Sometimes I rang and rang, at hours when Mother surely
would be nowhere but in her room, and got no answer. A few
days of this, and I would call the Home's office. "Was Mrs
Bruser all right? Yes, surely. The speaker had just seen her in
the dining room. Ask her to call her daughter, I would say. She
did not call. When at last I reached her — "Mother, where *were*
you? I was worried" — she would say, "Some man has been
ringing up, bothering me. So I don't answer."

She almost never, any more, took the initiative. So I was
surprised when I picked up the telephone one morning —
during the full-rate period — and heard my mother's voice. "I'm
going into the hospital," she said. "What's wrong?" I asked.
"Nothing," she said. "I feel all right. The doctor says I have to
go." Had she asked why? No.

I telephoned Dr Kettner. "Your mother has jaundice," he said.
"Well, that's not so bad," I said. "At your mother's age, jaundice
can be a very bad sign," he said. "There's an obstruction of the
bile duct," I asked the question to which I instinctively knew
the answer. Probably cancer. He had taken X-rays, would let
me know. That week I read up on jaundice. "A symptom rather
than a disease, commonly caused by an obstruction of the
passages through which bile pigment is normally excreted by
the liver into the intestines. If the blockage is not removed, the
liver enlarges and its function gradually fails…. The liver stores
the products of digestion, detoxifies certain poisons, partly
regulates the volume of blood in the body. It is the largest gland
in the body and its function is absolutely essential to life."

The X-rays came back, revealing ominous shadows in the pancreas. "Of course we won't know for sure," he said, "until we go in." *Go in.* How deceptively casual that sounds. I thought of my mother's long history of surgery: ruptured appendix, hysterectomy, hernia. Last time she said *Never again.* I don't think Mother would agree to an operation," I said. "And anyway — if it's cancer — what's the use?"

My mother's doctor was a kind man, and patient. He explained. Surgery could create a passage for the bile, relieve the jaundice. And then? I prodded. Well, there was always — theoretically — the chance that the shadow in the pancreas was innocent. If not: Mother would live three, four months, relatively comfortable. If nothing were done, the jaundice would get worse. She would suffer itching, extreme discomfort, eventually pain; without liver function she couldn't last more than two months. "Your mother's a strong-minded woman," the doctor said. "But I think you could talk her into the operation." I asked about post-operative pain. Couldn't that be as bad as jaundice? What about the chance that she might not survive surgery? "My dear," he said, "There are no guarantees. I've given my opinion. You make the choice."

I found her at the Misericordia Hospital, hooked up to tubes — an IV in the arm, a catheter tied to the bed's foot. "You'll be shocked at her colour," the doctor warned. Her skin had turned poisonous yellow-green. They had taken away her teeth, and her glasses. Sleeping, she lay with an aureole of thistledown hair on the pillow, eyelids a sore purple like a hooded bird's. I studied the bulk of the body, and saw that my mother was actually a small woman. It was her corsets, her assertive walk, that gave the impression of size. The cineraria I had sent stood on the stand next to a water pitcher and a gift basket of candy, tartan-bowed.

Remembering other meetings and partings, I had dreaded

this moment, my mother's embrace like a claim. She had never left without tears, without creating an atmosphere of final farewell. This time, when she wakened, there was no high drama. She contemplated me approvingly. "Your hair is turning so nicely," she said. "I always thought you looked like me." And then, summoning up a vision of all those occasions when she filled cookie tins in anticipation of my visit, she shook her head ruefully. "Such a wonderful guest, and I didn't even bake a cake."

Confident of my influence, I presented the case for surgery. I did not explain why the bile duct was blocked, and she didn't ask. I am sure she made her decision not realizing she had cancer. She understood that the "small procedure" proposed by the doctor would relieve her jaundice. She thought the choice lay, not between two months' life and four, but between cure and no cure. And she chose unhesitatingly. "Dr Kettner's a good man," she said. "We're close friends, but on surgery he's not a friend. I use my own judgment. He sends other doctors who approve of surgery. But it's not their stomach that's going to be cut open, it's mine. *Der vile vil ze machen gelt.* Meantime they want to make a little money."

"It's a small operation, Mum," I began. She silenced me.

"I'm eighty-seven," she said. "Can I live forever? Why would I let them cut into me? It's ridiculous. This is my body. Who knows? I might just go *poof* in the night."

For my mother's voice, I have always had perfect pitch. I knew that tone. I took out my pen and began to make notes. She smiled. "*Die schribst viter*, you're writing again....Kettner will be disappointed. He thought you would convince me, but it's me who has to do the convincing of myself — and I'm not convinced."

We sat silent. She pointed to the potted plant. "Take home

that container when I go," she said. "It's a good basket. And maybe that little candy basket for Audrey, for her shelf?"

Cancer of the pancreas is a slow death, and hard. Entering her room unobserved I might glimpse my mother inundated by waves of pain; the moment she saw me, she summoned mysterious reserves of strength. Always something of an actress, she ran through the old roles. "I'm sorry I'm not having a good day" (my mother the gracious hostess), and when I said, "Any day I see you is a good day" responding with "Ah, that's well put" (my mother the discriminating judge). A woman in labour, giving birth to death, she closed her eyes during a particularly fierce contraction, blinked and shook her head. "It's good I don't have a date tonight" (my mother the coquette). "I'm not up for boyfriends." "Not even Harry Belafonte?" I asked. (An old joke, this, my mother's passion for the man who sang, "For your true love, my darling, I'd walk on my head....") She mimed astonishment. "Harry Belafonte? Didn't you know? I gave him up."

In those last days, as I sat by her bed, making notes because I wanted to remember everything, she would peer over the guard rails — shockingly wasted now, nose thinner and sharper, cheekbones distinct and harsh, but the sunken eyes bright. Once a great beauty, strong and proud, now she contemplated her jaundiced body and said, "I always prided myself on being different. Well, I *am* different now." Amused, indulgent, she watched me with my notepad. "It's really handy when you have your very own writer. That way it doesn't cost anything." Death at the door, she retained a youthful jauntiness. When I offered to remove the cross that hung above her bed in a Catholic hospital, she laughed. "Some people say, 'Jesus Christ on the wall! I wouldn't have it.' I tell them, 'Why not? Is he bothering me?'" Towards the end, having to leave for a few days, I said, "I'll see you soon." She glanced briefly, with careful nonchalance, into the abyss. "There may be nothing to see." I winced at the bitter joke. She touched my hand and, uncharacteristically for a lifetime agnostic, whispered, "I'll pray for you." Pause, rueful smile. "I guess it's a little late to start praying," she said. "But maybe God will consider it." All day, every day, we sat together, waiting. Once I filled a silence by telling her about a woman who, when her daughter married a *goy*, cut off her only child, sat *shiva* as for the dead. "There is nothing you could do, dear," my mother said, "that would make me turn against you." I pushed a little. What if I had killed someone? She considered that carefully. "I would know you must have had a very good reason."

On the last day, as we sat quiet together, a nurse entered, carrying a dish of jello. "Please, Mrs Bruser, take a little. You haven't eaten for days." "I'm not hungry," my mother said. "I look at my daughter, and I'm *full*." She removed her heavy gold wedding band — it slipped off easily — and studied the inscription briefly. "1916. *RONA MY LIFE*. Well, it's all over now." She laid the ring in my hand. Never one for self-pity, she allowed herself a moment's grief, reverting to Yiddish and my baby name. "*Meine teira Freidele, meine kluge Freidele* — my dear, my clever Freidele, O, I will miss you!" Then she laughed her young girl's laugh. "That's silly. Where I'm going, I won't miss anybody." Once again my strong practical mother, she indicated the key to her safe-deposit box. "You shouldn't lose more time. There's a receipt from the synagogue. I've paid for everything — the cemetery plot, the box. You get a bronze plaque too." And then — my mother the shopper — "I bought before the price went up."

On April 29, 1979, in the Sharon Home, Winnipeg, in the eighty-seventh year of her age, Rona Bruser, daughter of Abraham and Freidel Slobinsky, dearly beloved wife of Boris Bruser.

Born in Russia, Rona Bruser created a home for her family in a succession of prairie towns – Lanagan, Foam Lake, Birch Hills, Gretna, Plum Coulee, Altona, Grandview – settling eventually with her husband in Winnipeg. Wherever she lived, she made friends and gardens. Beautiful, brave, resolute, blithe, dignified, humorous, generous and wise, she possessed to a remarkable degree the power to nurture creativity and joy in those she loved. She leaves two daughters, four granddaughters, four great-grandchildren, and the memory of a fruitful life.

Yisgadal v'yiskadash sh'may rabo…Baagolo uvizman koreev, v'imru Omayn. And this is the mourner's kaddish. The shofar sounds. The ark is closed.

I am sixty-five now. My mother, had she lived, would be ninety-five. I have been writing about her almost all my life, from mawkish childhood eulogies to the sometimes strained set pieces of my young womanhood. I could say now, as she said once of her mother, "There is no day I don't think of her." I reach for the wooden mixing spoon – and am back in my mother's kitchen, amid the fragrance of baking bread. I set a festive table with her linens, china, silver. Sometimes, on the street, I see what looks like a familiar figure – a woman short and stout and corseted, wearing heavy sensible oxfords with her best clothes, and I walk behind a ways, remembering. At one time or another, I have felt for my mother a bewildering range of emotions — tenderness, awe, gratitude, exasperation, pride, delight, disappointment, bitterness, fear, rage — and love. I see her now as flawed but remarkable — oh, always that — and rich in spirit, more complicated by far than she appeared. Once, as she lay dying, I asked a hard question and she said, with a rare literary flourish, "I'm taking my mysteries with me." Of course she did.

"After Great Pain…"

◦━◇━◦

Looking back, I can say that Max and I had a good divorce: we found, each of us, a new freer life. But the decision to part, and the period that followed that decision, felt like death. Long after the passion, sworn commitment and high romance of our early years together were gone, long after I stopped loving Max Maynard, I remained powerfully *attached*. I could say, almost until the end, "When things are good, he is still the most interesting (or the most original, or the most gifted) man I know." At any time I thought, "This may be a terribly difficult marriage, but it's still better than most." In spite of fears, anxieties and deepening problems, I did not want to lose my marriage. Over the years, I had played with the idea of divorce. Drunk, Max would insult a guest, fall downstairs, collapse at a friend's dinner table with his face in the lobster Newburg — and I would think, "This can't go on." Public humiliation, more often than private pain, triggered this response. But I could not imagine a life without Max.

The end came suddenly. At least, that's how it seemed. One day I moved through the small daily rituals, morning coffee to nightly news, a married woman on a journey to oblivion. The next, I had cut myself adrift, alone in a rowboat on rough seas while the unsinkable ship that was my marriage shuddered and sank. "After great pain a formal feeling comes, The nerves sit ceremonious, like tombs…." Emily Dickinson had it just right. In the first hours after decision, I remained frozen, suspended in time. Feeling, when it returned, was not primarily sorrow and certainly not (as it was to become) relief. It was pure panic, a childlike terror of being unsupported and unloved – Hansel and Gretel in the forest, Tom Thumb and his brothers abandoned by their parents.

I have thought a lot, in the years since I left my marriage, about the pain of divorce, devastating even when it ends a relationship that is dead or life-destroying. One source of that pain is the outside world. In a society which regards happy marriage as one measure of success, marital breakdown brings with it a terrible sense of defeat. This is particularly true for women brought up, as I was, to see getting and keeping a husband as a life goal. When I couldn't secure a university position, I could blame a sterile and prejudiced administration. When my children encountered setbacks, I could blame teachers, or Fate. But when my marriage collapsed, ultimately I blamed myself. In the central human task – loving and being loved – I had most spectacularly failed. One of the reasons it feels so good to be engaged and newly married, I read somewhere, is the rewarding sensation that, out of the whole wide world, you have been selected. One of the reasons divorce feels so awful – regardless of who initiates the separation – is that you have been *de*-selected.

De-selection brings with it, almost inevitably, a sense of guilt and shame. Divorce took from my children the stubbornly cherished belief that they were part of a loving family. It took from my parents, in their declining years, the reassurance of a daughter well married, secure. At the same time, it gave me a new, unsettling vision of myself as a displaced person, odd woman out. Dinner-party invitations dwindled and then ceased altogether. I had become an embarrassment. Men now regarded me as fair game: respectable long-marrieds turning up at my door with leering suggestions that if I were hard up, not getting any....Old friends drew back, fearful of being drawn in and having to take sides. Some casual acquaintances appeared to take satisfaction in our distress, gathering on shore to observe the shipwreck or plunging into troubled waters, exacerbating resentments (*I never could stand that man*). I came to envy widows who, I observed, were universally treated with special deference, comforted with casseroles and wreathed in tributes to the glorious dead. No-one said to me, after Max left, "A wonderful man, how we will miss him!" What I often got, subtly or directly, was the judgment that he was not wonderful, that I had been a fool to marry him.

A husband and wife who have grown apart, as Max and I had, may imagine that divorce will not dramatically change their lives. Shaken though I was by our parting, I assumed my own life would continue much as before. I had an active professional life. I would stay on in the house. True, there wouldn't be anyone to bring me coffee in bed mornings, an old practice initiated by Max in the early days to prevent my sleeping late. Such small losses would be more than outweighed by the gains in serenity — no drunkenness, no depression.

So I thought. In actual fact, Max's leaving created a shocking vacuum. My dresses swung in the half-empty closet. The house became suddenly quiet: no slamming doors, no small companionable kitchen noises (toaster down, burner switch on, kettle boiling for tea). I missed the ritual exchanges, cool but civilized ("Care for some coffee?" "Want a drive to Portsmouth?") and the patterns that framed our world. Who turned off the alarm, who got up early winter mornings to turn up the heat, who plugged in the coffeepot and fed the cat — all these habitual rhythms, instinctive as breathing, gone.

New practical difficulties appeared. Though Max had never played worker-about-the-house, he was the one who replaced faucet washers and laid the fire in the fireplace. Changing a fuse for the first time, I expected swift electrocution. Once I had dreaded coming home nights to over-loud music and lights on everywhere with Max raging or semi-comatose. After the separation, it was hard to enter a dark empty house. (I learned to leave lights on, as a fake greeting.) Mealtimes were hardest of all. Determined not to settle for sandwiches or cold cereal, I would roast a chicken — and eat leftovers all week. A ham was forever. I took pains with the table setting: candles, wine — and one place mat. Even with the evening paper, I couldn't make the meal last half an hour. I'd carry my coffee to the living room for the TV news, and even that was melancholy, because we had always talked during commercials. I washed up by hand — it would have taken all week to fill the dishwasher with my few forks and plates — keeping the television set on for an illusion of life. Because I couldn't keep my mind on real books, I read things with titles like *How To Raise Better Begonias* or *Hawaiian Holiday*. I didn't listen to music because music made me cry.

I cried a lot that first year. After decades of practised control, dry-eyed before disaster, suddenly I dissolved over the smallest provocations: a broken cup, forsythia blooming indoors in December, an old photograph, a tube of dried oil paint, a child's drawing, a letter from Max. I wept for my aging husband, accustomed to comfort and indulgence, wandering through the world with his raving bacchante. I wept for his daughters, one moved by desperate anxious love and one by rage. Most of all I wept for myself. Having tried to control everything — Max *will* stop drinking, I *will* be happy — I found myself a person who had completely lost control. I could not keep from pouring out my story (the early version: my virtue, his incorrigible vice) to anyone I met. I told virtual strangers on the street if they asked, "How are you?" One day I told the fish man when he asked, "No cod today?" I said the man who loved boiled cod was gone, and then I told him about the young woman, and the drinking, and in the end he put his arms around me (sweater smelling powerfully of Gloucester mackerel) and said, "I've hit the booze myself, gave it up. I'm sorry about Mr Maynard. Lovely gentleman." And then I cried all the harder, because it seemed that of everyone who knew him, only the fish-seller had glimpsed the man I married.

Though I saw my marriage crisis as unique, and uniquely dreadful, I have since discovered that most women experience after divorce much the same chaos of feeling. Self-pity, pity for the divorced mate, rage, bitterness, self-reproach, fits of nostalgia and sentimental reminiscence, cold hatred, vindictiveness, guilt ….I thought I was coping well. When Rona suggested a therapist, I reacted with hurt and anger. I didn't need any help in putting my life together. Was I not running the household, carrying on with my career?

What finally persuaded me to seek help was a small but ominous incident. I had begun, in a half-hearted way, to consider the possibility of another man. Usually, after dinner with an unattached male, each of us tentatively assessing the other, I returned home with relief. This one was boring, that one arrogant. Then along came a man I found decidedly attractive. The courtship, if it was that, proceeded swiftly. A few lively dinners, a theatre evening, a visit to an art gallery. He proposed a weekend at his summer cottage. Though I made a show of hesitation, I surely intended to accept.

And then the man made a small shy confession. There were things I perhaps ought to know. He was an alcoholic, off the sauce just now. He suffered from — a little sexual difficulty. And, as a matter of fact, he was married. Separated from his wife, to be sure, planning to be divorced. I heard all this with astonishment — and alarm. Alcoholic, sexually strange, married. Also an Englishman, also elegant, sophisticated, charming. Not *like* Max, to be sure, but cut from the same cloth. Next day I made an appointment with a therapist.

When people ask me what my year of therapy accomplished, I always say, "It showed me what I was getting divorced *from*." The therapist I chose was no lofty, silent, pipe-smoking father figure. Young, playful, direct, quick-witted, intuitive and intellectually challenging, John could stop me in my tracks with a question or a single word, obliging me to see what I had done, where I was heading. My first visit, for instance, I started off with a polished, well-rehearsed summary and analysis of my marriage. John listened for perhaps ten minutes. Then he mimed bowled-over amazement, flashed a fake yokel's grin and said, "My, my. You're making me feel like a schoolboy."

After that, I spared him my insights. Indeed, I soon discovered the limitations of those insights. When I claimed, one day, that one of my problems was inability to express anger, he said, "Oh? But you would agree that irony is your natural mode?" "I've always had an ironical style," I said. "And you think there's no relationship between irony and anger?" The first time he suggested that I had supported Max's drinking — at least made possible its continuance — I flamed. "I loathe drunkenness." "I believe you do," he said, as always courteous, calm. "Remind me, now. That time, when you were out of town and the police came to the house because Max had left his car in the middle of the road. Did you, next day, call the station with a story about his being taken suddenly ill?" "Well, sure," I said. "I couldn't let them know that Professor Maynard was so drunk he couldn't negotiate the driveway." "Mm," he said. "Mmmm. You thought you were helping him."

My therapist never lectured, never underlined a point; he didn't have to. After he'd listened, he in effect played back the tape, but in such a way that patterns emerged. Once he literally videotaped a conversation between me and my daughters. "Talk about any issue between you," he prompted. So we talked and he taped and he ran the tape for us. "Would you say that sounds like a conversation between adults?" he asked of the exchange between me and Joyce. I flushed, seeing. "It's parent to child." "But which is the parent and which is the child?" Infallibly, he put his finger on the distortion that had occurred when, after the divorce, I set out to placate the daughter who was her father's darling. John helped me see how overwhelming – and destructive – was my need to control, even after the marriage ended. When Max and I divorced – he retired, I still earning money – I undertook to pay him alimony. Magnanimous, I thought. John asked, "How is this money paid – through the bank?" "No," I said. "I send cheques monthly." "That's not a nuisance?" When I said, "Not really," he smiled very faintly. "Perhaps there's some pleasure in dispensing bounty. And then you could always *not* dispense." Of that year's many revelations, the one that most freed me was realizing that Superwoman had been a costume, an act adopted to conceal deep feelings of inadequacy and worthlessness. "It's live or die," John said. "If you really want to live, you have to begin making I-statements." "I don't know what that means," I said. "Ah, that's just your problem," John said. "Start small. Next time you talk to Joyce or Rona – or anyone else, for that matter – forget about pleasing them. Think about what *you* want. Be quite clear about what you will or won't do — and don't apologize for what you don't wish to do. Believe it or not, that's more likely to please than those old let-me-help-you routines."

One of my persistent despairs in those days was the apparent impossibility of change. "Okay so I've been inflexible, dogmatic, insecure and at the same time controlling. Rona once said, 'You come on too strong.' Even my voice is an instrument of control. I can't change those things after fifty years." "You can change everything — your voice too — if you really want to," John said. "What I observe is that so far you're perpetuating the patterns of Life with Max."

Taking that clue, I set out, after the therapy ended, to change patterns. It was not easy. A person who has been married a long time is like a wagon going downhill; there's tremendous momentum to continue in the same way. Though Max had been gone a year, I still had coffee in bed, started work at nine, walked in mid-morning to meet the mailman, skimmed magazines with the noon soup, gave an hour to letters and phone calls — and so on, through food-shopping and library and a drink at five and the evening news. I worked weekends as well as weekdays. If I left Durham at all, it was for professional reasons — a quick trip, and back to safe familiar routines.

I never consciously decided that a real trip might launch a new life. That just happened. Over dinner one night, after many glasses of wine, a friend said, "I'd love to travel in the Soviet Union. I wish I knew someone who would go with me." I heard a voice, which I recognized as mine, say "I will." "Where would you like to go?" Evelyn asked. The voice — where did it come from? — said, "Samarkand." I knew absolutely nothing about Samarkand except that name's golden reverberations in nineteenth-century poetry, and next morning, remembering this conversation, I was appalled. Travel to distant places without the excuse of a dying relative? Stop work for weeks? I hadn't even asked about costs. I prayed that Evelyn would forget. By next day, however, she had made inquiries and booked a tour. And that is how, a year after my marriage ended, I embarked on a new adventure.

I did not deliberately choose the Soviet Union as a change-agent — but I could hardly have done better. There was first the breathtaking physical difference: the grey streets of Moscow, onion domes piercing a mauve sky; elegant Leningrad; the towers of Khiva and the desert sands and a centuries-old glacier in Dushanbe, from which we looked over to the mountains of Afghanistan. Even eating became a new experience — cucumbers and beets for breakfast, water ladled out in the streets, vodka that went down the throat like Siberian winter. Russia was strange, yet part of my buried heritage; my parents had loved these forests and fertile plains. In Russia I learned how to circumvent government restrictions on tourist activity, how to move about a large city and subway system where I couldn't read the signs. Above all, I learned in Russia that it was possible to reach people without language. Having been all my life a verbal person, using language often as weapon or defence, here I found myself mute, reduced to *spasibo* and *das vedanya*. I developed a whole new vocabulary of smiles, shrugs, quizzical eyebrows, hand gestures, even the odd little dance. I made crude sketches, showed photographs, pointed. One whole afternoon in Tashkent, I sat on a raised platform, gloriously carpeted, drinking pale green Russian tea with turbaned tribesmen who popped sweet biscuits into my mouth. I chattered, they chattered, neither side comprehending the other's words, yet understanding. This lesson I could never have learned in the west.

I came back to Durham tired yet refreshed, and believing in at least the possibility of change. I no longer brooded over my dead marriage or the once endless list of Max's iniquities. I turned in our heavy old Buick — Max had loved substantial cars — for a small Renault. I indulged in luxuries like fresh flowers in the kitchen and bedroom — anemones, flagrant gerbera, sweet peas. I shopped in those formerly intimidating salons — no garments on display — where salesladies glided across the rug bearing selections from mysterious inner depths. Here I discovered that though clothes don't make the woman, they certainly help. Dressed by Bergdorf Goodman, I cut a different figure from the woman who hunted bargains in Filene's basement. I embarked on a plan to lose weight. In a week at a fasting spa (water, water everywhere nor any crumb to eat) I lost twelve pounds, gaining in the process a different attitude towards food and a gratifying sense of being in charge of my body. So what if my mother was fat and my grandmother too? I need not be a helpless victim of heredity and poor metabolism; I had a choice. The discipline of fasting brought me, along with freedom from food obsessions, a new energy and confidence. At that moment, Fate knocked on the door — or, to be exact, rang me up on the phone.

I was turning over the compost pile one May day the year following my divorce, when the ringing began. Very insistent. What a nuisance! I threw down the spade and ran. On the phone, a voice I had never heard said, "Is this Freidele Bruser?" No-one had called me that — my baby name, my real name — for almost fifty years. "Well," the voice continued, very English, very assured. "I've just read your book. This is Sydney Bacon of Toronto." The manner implied *Of course you remember me*. I said, "Who?"

Actually, I knew. Decades earlier, Sydney Bacon of Toronto had courted Celia; I remembered her account of a dashing, intellectual English Jew. It was of Sydney that she had written to me, "He's mad about Pushkin. Tell me everything you know about Pushkin." Of course I wouldn't tell her a thing. In time — maybe because she didn't know about Pushkin — Sydney Bacon vanished from her life.

Now here he was, obviously calling the wrong girl. I didn't immediately tell him that. In my what-have-I-to-lose? mood, I played along. Yes, I had grown up in Saskatchewan. Yes, I had lived in Toronto during the early 1940s. "Do you remember," he said, "when I invited you to hear Tim Buck and you appeared in an evening gown because you thought Tim Buck was a band leader?" At that point I confessed. It was my sister he'd known, and *my* book he'd read. He didn't hang up. Cautiously we explored new ground. After that he began to phone nightly. The conversations were not particularly lively, certainly not romantic. Sydney Bacon told me all about his accountant, his lawyer, his banker; I thought this tedious and show-offish. Still, beyond the words, I heard something I rather liked — a clarity and earnestness, and a curious intriguing innocence. One day he said, "If you're ever in New York, I'd like to take you for dinner." "I've just been to New York," I said. "I won't be going again for ages." "Do you come to Toronto?" he asked. "I'm not going to Toronto," I said. And then, with a boldness that would once have seemed unthinkable, I said, "What a pity you're not asking me to dinner in Durham." "Who says I'm not?" he said. "Are you free the evening of June 24?" So I invited him to dinner at my house.

A few weeks before the arranged date, a visiting Toronto friend, overhearing the nightly telephone call, asked, "What was all that about?" "Some madman in Toronto," I said, carefully offhand. I told her the story — the original mistake, the man's unexpected persistence, my invitation. "What's his name?" she asked. "You wouldn't know him," I said. (Businessman. Not our world.) "It's Sydney Bacon." "*Sydney Bacon*," she repeated.

"Well, I don't know him — but I think I know someone who does. Let me check." The day before my dinner date, a note came from my friend. "Guess what? Sydney Bacon is *loaded*. He keeps a mistress on the island of St Martin and several other ladies besides. See that you at least get an island out of it."

A more experienced woman might have been agreeably titillated by this information. I felt pure panic. A wealthy lecher? A collector of women? I called my most worldly woman friend for advice. "Relax," she said. "He's read *Raisins and Almonds*. He can figure out your age, he's seen the jacket photo. So he knows you're not harem material. If he wanted another lady for tropical diversions, he wouldn't be on his way to New England."

Still, for our first meeting, I dressed with anxious circum-spection in my primmest navy-blue suit, buttoned up, with Peter Pan collar and demure tie. (Later he would ask, "Was that a *uniform* you wore when we met?") We were both in dis-guise, me as a combination schoolteacher-schoolgirl, he as a businessman-with-briefcase. At the dinner table, he politely sampled the gourmet creations I'd laboured over — the paté and stuffed mushrooms, the salmon mousse. "What I really like," he said, "is a good tin of sockeye salmon." He tried the white wine and registered shock. (Much later, I discovered he liked a purple-grapey flavour — shades of my grandfather's home-made Passover wine.) He talked about the import busi-ness, I talked about writing. He told me how successful he was, I implied I hadn't done too badly myself. The whole occasion would have seemed utterly dismal, hopeless, had it not been for two things. He told me about the woman on St Martin (the only woman, as it turned out) — a post-divorce fantasy that had just ended. And he asked, kindly but with obvious puzzle-ment, "Why do you wear those glasses?" "I'm short-sighted," I said, snappish. "I can't see without them." "When did you last change your frames?" When I asked why, he said, musing,

"Octagonal tortoiseshell….They must go back fifteen years." I realized he was right. I hadn't noticed — and neither had anyone else. I took off my glasses and looked at the frames — hideous — and Sydney said, "You have beautiful eyes." For the first time in years, I felt truly seen by a man. So I invited him to breakfast next morning.

Breakfast at home is, by its very nature, an informal occasion. The navy suit was out. So I dressed next morning in something long and white, with ruffles at the throat. I left off the tortoiseshell glasses — and found I could see quite well. Volunteering to help in the kitchen, my visitor looked at me in a new way. I was beating eggs, making small talk, when he took the bowl from me, put his hands on my shoulders and said, "I'm baffled. I heard your voice in the book. Where are you?" When I began to cry, he sat me down on the living-room couch and said, "Tell me about your marriage." Though I told him very little — he was, after all, a stranger — he made a swift intuitive leap. "My goodness, you really are a virgin, aren't you?" "I have two children," I sniffed. He didn't comment. Then he said, "Would you come upstairs and lie down on the bed beside me?" "Certainly not," I said. "I promise I won't touch you if you don't want me to," he said. "I'd like us to relax and talk."

I thought the suggestion astonishing, yet I scarcely hesitated. I was, after all, snugly dressed. As I turned into my bedroom, he asked, "What shall I wear?" "What kind of question is that?" I said. I had scarcely arranged myself decorously on top of the bedspread when Sydney Bacon walked in — wearing nothing at all. "Have you ever seen a naked man before?" he asked — and then, when I remained silent, "I thought not." So he lay beside me, on the bedspread, not touching me except at moments to hold my hand or turn my head to his. We had talked almost continuously for twelve hours when he said,

"The airport limousine leaves soon. Shall I come again next week?" And that is how it all began.

Sydney Bacon came to Durham most weekends after that. There were no bolts of lightning, no romantic storms of the kind I had always associated with falling in love. We walked on the beach and down country roads. Once, as a car whizzed past, I asked, only half playfully, "How would you feel if I were run over?" I felt his swift distancing. "I have a long history of forced declarations to women," he said. "That's over. If you don't see me for what I am, what's the good of protestations?" We talked and talked — about families, marriages, children, friends, books, films. When he found that I'd never been on an ocean liner, he took me to England on the Queen Elizabeth II. When he realized that I had hardly ever travelled except for business or family matters, he took me around the world: Hawaii, Australia, Hong Kong, India, Israel, Romania, Poland, Hungary, France, Italy, Spain. He made no protestations, never said "I love you" and certainly not "I can't live without you."

Once, as we sat silent together on the rocks by the ocean near Durham, I thought of Max's eloquence as a suitor — the poetry, the celebration. Insubstantial the words may have been, but I missed hearing them. "What's wrong?" Sydney asked. And then, "Don't tell me. Whatever it is, forgive me." We had been together, off and on, just over a year when he said, "We've reached a point where we either go forward or lose ground. If you will move to Toronto, I will buy you any house you choose, I will give you the key and never come unless you invite me."

That is how we live now — I in my row house, he in an apartment hotel twenty minutes away. I invite him to dinner very often; he brings his overnight case weekends. In the beginning, I assumed we would ultimately marry. Isn't that what you're supposed to do, when you love someone and want to be

with him? So when Sydney announced, as he did at the beginning, that he would never marry again, I thought he'd in time
see the light. What has happened is that I have seen what
works for us. Although I believe in marriage, I also think that
it's an incredibly difficult arrangement, and that if you're not
raising children the disadvantages may outweigh the advan-
tages. At this stage of life, privacy and freedom are prime
values. I like, often, to spend an entire day reading, working in
the garden, just thinking, without the pressure of another
person's presence. Though I love to cook, I like not being
bound by a three-meals-a-day routine. I like the freedom to
make plans — I will have my family come for a week, I will
renovate the kitchen, I will go to Mexico — without considering
anyone else's wishes. As for the relationship between a man
and a woman — it seems to me that, apart from the brief
euphoria of first love, this too goes better with some distance.
Sydney inhabits a setting that suits him perfectly; he doesn't
have to defend his preference for leather chairs with brass
studs. I surround myself with plants and bright pillows and a
clutter of folk art, all of which he likes fine — for the weekend.
Sydney comes to me at the end of a business day, eager for talk
and laughter. He comes still as a suitor; few husbands stop
regularly, on the way home, for a manicure, a blow-dry, flowers
and wine. If we have a difference, and that's rare, it will be over
something real, not the minor irritations that so often tangle
the lines in a marriage. (Who forgot to buy coffee, who left the
car lights on and burned out the battery *again*?) Our time
together is good time, saved up and prepared for. Time apart is
absolutely our own. After thirteen years together, we continue
to observe the courtesies natural in any good friendship. I
would not ask him to drive me on an errand where he might
have to wait. (My husband used to fume in the car while I

chose dress patterns and fabric.) I would never appear at his apartment door without calling first to see if he wanted a visitor. I don't do Sydney's laundry, he doesn't pay my bills.

Sydney and I met, thirteen years ago, as failed romantics. I had married and outlived a dream. He had a highly developed fantasy life inspired by oriental harems, Chekhovian heroines and memories of *Pygmalion*. We tried, briefly, the old games of projection and elaboration; this time the material proved intransigent. Sydney was not an artist well versed in English poetry; I was not an enchantress whose appearance in public would draw all men's eyes to her fortunate escort. We began, awkwardly and with some disappointment, to cope with what real life provided. I don't know just when this began to seem at least as good as the dream world. But if I were to choose a moment, it would be The Party For Men.

When I moved to Toronto in 1975, I carried with me a persistent fantasy. Wouldn't it be wonderful, wouldn't it be *fun* to give a party at which I would be the only woman present? I started compiling a list of potential guests: men whose works I'd read, men I'd seen and liked on TV, men encountered years before, when I was a graduate student at the University of Toronto. Also, of course, men I knew well — including my hairdresser, my accountant, the man from the health-food store. All in all, a list of ninety. At the Art Gallery, I chose ninety different postcard reproductions, each appropriate to a particular guest. The invitations read: "FOR MEN ONLY. Wine, cheese and conversation with Fredelle Maynard." Some invitees telephoned to ask, "Who are you? What's this about?" Some telephoned but did not appear. Some neither phoned nor appeared. But on the appointed day over seventy men showed up at my door — many bearing flowers, chocolates, wine. I wore a preposterous dress chosen for the occasion — a long coffee-coloured Mexican gown, flounced and pleated and lace-trimmed, with plunging bodice and hanging sleeves like a medieval angel's. The party roared on for hours: a houseful of men, and me.

When it was over, when the last guest but one had departed, that one said, "Let's not bother with the dishes." I changed into my flannel nightie and bathrobe. Sydney made a pot of tea and set out the Peak Freans. "Nice party," he said. And then, looking around, "Nice house. Nice life."

And Therefore I Have Sailed The Seas…

I know just when it came to me, the realization that I was growing old. There had been intimations earlier, like the time a shoe-store clerk called out to a fellow worker, "Would you help the lady with the glasses?" There was the unpleasant incident when I jumped into a taxicab at Los Angeles airport for a ride that proved to be about a hundred yards. The driver, a sullen late-adolescent, announced, "Five dollars." "For that?" I said, handing him three. He flung open the cab door. "Old lady, *you* mean." But that was vengeance, not justice.

The decisive moment came some years ago, in my mid-fifties. It is not irrelevant to this story that I was on my way home from an exhilarating conference, wearing what my daughters call my author suit, looking and feeling smart. In the airport lounge, where Boston passengers waited for a late plane, two individuals caught my attention. One was a charming young woman in a loose gauzy gown, ankle length, with flowing cornsilk hair and bare feet — Rossetti or Burne-Jones crossed with late sixties flower child. A little girl, just learning to walk, alternately nestled in her lap or staggered about the room. The other notable passenger, almost certainly European, was a middle-aged man who might have stepped out of the pages of *Town and Country* — impeccably groomed, wearing on this steamy day a soft grey Borsalino felt, creamy silk shirt with French cuffs and gold cufflinks, supple Italian shoes. Not handsome but what the French call a *joli laid*.

Once on the plane — open seating — the young woman settled herself and her baby in a bulkhead seat and began to spread out her gear. Diaper bag, bottle, doll, cracker snacks. The elegant European sat immediately behind these two; I took a seat across the aisle. As the young woman stood to place her bag in the overhead rack, the man jumped up. "Please let me help you." She looked surprised, shook her head, stowed the bag and sat down again without a backward look. Minutes later, the toddler came weaving down the aisle, gumming a cookie. The man reached out with winning smile and took one grubby paw in his own beautifully manicured hand. The little girl squawked and the mother turned, gathering her child up as if to protect against imminent abduction. The man bowed to her back. As the plane neared its destination, he made one further attempt, tapping her shoulder. "Would you allow me to assist with your baggage when we reach Boston?" The young woman turned and stared. It was not a rejecting stare, the kind that would have acknowledged, while refusing, a romantic advance. It was merely incredulous. (Why on earth is this old fellow bothering me?) "My husband is meeting us," she said. In some embarrassment now — several passengers obviously listening in — the man looked about with a shrug which assured us all he was only trying to help. For the first time our eyes met. I smiled. I suppose my look might have translated as "You know what young women are like" with overtones of "Well, aren't you an attractive man!" I certainly didn't intend it to be flirtatious. The European stared — (Why on earth…) — and in that moment I knew I was no longer young.

"And therefore I have sailed the seas and come To the holy city of Byzantium." I like the place I am now. Observing women my age who dye their hair or undergo cosmetic surgery, I am honestly amazed. How — after what they must by now have endured — how can they imagine that female power resides in a rag or a bone or a hank of hair? "Brightness falls from the air; Queens have died young and fair; Dust hath closed Helen's eye…but the spirit endures." I am old enough now to have known loss and pain, rejection and failure, grief and devastation. I have learned the difficulty and necessity of change. I have reordered my priorities. At twenty I wanted a man handsome, charming, witty, sophisticated, artistic — and a good dancer. Now the man I choose must be responsible, compassionate, honest, independent, generous-hearted…and must love women. That I now *choose* is an important difference. Literally and metaphorically, I do not wait for the phone to ring.

When I look for origins of my later-life confidence, I see that it comes, not from years of achievements, but from the way I am treated by those closest to me. This is not a simple matter of being "loved." My parents surely loved me. My husband may have done so. My daughters, growing up, offered the love born of need. What has changed my feeling about myself, and so my life, has come partly from friends but mostly from being with a man who from the first respected me more than I could then respect myself. Days after our meeting, Sydney Bacon, still an eccentric stranger, said, "Have you any idea how often you say '*Sure*'?" and then, startlingly, "I don't know where your boundaries are. You seem prepared to accept invasion at any point." Fiercely protective of his own boundaries, he showed me how to protect mine. "Who is Sheila?" I asked one day, picking up a birthday card from his desk. "Why do you ask?" he countered. When I said, "Idle curiosity," he said, "There is no such thing as idle curiosity," and then, with finality, returning the card to its envelope: "Sheila is the person who sent me the card." When we travelled together, he would never allow me to put *my* things into *his* suitcase. "But you've got lots of room," I'd protest, gesturing towards my bulging luggage. "If you can't manage, throw something out − or buy another suitcase," he said. Not unkind, just firm, the door marked PRIVATE. The first time I asked, "Do you love me?" he said, "You know the Tantric definition of love: *I recognize and respect your essence.*"

The physical changes of aging − some seem to happen overnight − come as a shock. Sometimes I feel I am travelling in disguise, a young girl inexplicably trapped in that body I glimpse as I pass reflecting windows. Grey hair, thickened middle, round where one hopes for flat and flat where one hopes for round.... Recent acquaintances, seeing a studio portrait of me at twenty, ripe against a background of leaves and flowers, ask, "Who's that?" I have become accustomed, though not resigned, to the camera's current images of someone with jowls and lines. (The worst comes when a well-meaning friend says, "Here's a great picture of you!")

These are the inevitable losses of age, to be borne as well as possible with Hemingway-style courage, grace under pressure. It is certainly true, however, that some losses are gains. Vanity no longer stands in the way of comfort and good sense. Was that really me, the girl who wore waist cinchers so tightly laced that I could not have swallowed a marshmallow? Who, like Cinderella's sisters, squeezed her feet into agonizingly tight shoes and teetered about on three-inch heels hoping to attract the prince? Once I wore corselets and nylons in the hottest weather. It has been decades now since I owned a girdle; I go bare-legged and sandalled or barefoot all summer. I have accepted the fact that I will never be thin — that, regardless of diets, certain unwelcome redistributions of flesh have occurred. I would have liked a different figure. But I have, after decades of dissatisfaction, come to terms with my face. Young, I sighed for this one's eyes and that one's perfect nose. At sixty-past, I look in the mirror and, without vanity, am on the whole pleased with what I see. I have made this face. It is mine.

Along with youthful vanity, I am losing — have perhaps finally lost — the vision of life as competition. Looking back at my growing years, I can't remember a time when I didn't think it important to be best. This may be typical for a child of first-generation immigrants; certainly I observed, when I left my parents' insular world, that WASP friends did not run so hard. In our family, I longed to be best loved, never guessing how costly success would be. By the age of three, I had become self-consciously good, working for those moments when my mother would say to my older sister, "Look at Freidele! She never gives me any trouble." At five I discovered school and a new, grander arena where I might be best at reading, best in composition, best in behaviour. I rejoiced the day the school nurse weighed all the second graders. "I'm overweight!" I reported happily to my mother. "I'm more overweight than anybody in the room!" Being first in class, most admired elocutionist, teacher's pet (chosen to distribute ink and clap blackboard erasers) — for years I saw these as worthy goals, prizes to lay at my parents' feet.

Graduating from Harvard with a Ph.D., Phi Beta Kappa, provided a satisfactory close to academic competition; I mailed the diploma to my parents, another trophy of the hunt. Married the following year, I became once more a runner, toe poised at the starting line for the homemaker marathon. *Get ready, get set....* With no hope, in a New England town, of entering the "best family" race, already determined by birth and old money, I set my own terms for social success. I would be best hostess. Had prizes been given, during those early married years, for complication of menu and multiplicity of occasion, I would have taken all the blue ribbons. I gave parties when people arrived in Durham and when they left; I entertained groups of ten, twenty, thirty at dinners where every ingredient had been tormented into a new shape or flavour. Preparing for a party, I pored over cookbooks in search of novelty. Should I purée the green beans with nutmeg and mace, or sauté them with onions and almonds? I made seven-layer tortes and ratatouille involving separate preparation of a dozen different vegetables. I prided myself on the range and absolute originality of my *hors d'oeuvres*, serving the first chocolate-covered ants ever offered at a Durham soirée. I once prefaced a dinner with thirteen appetizers, six hot and seven cold.

At the age I am now, I look back at the run farther, faster period of my life with astonishment. Partly the difference is a matter of my having less energy. But mostly it's a shift in perspective. The notion of life as open competition has come to seem absurd. There will always be women more popular and more accomplished, who give better parties, write better books. This realization comes not as defeat but as blessed relief. At last I can forget about coming first in class. I take time now to read, reflect, sew, garden, walk, talk with friends, play with my grandchildren.

My daughters, grown, continue to mystify, delight, amaze. Rona, the straggly plump schoolgirl, has become an exquisite woman whose closets and drawers, once a scandal, are far tidier than mine. As a child, she seemed unco-ordinated, physically lethargic; today, she runs before breakfast and works out on an exercise bike. Joyce, our problem eater who dreaded mealtimes and subsisted largely on a diet of popcorn and fried chicken

wings, is a superb cook and hostess. Growing up in rural New
Hampshire, she longed for the brighter lights and prospects of
cities; today she lives happily in rural New Hampshire with a
pond, a meadow, a wood, and an orchard of her own. These
things I could not have foreseen. Still, I can look at two poised,
competent women and recognize my babies. Rona was a remote,
almost regal infant. The reticent cool remains; it no longer feels
hostile. Joyce, a cuddly baby, was all confidence and energy;
she has carried those qualities into adult life. Both daughters
smile at my writing and lecturing about child care. "*You* a
parenting expert?" one said, not without affection. "*You* will tell
other people how to raise their children?" It's true I was a most
imperfect mother — overprotective, overambitious, overinvolved.
But when I consider Rona and Joyce — as mothers, as writers,
as unique individuals — I think I must have done something
right. I cherish the memory of Rona in a fury of adolescent
rebellion, shouting as she slammed the door: "I'll say one thing
for you. You gave me the strength to fight you!"

Given my experience, the pure pleasure of grandparenting
has taken me by surprise. I was never the kind of parent who
asks, "When are you going to make me a grandma?", could not
have imagined myself wearing a charm bracelet with dangling
grandchild silhouettes. When Rona announced her pregnancy,
I felt not rapture but dismay. So young, newly married, still a
student — and the world waiting to be explored. What did she
need a baby for? The actual child produced no swift instinctive
rush of tenderness. I remember looking down at the rosy
fragrant newborn, a blue-eyed stranger, and thinking, "I have
no room for him in my life." As it happened, I had to make
room. A year later, Benjamin and his mother came to visit me.
After my own recent divorce, I saw an active small boy as one
more complication. He rushed about the rooms, imperilling
Mexican pottery. He scribbled on the walls. He woke early and

stayed up late. He *needed* — Pampers, drives to day care, comfort, toast. Gradually, that need became less irritant than bond, but a bond quite different from what I had experienced in mothering. My daughters for years had seemed flesh of my flesh, an extension of my being; their pain was mine. This first grandchild made possible a love almost wholly free from narcissism. I love Benjamin — as I have come to love Joyce's children, Audrey, Charlie, Willie — with a passion born of the blood tie but also, purely, for the person he is.

Benjamin has never called me Grandma. He was a year or so — just beginning to talk, having trouble with his Gs — when I walked into the kitchen where he sat banging on his high-chair tray. At the sound of my footsteps, he stopped banging, grinned, held out his arms to be picked up and said, "*Das. Das.*" And Das I have remained. Das is a personality different both from Fredelle Maynard and from Rona and Joyce's mother. She is freer, less dogmatic, less intrusive. She makes fewer demands. She is more generous, eager to give whatever will be useful without looking for returns. Above all, she pays attention.

At fourteen, Benjamin is taller than I. He speaks Computer while I, hopelessly mired in the Neanderthal simplicities of typewriter and ballpoint pen, don't know a modem from a floppy disk. It has been years now since I could beat him, or even hold my own, in a game of Big Boggle. (I am not so reckless as to try chess.) But still, when he comes to my house for the weekly sleepover, he reaches for the coloured plastic drinking glasses I bought when he was in nursery school. Scarcely a detail has changed in our long-established rituals. I hug him; he manages to not quite evade the embrace. He heads first for the kitchen, opens the fridge and leans on the door taking stock. He pours himself a glass of ginger ale and we talk — not a connected conversation, just bits and pieces. Anything really important will emerge later if at all. "Is there soup? Can I have it at 4:30 — and supper at 6?" Then he's off. He fits in his braces retainer, stretches out on the couch, reads, does his homework, watches television. Sometimes he invites me to watch a program with him; sometimes he's up for a board game. If he finds a pretext to come into the room where I'm working, I try to help him towards the conversational opening he needs. That's when I might hear that he's unhappy at the new school. Very, very occasionally now, he'll ask me to read him a story. I never have to ask, "Which book?" This silent guarded boy, a Dungeons and Dragons devotee, a fan of Stephen King, wants once again the stories we have read together since he was a small child: "Clever Gretchen," "The Little Mermaid," The Ugly Duckling."

With Audrey, Joyce's eight-year old, the relationship is qualitatively very different. She's a girl, after all, a girl who shares something of my temperament and most of my interests. But one element in the pattern seems to me absolutely the same. For both Audrey and Benjamin, my house is safe territory — like goal in a children's game, a place where you can't be tagged, you're home free. What happens here — again like a children's game — is ritual, ordered, exactly as it has always been. Audrey still brings to my house the Mexican wax dolls I gave her on her first overnight visit years ago. They're sadly deteriorated, short on fingers and feet. She doesn't really play with them any more but they're part of the scene. I always have Lipton's chicken noodle soup on hand. It's no longer her favourite, but she likes knowing it's there.

I read once, in a book called *The Vital Connection*, that no matter what they do or don't do, grandparents affect the emotional wellbeing of their grandchildren simply because they exist. I understand that. My own grandparents were not, from a child's point of view, ideal. (Too old, too strange.) But they *mattered*.

The only surviving pair, my father's parents, were separated from me by experience, culture and, most definitively, language. They spoke not a word of English; I knew very little Yiddish — not enough, certainly to follow Zaida's discourses on the nature of the universe. What I remember, though, is how hard I tried. "Can there be a watch without a watchmaker?" he would ask. "A world without God?" Though theological-philosophical argument had never much interested me, I hung on my grandfather's words. This gentle old man in yarmulka and rusty caftan, bent reverently over the Talmud, was my father's father. He had known my father as a little boy, a young man, and had himself once been a young man, a lover. My grandfather was living history — spirit of the *shtetl*, survivor of the Tsar's pogroms, evidence of Diaspora. I wanted his secrets, and my grandmother's, but had to settle for Russian tea sweetened with *veranya*, cherry jam, and thin dry poppyseed cookies tasting of flour. Brought to alien Winnipeg by their grown sons, my grandparents knew nothing of the world beyond their curtains. When I wore fashionable toeless shoes, my grandmother wept and pressed a crumpled dollar bill into my hand. When I acquired a bicycle, my grandfather said, "Now we need a radio," an apparent *non sequitur* later elucidated by my father. "Zaida's afraid you might get hurt on the bike. He thinks if anything happened to you, the news would be flashed on the air at once." Since in all my years of visiting, my grandparents and I never had anything approaching a real conversation, it is perhaps true that they did not know me. Yet I felt loved. Precisely because our chief communication was non-verbal, their tender affection had a special quality, unconnected with character or achievement. My grandparents loved my *being*.

So I think now that this purity of feeling — you are, therefore I love — is a grandparent's most precious gift. Parents love, of course, but in complicated ways, the love so often shot through with need, ambition, exasperation, anger, disappointment, pride. To the parent, a child represents a second chance at being a perfect person. Inevitably, there's pressure on the child to go farther, achieve more. To a grandparent, the child represents a second chance at being a perfect *parent*. The result, at least in my experience, is uniquely liberating. I wanted my daughters to be successful writers and – successfully, but at some cost – pushed them towards that goal. I want my grandchildren to be happy. If Benjamin were to prove a computer genius I would be gratified, no doubt. But if he were to become a chef or a bicycle mechanic (possibilities suggested by his interests, not mine), I would be equally pleased so long as he enjoyed his work and did it well.

On Parents' Night, I used to appear at school like a horse trainer at the racetrack. How is my entry doing – compared with the others, compared with previous performance? What could we do to improve distance and speed? I thought of this when I had occasion, once again, to line up at the teacher's desk. Benjamin was spending a week with me during his parents' absence; I was attending Parents' Night on their behalf. In the high-school auditorium, mothers and fathers milled about or stood in line to get the latest report on their children. Waiting, I remembered all the times I had performed this ritual, the usual reward being a tribute to my daughters' good behaviour and brains. As I moved up the line I caught familiar drifting murmurs: "She's doing beautifully." "Great improvement." "We really enjoy him." As my turn arrived and I identified myself to each teacher, the smiles faded. Benjamin was a very bright boy, no question. Likable. Academically a disaster. He came to class without his textbook, paid no attention, clowned, distracted classmates, failed to hand in homework, appeared indifferent to either encouragement or reproof.

Had I received such a report on my children, I would, I fear, have first questioned the teacher's capacity. How could she have failed to stimulate or appreciate my brilliant daughters? Then I would have gone raging home. *Do you realize your whole future is at stake? What has come over you? If you don't pick up those grades, there'll be no movies, no trips to Boston, no new guitar.* And finally, *How can you do this to me?* To me. My children were my representatives in the world; their failure would be mine. As Benjamin's grandmother, I felt none of these things. I saw his teachers as allies, not adversaries. Riding home on the bus, I was overwhelmed with anxiety and grief. What I had heard revealed not a bad boy or an indolent one, but a troubled child. How could I have wished to reprove, or to punish? The important thing was to help.

Mostly, as a grandparent, I keep a sense of perspective. This child is not me, not mine. I have no right to impose on him my wants, my expectations.

When I was a young mother, I knew all about the dangers of spoiling a child. Picking up a crying baby, allowing just one more turn on the swing, giving cookies to a child who hadn't finished his spinach — in effect, giving children what they wanted — all that was spoiling, and led to No Good End. Spoiled children became difficult, demanding adults. So I made, and tried to keep, a lot of rules. I ran a tight ship.

Over the years, I've changed my mind about the dangers of giving children, within reason, what they want. I think truly "spoiled" individuals, selfish and self-absorbed, are those whose needs, in childhood, were never met. And in any case, spoiling seems to me a grandparent's prerogative. With Benjamin, Audrey, Charlie and Willie I run a loose ship. I let Audrey spend an entire day in nightgown and bathrobe if she feels like taking things easy. I allow Benjamin to glut on raw cookie dough and TV. I have on occasion shared my bed with *three* grandchildren (all wiggly, one damp) to settle a squabble over *whose turn.*

When Charlie scatters blocks over the living-room floor I can say, "I'll pick them up tomorrow." I have been known to agree with a tired child that it's too late for toothbrushing. And none of this matters, or will corrupt their characters, because the children draw no conclusions from what goes on in Grandma's house to what's permissible in the real world. My house is Liberty Hall, Queen for a Day, Name Your Tune.

My eagerness to give my grandchildren time has, I suppose, a melancholy undernote. I won't always be here for them. As a young mother, I felt immortal. Right into my thirties and forties, the age at which I began to lose people dear to me, I would say, "*If* I die," not "*When* I die." I still feel immortal in flashes — when crocuses push through the frozen earth, when Audrey hugs, giggles and whispers all at once. But mostly I'm very aware of the fact that I don't have forever with these flowers, my children's children. I want, in whatever time we have together, to give them strength for the road ahead, tell them what I know. I show Audrey how to roll piecrust and how to root a new African violet from one furry leaf. I teach Benjamin to operate the sewing machine. When Joyce's Charlie asks, "Why did God let the airplane crash and kill people?" I take that very seriously; I try to explain. I want to pass on skills that have served me well, along with a sense of who I am, that being a part of who *they* are. I tell my grandchildren stories about their parents and my parents, and about my own unimaginable childhood in a world without television. When Audrey asks, "What's Jewish?" I try to explain in terms meaningful to eight-year-olds — about Jewish food, Jewish holidays, about the wineglass ground underfoot at a Jewish wedding and the solemn bar mitzvah processions, following the Torah in its tasselled, filigreed silver case, that celebrates a Jewish male's coming of age.

When I think of my hopes for my grandchildren, what comes

to me is a film called *The Triumph of Job*. Set in wartime Hungary, it tells the story of an elderly Jewish couple whose children, all seven of them, died at birth. Now, in the shadow of death, the old man determines to realize a lifelong dream. He will "raise a man for the Lord." The couple adopts a child — Christian, since only a Christian can inherit their small substance, survive the coming catastrophe. In their brief time together — it's perhaps a year, a year during which love grows painfully, powerfully, between these grandparent figures and their wild child — Job and his wife prepare the boy for survival. This you must remember, this you must do. One day the father begins, "When you are alone —" and the child bursts out, "I don't want to be alone, I want to be with you." "The old cannot always remain with the young," Job says gently. "So now you must learn to be alone."

I thought of that film the day Audrey and I walked along the Toronto lakefront, eating ice cream and popcorn simultaneously, planning the next adventure. Out of nowhere, Audrey said, "Grandma, I wish you could always be just the way you are now." Startling at the adult prescience in that wish, looking at Audrey with her wild-honey-coloured skin and huge dark Yemenite eyes, I thought of a scene in *The Triumph of Job*. With the Germans on the march, their fatal trucks advancing, the old woman packs a chest of linens and silver for the child who will be left behind. Then she lights the candles; it is Sabbath eve. "Dear God," she prays, "only let me live to bake his wedding bread."

Time. Ay, there's the rub. Between the desire and the reality falls the shadow. I have never feared death, because death is not real on my pulses. But the recognition that time is finite — that has come. I remember when I was in my forties, an elderly friend brought flowers for my garden saying, "So you'll think of me when I'm gone." As we walked to her car, a new one, she gestured. "This will be our last car." I wondered then at her serene acceptance. Wouldn't there always be another car, another visit? Mrs Phillips is long gone now; her Canterbury bells blow about my yard, seeded everywhere, and I think of her and I think of my own ending. I feel a sense of waste, also some outrage, that life won't go on forever – just when I'm getting the hang of it.

One day recently, when I was summering in New Hampshire, a real-estate agent called. "Do you own property in Durham?" "Yes," I said, proprietary. "I'm standing on it right now." "Would you be interested in selling?" the voice asked. I was surprised at my irrational rage. Selling *my house*? Someone else swinging on my porch, picking my crimson tulips, cutting down the lilac? Obliterating the pencil marks that show my children's heights as they grew? Obliterating *me*? I put down the phone trembling.

These days, when I glance at obituaries (a recent interest), I see that most of the departed are my age or younger. Cancer, heart, after long illness.... On annual trips to New Hampshire, I see old people who were once members of our kindergarten car pool. My parents have died, the love of my youth has died. I am at the top of the tree, beyond the fruiting branches. But I am still here, still looking skyward.